I0547581

Spirit Quest

By Paul Lentz

Ty Ty Press, Peachtree City, GA
Earth Analogue III

ISBN: 978-1-7355617-0-7

Cover design and realization by J.R.C. Dyer, jrcdyer.com

Illustrations on Pages 39, 45, 57, 95, 115, 119, 121, 130, 178, and 234 by Janine Rhodes, illustrator of "Cindi the Teenie Chiweenie" janinerhodesillustrator@yahoo.com.

Maps of Chaco Canyon on Pages 43 and 232 were produced by the National Park Service and are in the public domain.

Photographs of Anazazi pictographs ("rock art") and illustrations not listed above were made by the author.

This narrative is a sequel to "The Cry of the Innocents." Familiarity with that narrative, while useful, is not essential.

All royalties from the sales of this author's books go directly to the Friends of the Peachtree City (Georgia) Library, a 501(c)3 corporation.

www.PaulLentzAuthor.com

Amazon Author Page: amazon.com/author/paullentz

10 9 8 7 6 5 4 3 2 1

Dedication

This narrative is dedicated to the Native Americans of this Earth Analogue who more than most suffer greatly from the Covid-19 pandemic.

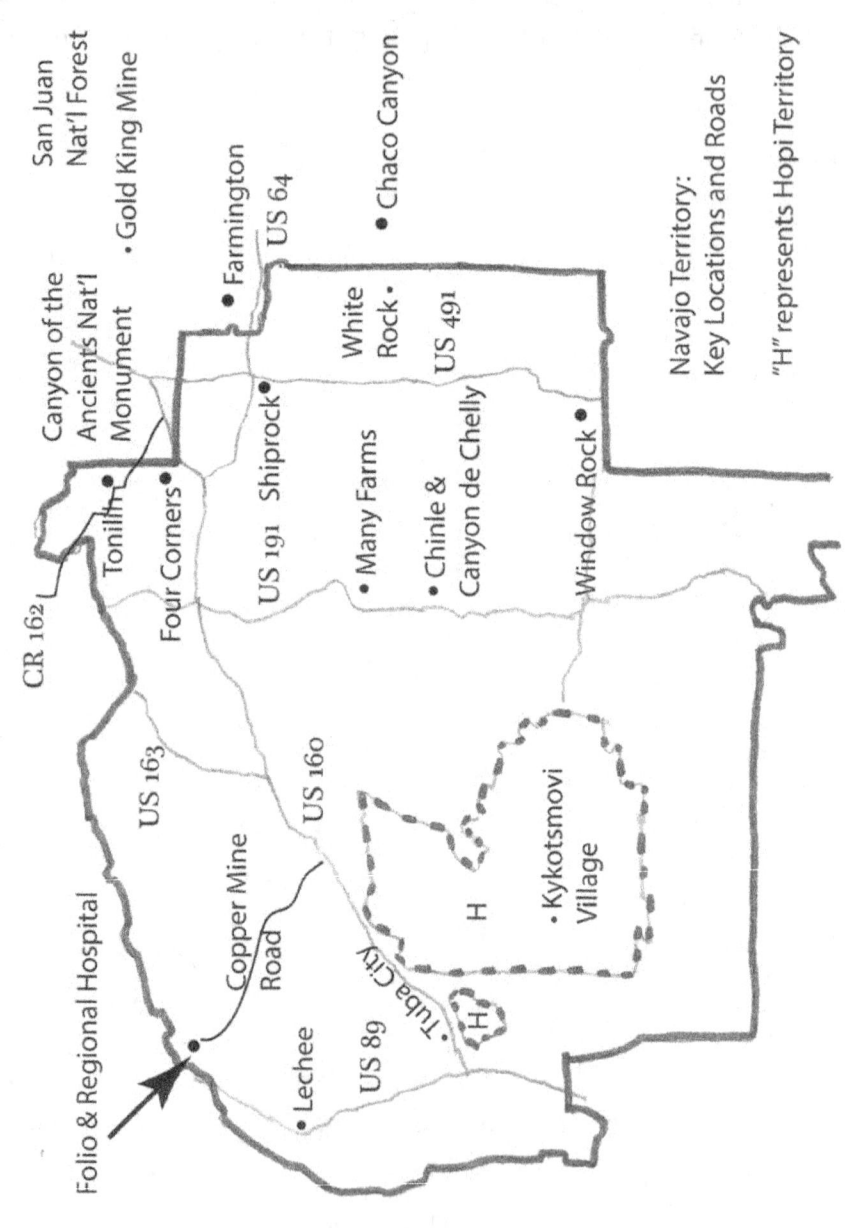

San Juan
Nat'l Forest

• Gold King Mine

Canyon of the
Ancients Nat'l
Monument

Farmington •

US 64

• Chaco Canyon

CR 162

Tonili

Four Corners

White
Rock •

US 491

Shiprock •

US 191

• Many Farms

• Chinle &
Canyon de Chelly

• Window Rock

US 163

US 160

Folio & Regional Hospital

Copper Mine
Road

Tuba City •

Kykotsmovi
Village

H

• Lechee

US 89

H

Navajo Territory:
Key Locations and Roads

"H" represents Hopi Territory

iv

Kiva Members

Ahiga [ah HEE gah] (Navajo, part-time hospital orderly)

Ahote [ah HOE tea] (Hopi; police deputy)

Chatima (Cha′tima) [chah TEA mah] (Hopi, student Medicine Elder)

Cheveyo [chev ē ō] (Hopi, works for a telephone company)

Chuchip [chew chip] (Hopi, autopsy technician)

Dr. Nastas Deschene [nahs tas de SHANE] (Navajo, coroner)

Gaagii [gah gē] (Navajo, student Medicine Elder)

Hokee [hoe kēy] (Navajo, police deputy, pilot)

Joseph White Eagle (honorary uncle, Chief of Police)

Niyol [Nī ōhl]] (Navajo, police deputy, computer hacker)

Spencer Hansen (Norwegian-American; medical student)

Susan Calvin (Anglo-American, journalist, author)

Tommy Chee (Navajo, nephew of Chief Joe, civilian)

Table of Contents

Chapter 1 Murder of Ton Yah

A gunshot crackles through the dry desert air. Among the sagebrush, a rabbit's ears stand erect and twitch. The desert blurs for a moment as a small cloud in the otherwise cloudless sky passes across the sun. A young man wearing blue jeans, moccasins, and a doeskin vest walks toward the east. The beads of his necklace – blue-green turquoise, yellow garnet, black obsidian, and white shell – shine in the rising sun.

~~~~~

Hokee puts the de Havilland Beaver DHC-2 aircraft into a slow right turn centered on a pickup truck in the desert two hundred fifty meters below. The truck is ten kilometers from the nearest road and surrounded by sagebrush. In the right seat, Niyol presses binoculars against the bubble window. "There's a body two hundred meters south of the truck," the Navajo Police Deputy announces.

Hokee banks the plane to the left and looks out his window. The high wing of the Beaver makes observation easy. He widens the turn and scans the ground. "I see it and I can land nearby. Call Chief Joe and ask if we should."

Niyol selects the preset radio channel and thumbs the talk button on his headset. The Nation's Police Chief answers. The chief has confidence in his young deputies and approves the landing.

A few tumbleweeds propelled by the breeze roll slowly across the desert floor, giving Hokee wind speed and direction.

He aligns the plane with a strip of desert speckled with sagebrush. He reduces power and slows to 70 knots, turns on carburetor heat to prevent icing – even in the hot and dry desert air – checks the hydraulic flap selector valve beside his seat, and pumps the handle. The flaps drop 48 degrees and both ailerons droop five degrees – part of the short take-off and landing, or STOL, capability of the plane.

Four-point harnesses hold the two deputies while 36-inch bush wheels bump over the desert. Hokee reports touchdown and GPS coordinates to the police dispatcher, then shuts down the engine and avionics.

"The body is about a hundred meters due east of us." Niyol looks through the sighting slots of his lensatic compass. "I'm centered on the top of the hill, there." The deputies walk toward the hill and reach the body minutes later.

"Old man, looks Navajo, lying on his back. An entry wound in his chest and a dried blood pool under him."

The wound and blood are not as striking as the man's clothes. "He's got on traditional stuff," Niyol says. "Knee-length moccasins, loincloth, and a bead necklace."

"And two raven feathers braided into his hair. He's a Medicine Elder," Hokee asserts. "See the canvas duffle bag? It's full, with sage spilling from the top. He was gathering sage for smudging."

The deputies are familiar with the rituals of both Navajo and Hopi Medicine Elders. Two members of their kiva society – one Navajo and one Hopi – study to become Medicine Elders. They weave the traditions of both cultures into ceremonies. Few people know kiva membership includes young men from both nations. Their elders would not approve. Even fewer know the kiva includes two Bilagáana – non-Indians – one of whom is a woman. No one outside the kiva knows about the mixed ceremonies.

Niyol uses his cell phone to take photos of the body while Hokee walks to the truck. He notes the license number and searches for registration, but does not find it.

~~~~~

"It was a high-velocity bullet that tumbled before it hit. The exit wound is bigger than a baseball." Niyol rolls the body only far enough to see this.

"Through and through, then." Chief Joe's voice crackles from the boy's cell phone.

"Yes, sir."

"I've dispatched a crime scene team. ETA four hours. Will you wait for them and secure the site?"

Niyol and Hokee exchange looks and nods. "Yes, sir."

The wings of the Beaver shade them, and the deputies have plenty of water and—

"MREs? You're not going to eat that, are you?" Hokee asks.

Niyol removes the contents of a *Meal Ready to Eat* pouch. "This one is good – beef in gravy and potatoes with cheese. Not as good as mutton – or as tough as goat. You can open another one or have the wheat crackers and peanut butter from this one."

Hokee snorts. "Gimme. Even the U.S. Army can't mess up peanut butter."

Hours later, Hokee sees a bright yellow crew-cab pickup lurching over the desert. He pokes Niyol, who is napping in the shade of the wing. "They're here."

The first person out of the truck is Dr. Deschene, the nation's coroner and a member of their kiva society. Chuchip, another kiva member, and two police technicians follow. Hokee and Niyol report to Dr. Deschene while the two technicians take metal detectors from the equipment boxes that sprout from the back of the truck and begin scanning the ground in the direction the bullet might have gone.

"Jaw and neck are in rigor," Dr. D says. "Fingers are; arms are not. He was likely killed around dawn. The entrance wound is high in his chest; the exit wound, lower in his back, so the shot may have come from above. Put him in a body bag, please – with his medicine bag. Anything in the truck?"

"Three hundred meters away from here in that direction," Hokee says as he points. "Key is in the ignition and there's no registration. The truck has automatic transmission and hand controls for gas and brakes. That's unusual, and there's no sign he needed them."

"Lock the duffle bag he filled with sage in the truck and bring the keys. Chief Joe will send someone to retrieve it."

The two technicians with the metal detectors return. One is holding a clear plastic evidence bag. "Found the bullet – it's in good condition and has some organic material that should match the victim."

"Did you mark where you found it?" Dr. D asks.

The two technicians pretend to be offended before pointing to a stake set among the sagebrush about sixty meters behind the body.

The technicians unload a theodolite and a bright yellow pole from the truck. A few minutes later, they report. "There are some inaccuracies, but given the trajectory of the bullet – where it hit the ground and how it passed through the body, the person who fired the shot was—" He points toward a ridge some 1200 meters away "—behind those rocks."

"Good thing he didn't stay around," Hokee mutters.

Niyol and the two technicians walk to the hill. More work with the metal detectors finds a shell casing, which a technician picks up with plastic tweezers and puts in an evidence bag. "Seven point six two NATO cartridge. Favorite bullet for snipers. He was sure no one would find this."

"Not a Navajo; not one of us," Niyol says. "Someone who thinks we are backward. Someone too confident."

Or someone who thinks he is invulnerable, the second tech thinks. "There are tire tracks, here. The two pairs of tracks are too regular to be anything but a dually – a fat-assed pickup with four rear wheels."

"It will be hard to get an impression from the sand," Niyol says.

The tech pulls a large, two-barreled caulk gun from his kit. "Not with this stuff. It's a dual-component casting plastic. Very liquid. The two parts mix when I squeeze them out, they flow into the track and harden quickly enough they won't sink into the sand." Within minutes, he lifts a cast of the tire tracks. "We carry only enough polyurethane for one cast of this size. I picked the track that showed a nick in one tire."

Dr. Deschene has wrapped up the crime scene investigation when they return. "Excellent work everyone. You remembered what you learned. *Ahéhee',* thank you. Chuchip and I will do the autopsy tomorrow."

~~~~~

Two young men, members of the Eastward Kiva Society, spend the rest of the day and the night fasting, preparing themselves to help the spirit of the murdered Medicine Elder find his way through the mist to Creator. The sun is still below the hills the next morning when Gaagii, whose name means *Raven*, and Chatima, *The Caller*, draw a circle in the desert near the hospital. In the center, they build a small fire on which Gaagii sprinkles *dził nát'oh*, mountain smoke. Although called tobacco, it is a mixture of plants carefully harvested from throughout the territory bounded by the sacred mountains. The mountain smoke will carry the words of their song high into the air so Creator may receive them.

Their song would sound familiar to both a Medicine Elder of the Navajo and a Master of Knowledge of the Hopi. The song would also sound strange, for the two young men have studied with Elders of their own nations – Gaagii the Navajo and Chatima the Hopi. Except for differences in language, they found many rituals of both nations to be similar, and merged them into a power greater than either, alone.

When the sun breaks over the hills and pierces the dark of night, the young men quench the fire and erase the circle before breaking their fast in the hospital cafeteria.

≈≈≈≈≈

Dr. Deschene closes the pathology laboratory to all but Chuchip. From an observation window above the lab, Joseph White Eagle, Chief of the Navajo Nation's Police, watches.

Dr. D begins the autopsy, speaking toward the microphone hanging over the stainless-steel table. "We are presented with the body of a man aged 82 years, Ton Yah, born to Tall House Clan, born for Silent Walker Clan. The Nation's Police provided identification. Weight and height have been recorded and are within normal limits. The apparent cause of death is a single bullet wound which entered the chest and exited the back. The size of the exit wound suggests a high-velocity bullet. A bullet and shell casing were recovered at the scene and are undergoing tests."

Because of the manner of death and at Chief Joseph's request, Dr. D conducts a forensic autopsy, which includes opening the skull and removing the brain.

"Other than the bullet wound, there is only one sign of trauma. The occipital bone has a depressed fracture with cracks radiating to the lambdoid suture. There is no remodeling of the bones. That and a small endocranial stain suggest the fracture is peri-mortem and resulted from falling backwards after being shot, with the back of his head striking the hard caliche of the desert surface."

Chief Joe pushes the intercom button. "In English, please?"

Dr. Deschene nods. "There is a fracture on the back of his skull that suggests a blow to the head, but it's not serious. I think the bullet drove him backwards, and he hit his head on the hard ground. There's some blood on the underside of the skull at that point, suggesting a slight brain bleed before his heart stopped beating. However, the size of the bullet wound marks it as the proximate cause of death."

Dr. D is both a forensic pathologist and the Navajo Nation's coroner. Three hours after the autopsy began, he announces the official findings. "Cause of death – gunshot wound; manner of death – homicide." Then, he directs Chuchip to close the Y-incision on the man's chest and wash the body. Both Dr. D and Chief Joe watch Gaagii and Chatima enter the lab and prepare the body for the man's final journey. They have safeguarded Ton Yah's medicine bag and cleaned his clothing. They dress the man and sprinkle herbs over him, clean his hair

7

and weave raven feathers into it, and wrap him in a wool blanket with his medicine bag before summoning the elders of his clan.

"Why do you not call a Medicine Elder to do this?" Chuchip asks.

"He was the last of the true Navajo medicine elders," Gaagii answers. "Those who now claim to be Medicine Elders imitate the songs, sand paintings, and rituals. They pretend to have power. They may even believe they have power, but the only power they have is the ability to take money from tourists and from their own people."

Dr. Deschene interrupts and speaks into the microphone that carries his words to the recorder and to Chief Joe. "I'll need lab results to be sure, but while the proximate cause of death is the bullet wound, his body is riddled with lymphoma – a cancer. He would likely have died in months, if not weeks."

Chief Joseph triggers the intercom in the observation room. "We have found only one close relative – a boy, the man's grandson. He is *Tsela* born to Bitter Weed Clan, born for Roan Horse Clan. He was crippled by polio and the boys at the school gave him a cruel nickname – Gahtsoh, meaning Rabbit."

~~~~~

Gahtsoh's grandfather, Ton Yah, was a Medicine Elder who told the boy the history of his people and stories of Creator. "Creator made the sky and the earth, and the things that live on the earth and in the waters. Creator made Father Sky and Earth Mother to protect us and give us Summer, Fall, Winter, and Spring to plant, harvest, and hunt. He made others to be our teachers and spirit guides."

Grandfather taught Gahtsoh the dances and the drum. "Most people hear only the four-four beat with the accent on the first beat. They do not hear the subtle changes in loudness and rhythm. These you will learn."

When the boy is eight, polio strikes and freezes his arms and legs and stops his breathing, his drumming, and his dancing. For two weeks, Grandfather Ton Yah sits in his hogan with Gahtsoh and lifts songs and prayers to Creator over the wheeze of the iron lung. The boy labors to speak a few words each time the machine exhales for him. "Grandfather, if Creator is ... so powerful why ... do I have the polio?" For a moment, he thinks Grandfather is angry. Grandfather told him that *why* is a word for someone who does not want to believe, and he forbade the boy to say it.

Ton Yah looks at the small boy in the huge, clanking machine and fashions an answer which will give the boy a deeper understanding of his culture. "Unlike the Hispanglo god, none of our teachers, not even Creator – our First Teacher – claim to be all-powerful. One of the Bilagáana elders said about their god thousands of years ago, *If god is good, he is not omnipotent; if god is omnipotent, he is not good.* That person captured an important difference between the Hispanglos, the Bilagáana, and The People.

"But we will thank Creator, because your doctor says you are recovering, and you will breathe by yourself, soon. The doctor is a Bilagáana, a Catholic, and believes it is a miracle."

"What do you belicve ... Grandfather?"

"I believe Creator may have a task for you. Now go to sleep. It is nearly midnight."

~~~~~

The boy recovers enough to leave the iron lung and regain control of his upper body, but his legs remain paralyzed.

9

After months of therapy, and with the aid of braces that extend from the soles of his feet to his hips and crutches that clamp onto his arms, he can walk. The braces lock his ankles and knees, forcing him to twist his body with every step and turning his walk into a lurch. It is a year before he can use the drum with the touch and skill his grandfather taught him. He can never again perform the dances.

Gahtsoh is too young to undertake a Spirit Quest and meet the totem animal who will become his spirit guide. He is too young to be initiated into his grandfather's kiva, but waits outside in Ton Yah's truck and listens to the drums and songs which tug at something deep inside him. *I am meant to be there*, he thinks.

Chapter 2 Vigil & Vision

Five years after polio struck, Gahtsoh attends his grandfather's funeral. A dozen men walk from the kiva. The first four carry on their shoulders a catafalque on which Gahtsoh's grandfather lies. Gaagii and Chatima wrapped the old man in a wool blanket. There are not enough buffalo to provide the traditional hide – even for the last Navajo Medicine Elder. Most buffalo herds are on land owned by Bilagáana or the US Park Service. Gahtsoh recognizes everyone except the two young men who walk behind the procession. They wear deerskin moccasins, leggings, and vests decorated with beads in patterns Gahtsoh does not recognize.

Gahtsoh struggles to follow the procession, lurching from foot to foot, his feet and crutches sliding on the shale. The two strangers drop back.

"The path to the sacred ground is treacherous, even for us. My name is Gaagii, of the Navajo."

The second stranger speaks. "I am Chatima of the Hopi. May we help you? How can we help?"

"Yes, please," Gahtsoh responds. "Will you hold my belt, one on each side? Don't pull hard unless you feel me falling. My name is *Tsela*, born to Bitter Weed, born for Roan Horse, but everyone calls me Gahtsoh." He does not see Gaagii and Chatima lift their eyebrows and look over his head at one another.

The trail is long. Gaagii speaks to the wind. "Gahtsoh's grandfather was the last true medicine elder of his clan and of the Navajo."

11

Chatima picks up the narrative. "Gaagii studied the Navajo ways of knowledge with a Medicine Elder, a true one, but Gaagii's teacher died six moons ago. I study with a Master of Knowledge of the Hopi, but he is old. His mind wanders and he will soon journey through the mist. Then, of our people's Masters of Knowledge, only I will remain."

Gaagii completes the story. "Chatima and I are – or will be soon – the only Medicine Elders of either the Navajo or the Hopi. But we have only partial and imperfect knowledge and no teachers."

Before Gahtsoh can question Gaagii and Chatima, the procession reaches a sacred place where a platform stands two meters above the ground. Men place the catafalque atop the platform, then turn and begin the return journey. Gaagii sees tears in Gahtsoh's eyes.

"Even a warrior may cry," Gaagii says. "You cry for your grandfather."

"No," the boy asserts. "I cry because no one of his clan stays to honor him. You are not of our clan and must leave. I will stand watch alone."

"We are not of your clan, but we are of something greater than any clan or nation; we will stay with you," Chatima says. "Creator will understand. Sit here." He and Gaagii gather sticks and build a small fire near the platform. Gaagii sprinkles the traditional herbs called mountain smoke on the fire. Gaagii's spirit guide, Raven, circles the platform and cries as he flies over the three watchers. First, Raven circles counterclockwise – the direction of the setting sun. Then Raven reverses his path and flies in the direction of the rising sun. Chatima sprinkles more pungent herbs on the fire. He and Gaagii begin a song. The words are not the words Gahtsoh's grandfather taught him, but the rhythm echoes in his chest, and he takes up two sticks to beat together. He feels Chatima's approval. After hearing the song through twice, Gahtsoh joins with the two older boys.

They continue to chant until the shadows of sunset cross the sacred ground. The sky becomes purple and then black, and the fire exhausts its fuel.

"It will be cold tonight," Chatima says. "Lie between us and share our warmth."

The next morning, the boys resume their song. Gahtsoh remembers the words from yesterday and joins with his voice and the sticks. Even though they have no food or water, they continue their call to Creator.

Night falls, and the three make ready for sleep.

Gahtsoh finds it hard to sleep. The desert's dry air has parched his mouth; his lips have cracked. His legs hurt. The polio robbed him of motor nerves but not sensory nerves, and he brought none of the pain pills he receives at the Chapter Health Service. He lies quietly and watches the stars until a presence interrupts his vigil.

The moon – nearly full – has risen and provides enough light for Gahtsoh to see a man standing beside the platform that holds his grandfather's body. Gray streaks the man's hair. Feathers are woven into it – eagle, raven, condor, and owl. A shield made from the thin, long leg bones of *naatsédlózii* – the roadrunner – covers his chest from neck to navel. A cloak of buffalo skin lies over his shoulders.

The man raises his hand and sprinkles stardust over the platform that holds Gahtsoh's grandfather. Gahtsoh gasps when he sees that the man is a giant – a giant who turns and puts his hand over his mouth to signal silence. A voice speaks only in Gahtsoh's head. "Hold out your hand."

A few of the stars land in Gahtsoh's hand. The man gestures, and Gahtsoh touches them with his tongue.

13

"Corn pollen, to feed him on his journey through the mist. Your grandfather was right. Creator has a task for you. You have done what you must do here. Depart to your home with the dawn." The figure disappears.

When Gahtsoh wakes, he sees no corn pollen. He accepts Gaagii and Chatima's help to travel the rocky trail and return to the place he had left his grandfather's truck.

~~~~~

Chuchip sets up a video conference between the offices of Dr. Deschene and Chief Joseph. Niyol, who stands by Chief Joe, greets Chuchip in Navajo; Chuchip responds in Hopi. Dr. Deschene and Chief Joe greet each other by first names.

"DNA from tissues on the bullet matches Ton Yah's DNA," Dr. D reports.

Chief Joe lifts the evidence bags holding the bullet and the shell casing. "The FBI matched these to a sniper rifle missing from a Drug Enforcement Agency armory in Tucson. The DEA reported the rifle missing two months ago. They think it got into the hands of one of the Mexican drug cartels."

The four conferees exchange looks. Niyol is first to speak. "Someone in the DEA sold the rifle to a *cartéle*. But why kill an old Medicine Elder?"

None of the answers offered are satisfactory. Chief Joe ends the conference.

~~~~~

The Eastward Kiva meets in the back room of the Tuba City Diner with iced tea and Navajo Tacos, which are both generous and inexpensive. This is important since only half of the twelve kiva members have proper jobs. The others find occasional work as day laborers or other part-time, minimum-wage jobs.

Chatima describes Ton Yah's funeral vigil and what Gahtsoh saw. "It is quite a story, and I wonder how real it is."

"He saw what he wanted to see," Niyol says. "Mixed with what his grandfather taught him."

"Or, Creator sent a real Medicine Elder," Gaagii says. "Or came, himself."

"You think?"

"Is there any way to tell? What about Gahtsoh's description of the man?"

"His grandfather would have told him what a Medicine Elder would wear."

"My teacher never wore that kind of necklace or breastplate," Gaagii says.

"Nor mine," Chatima adds.

Gaagii pushes his plate aside. He fiddles with his iced tea glass while gathering courage to speak. "Raven flew over us. First, counter-clockwise, a closing, proper for the vigil. Then clockwise, signaling an opening or beginning. That means something."

"At least we can help Gahtsoh, and he knows he can call us if he needs anything."

"Which is likely, considering how little help his clan was," Niyol grumbles. "You know they turned him over to juvie."

There is no answer to this accusation, but Susan Calvin smells a story. "Gahtsoh's grandfather was the last Navajo Medicine Elder. Someone murdered him. His grandson saw a vision of a Medicine Elder. Raven signaled a beginning. That would make a fine story for the Sunday supplements."

15

"It would paint us as ignorant savages, believing in what science is unable or unwilling to explain," Niyol says. "I am sorry, Ms. Susan, but I do not like it."

"I never want to offend you, Niyol," Susan says. "Would you help me turn this into a teaching story for children? The People have lost so much history and so many stories. You and I might help rebuild them."

Niyol knows Susan Calvin was an investigative reporter until one of her investigations came too close to the President. The paper's owner bowed to pressure and fired her. She has turned her journalistic talents into a project to preserve Navajo culture and history. Niyol agrees to her proposal, and conversation turns to another event.

"Spencer will get here tomorrow," Ahiga mumbles through a mouthful of food. Spencer is Dr. Deschene's protégé, the white-haired Norwegian, son of mining engineers and the first of the kiva society members to have been disfellowshipped by their church and scout troop. When they initiated Spencer into the kiva, they named him Atsa, *Eagle*, because he had flown ahead of them.

Now, his kiva has plans for him.

~~~~~

Spencer's flight from Boston is a milk-run, stopping at Buffalo, St. Louis, Omaha, and Denver before reaching Phoenix. It is the cheapest flight he can find. The Navajo Nation pays Spencer's college expenses and they expect him to become a doctor and serve The People. Although not adopted by the Navajo, he is a member of a kiva society and knows the obligation his education will create. He understands this completely.

16

What he does not understand is the Air Marshall who accosts him and presents his badge before Spencer can leave the plane at Phoenix. "Mr. Hansen, someone will intercept your baggage at the carousel. Remove your carry-on from the overhead and keep your hands where I can see them."

Spencer wants to run, but he knows the power of the Air Marshalls since they became a cog in the gears of Homeland Security. He has dual citizenship, but the only passport he has is Norwegian, the country of his birth. He fights tremors as he removes his small duffle from the overhead and precedes the Air Marshall from the plane.

Two young men wearing the khaki uniforms of the Navajo Nation Police are waiting. Their web belts hold nine-millimeter pistols on one side, Tasers on the other. Pouches and pockets hold ammunition and handcuffs. "This the one you want?" the Air Marshall asks.

"Yes, and thank you," one of the uniformed figures replies. "We'll take it from here."

The Air Marshall melts into the crowd.

"You guys scared the pee out of me," Spencer says.

Niyol and Hokee grin and then push and shove one another to greet Spencer.

"We're glad you're home, *Atsa*," Hokee says, using Spencer's kiva society name. "Remember when you pranked me at that autopsy? Are we even, now? I hope so, because we need you more than ever."

Spencer remembers the prank that left Hokee alone in the pathology lab holding the stomach of a corpse, but before he can ask Hokee why they need him, the young man grabs Spencer's duffel from the carousel. Niyol leads them toward an alarmed exit door. "Don't worry. We're cleared for this." He punches buttons on a keypad, and the door opens without alarm.

At the foot of the stairs, an airplane is waiting. It is a single-engine tail-dragger, with main landing gear under the cockpit and a third wheel in the rear. The vertical stabilizer is painted with the insignia of the Nation's police. Hokee is breathless with excitement, and gasps between sentences. "Chief Joe got this in a drug raid. A company in Canada overhauled it. I went to Vancouver for a check ride. Since I'm the only qualified pilot, it's pretty much my plane. Do you like it?"

"It's a beauty! What is it?"

"1950 De Havilland DHC-2, Beaver. It belonged to the Bilagáana Air Force, but they mothballed it in 1952 with only a hundred hours on the engine."

~~~~~

Hokee ties down the plane at the Folio Airport and locks the control surfaces to keep wind from moving the rudder, ailerons, and elevator. "Chief Joe doesn't want me to fly at night in a single-engine plane," he says. "How about supper at the Tuba City Diner?"

Spencer looks around the deserted airport parking area. "Dr. D said he would meet me and tell me where I'll be staying."

"He'll be at the diner. It's supposed to be a surprise, though."

"I'll act surprised."

Spencer recognizes Chief Joe's Humvee parked outside the Tuba City Diner. Although the military model is not marked as a police vehicle, it's hard to miss the forest of antennas on the roof. "Is the chief here or is he letting Tommy drive the Hummer?"

"Chief's kind of busy … you'll learn more later. And Tommy has grown a lot since you left," Hokee says.

"Three inches, at least, and he's all legs, so no problem reaching the pedals." Niyol says and laughs.

Banners of civic clubs – Lions, Rotary, Kiwanis, and others – decorate the back room of the Tuba City Diner. Spencer chokes with emotion when he sees members of the kiva society waiting for him. A waitress follows Spencer into the room with a cart loaded with plates of Navajo Tacos and glasses of iced tea. Boys and young men vie with one another to greet Spencer with hands clasped at wrists in the manner of warriors. Spencer's eyes widen when Susan Calvin stands to hug him. She's pregnant – about five months, Spencer estimates. He looks around, but does not see Dr. Deschene.

Chatima knows who Spencer is looking for. "He called a few minutes ago. Must have been right behind you. He'll be here—"

At that moment, Dr. D steps into the room. He greets Spencer as an uncle to his nephew. "Shiye´."

Spencer replies with a word from the Navajo kinship system, the word for maternal uncle, "Shidá´í." Those two simple words are enough to acknowledge and affirm the depth of their relationship. They acknowledge that Dr. D adopted Spencer under Navajo law to prevent him from being deported when his parents disfellowshipped him. The words keep alive the memory of the doctor becoming Spencer's mentor and enrolling the young man in a prestigious eastern medical school.

~~~~~

"It looks like Spencer missed fry bread more than he missed us," Susan teases minutes after the food is served.

"There's not an authentic Navajo Taco in Boston," Spencer says. "And pizza is not an acceptable substitute."

19

"What did you study this year?" The question comes from Niyol. He was a computer hacker before joining the police force; now, he hacks on the side of the law. After Spencer, he's the person most interested in science.

"So far, anatomy is easiest. It's all from a book, and I learned more anatomy than that from Dr. D.

"The 'Population Health' course might be useful. We learned many diseases occur in small populations because of gene mutations inherited from common ancestors – Ashkenazim and Sephardic Jews in Eastern Europe and New York, Amish and Mennonites in Pennsylvania. Someday, we may face something like that."

Spencer realizes he's lost everyone's interest except Dr. Deschene's, and changes the subject. "Hokee said Chief Joe has been busy, and that you would tell me what's going on."

"Supper is not the place for details," Dr. D says. "But in the past eight months, too many people have died with an assortment of strange symptoms. We may be facing something genetic. We may be catching up with the Ashkenazim and the Amish."

Chapter 3 Trip to Tonilih

On the drive back to Folio, Dr. Deschene outlines the first tasks of Spencer's summer. "I enrolled you and Chuchip in a course of independent study in forensic pathology at the community college. You will live in a suite in the student dormitory. Chuchip lives in the other bedroom and will drive you wherever you need to go, including the grocery store. Your suite has a kitchen. We have an autopsy tomorrow. The next day, Hokee will fly us and Chuchip to the Tonilih Airport where Tommy will meet us with his uncle's Humvee. Pack sturdy clothes for two weeks."

"I probably shouldn't ask why," Spencer says.

"You'll find out when we get there, and I don't want to prejudice your thinking."

Susan's laugh is melodic and light. "Dear, give the boy a break. He's been at medical school for nearly nine months! Doesn't he deserve a little time to himself?"

"Thank you, Ms. Susan," Spencer says, "but that can wait. If Dr. D has assignments, they're going to be much more … maybe, 'fun' seems like the wrong word, but it works for me."

≈≈≈≈≈

Chuchip knocks on Spencer's door at 5:30 AM the next morning. Thirty minutes later, they are first in line at the hospital cafeteria. Their employee ID cards give them a discount, and the food is pretty good for hospital food. At seven, they reach the pathology lab. It is already unlocked and Dr. D has rolled in a gurney with the body. Chuchip and Spencer unzip the body bag and transfer the body to a stainless-steel table.

Dr. D turns on the microphone and begins. "We are presented with the body of an elderly woman of obvious and known Athabascan ancestry. Her weight is 125 kilograms; height 160 centimeters. Body mass index of 49 plus appearance confirms clinical obesity. She died in the hospital two days ago after being in care for four days. This will be a clinical autopsy." He adds the identification and details provided by the hospital records department.

Chuchip continues the initial external exam. "Her skin and eyes are yellow – jaundiced – suggesting cirrhosis. She has no visible surgical scars, but does have a tattoo that looks like barbed wire around her left ankle."

Dr. D hands Spencer the scalpel. Spencer begins the Y-cut at the acromia, the bony bumps at the top of the shoulders, and cuts to the bottom of the sternum, moving aside her pendulous breasts as he does so. Then, he cuts downward toward the pubis, making a detour around the navel. After folding the V from the top of the cut upward and over the woman's face he separates the lower part of the skin, cutting it away from the rib cage and pulling it back from the midline, exposing the peritoneum.

Chuchip uses pruning shears from a garden-supply store to clip the ribs and remove them and the sternum. Dr. D makes a small incision in the peritoneum. There is a hiss. Spencer switches the exhaust fan to *high*.

"What would make a body smell like a … a fart?" Chuchip asks, and blushes because he doesn't have a better word.

"Flatulence, is the word you want," Dr. D says without censure. "Spencer? What might be the answer?"

Spencer begins by talking around the question. "It's too soon after death for any significant putrefaction to occur and she's been in a refrigerated drawer. The peritoneum deflated a couple of inches when you cut it. I think the intestinal tract was compromised and gas leaked from the large intestine into the abdominal cavity."

Dr. D continues to open the peritoneum, the membrane that covers internal organs, and gestures for Spencer to take over. Spencer cuts the liver's three blood vessels and its ligaments and removes the liver. He removes and weighs the adrenal gland, heart, kidneys, pancreas, and spleen, then hands them to Chuchip who takes samples, which he puts in bottles with preservative.

"The liver is large, yellowish, and greasy," Dr. D says as he slices across the smaller, left lobe. "And visibly fatty. Because she was under treatment for cirrhosis and died after four days in the hospital, we will not do a tox screen.

"We will save samples of the organs in formalin in case there are questions, later. Take an additional sample of the liver and the pancreas. Spencer will prepare microscope slides, and you both will write a report of what you see." Dr. Deschene is in teaching mode. He sees the surprise on his two assistants faces. "Your summer internship will count toward graduation credits. Even Spencer's fancy medical school in Boston agreed to transfer credits from an obscure community college." Chuchip and Spencer exchange glances. They know it is Dr. D's reputation rather than that of the college which guarantees the credits.

Spencer spots something and grabs a small plastic ruler. "Sir, it's hard to tell without a point of comparison, but the lymph nodes in the cavity – they all seem larger than they should be."

While Spencer measures, Chuchip takes photos. "All are bigger than one point five centimeters; some nearly three centimeters. That suggests lymphoma, but she was a big woman. Would her size make that much difference?"

Dr. D looks at Spencer through the top of his goggles. "Did anyone tell you about the Medicine Elder's autopsy? Anyone?"

"No, sir."

"Did anyone say anything about lymphoma?"

"No, sir."

"That is what I wasn't going to tell you until you discovered it for yourself. It seems you have. Sample several lymph nodes – try for matching pairs or clusters from each side of the body. And get another sample of the spleen. We don't have the equipment to do the tests we need to do, but I will send the samples to the forensic laboratory at James Holomon University. Their lab is equipped for it, and they'll enjoy a chance to use their new MRI machine."

Chuchip pushes aside the large intestine, preparing to detach it from the rectum when it rolls to show a split about half-way down the descending colon. This time, it is he who kicks the exhaust fan speed to high. "This must have been where the break was."

Dr. D nods agreement, and then asks, "What was the TOD – the time of death? Can we determine if the damage to the intestine was ante-mortem, peri-mortem, or post-mortem?"

Spencer gives Chuchip a chance to answer before he says, "If it had been ante-mortem, she would have died of peritonitis pretty quickly. Since the only sign of infection are the enlarged lymph nodes – wait a minute." He strips off his gloves and begins typing on a nearby computer terminal. "Her hospital chart doesn't show either above normal temperature or a high white cell count. Likely, not peritonitis."

"I agree," Dr. D says. "The damage to the intestine was post-mortem, and probably an artifact of handling the body – compounded by over-eating for years. Cause of death – cirrhosis of the liver; manner of death – natural."

Dr. D concludes the autopsy, leaving Spencer and Chuchip to close the incision and wash the body. When they are finished, Dr. D announces. "We leave early tomorrow for Tonilih."

Chuchip interrupts. "Awesome! A field trip!" He and Spencer exchange high-fives.

Dr. D smiles at his young assistants' enthusiasm, but tries otherwise to ignore the interruption. "Don't forget – pack for a couple of weeks in the backcountry. We will be guests at the Tonilih Chapter House, but Tommy will bring canteens, water, MREs, and sleeping bags in case there's some field work. Hokee will meet us at the Folio airport. An orderly will take us there at five o'clock tomorrow morning."

That afternoon, Chuchip puts bags of groceries on the kitchen counter. "You knew I couldn't answer his question about time of death. You covered for me."

"Time of death is the first thing the police want to know, and the hardest thing for the pathologist or medical examiner to determine," Spencer says. "Sorry, that sounds like Dr. D lecturing."

"Yeah, that's what he says. But body temperature—"

"You stick a liver thermometer – that's the dial on a sharp, long probe – in one place and a rectal thermometer in … in another place, you're going to get two different readings. There are too many variables, including air temperature, how long the body has been exposed, clothing, how fat the person was. If we get there quickly, and are sure nothing changed since death, we can come up with a pretty good estimate. But, at a murder scene, that's not likely what we will find.

"Dr. D wasn't trying to prank you on body temperature – he wants us to know it's not always easy to figure out.

"I have a question for you – something I didn't learn last summer working for Dr. D," Spencer says. "He said the autopsy today was a clinical autopsy, but the notes you showed me on the shooting victim say, 'forensic autopsy.' I know the difference. At least, I know a forensic autopsy is more thorough and is done when the person is the victim of a crime. I know a clinical autopsy is less invasive and less thorough. But how does Dr. D decide?"

Chuchip is pleased Spencer asks him this question. Spencer is the smart one, the scientific one, and the one who is going to college to become a real doctor. Chuchip was educated in a school that lacked indoor plumbing and whose textbooks and teachers were years out of date. He is content to be a technician, although he is happy that Dr. D enrolled him in the community college.

Chuchip answers Spencer as he sorts groceries into cabinets. "Dr. D is the coroner, and he can order a clinical autopsy anytime he thinks the person may have died from a contagious disease. He also performs clinical autopsies at the request of the family or if the hospital administrator has a question about the cause of death of someone who dies in the hospital."

Spencer is dividing his time between what Chuchip is saying and making mental lists of meals he will prepare using the groceries when they return from Tonilih.

"Our law requires a forensic autopsy of anyone in official custody," Chuchip says. "That law was made for people in police custody, but Dr. D says it also covers children in custody of Family Services or an FS guardian." Chuchip wraps up his explanation by saying, "Chief Joe can order a forensic autopsy any time there's a suspicious death, and they are automatic when a death is associated with a crime."

"That's the first time this has made sense to me," Spencer says. "Thanks! And, will the other autopsy techs – the ones from last year – will they go with us tomorrow?"

Chuchip shakes his head. "One got a job as an EMT at Four Corners. The other two are working somewhere else. I've lost track of them. Besides, the hospital administrator is pressuring Dr. D to justify my pay – and yours. If Dr. D wasn't a good friend of the college provost, we'd be sleeping in one of the abandoned trailers out in the desert."

~~~~~

A year ago, Spencer had flown with Dr. Deschene to a body farm in Colorado and to the Mescalero Apache Reservation. Both trips were to investigate suspicious deaths. But this is Chuchip's first time in an airplane. Spencer and Niyol throw their duffels in the cargo space behind the rear seat and gesture for Chuchip to take the copilot's seat. Dr. D curls up on the rear bench seat and seems to be asleep before takeoff.

Chuchip spends the first half hour with his face pressed to the bubble window, watching the terrain passing below. Then he sits back. "Hmph! Nothing to see except geologies. I get enough of that driving Dr. D around in the coroner's truck." He leans back and tries to nap, but only twenty minutes later Hokee's voice comes over everyone's headphones. "Please place your seats and tray tables in their upright and locked positions. And somebody wake up Dr. D and get him in a seat belt. That would be you, Spencer. We're about to land at Tonilih."

He switches the intercom to a radio frequency. "Tonilih Unicom, this is Navajo Police DHC-2 Beaver one-mile west, crossing midfield." There is no reply.

"Not surprising," Hokee tells Chuchip on the intercom. "There's not much traffic and no fixed base operator. But if there's anyone in the air nearby, they'll know where we are and be on the lookout for us. See the windsock? Wind is from the north-north-west. We'll land on Runway 36." He switches to the radio. "Tonilih traffic, DHC-2 crossing midfield from the west for right downwind Runway 36."

There is still no answer.

The plane touches down just past the numbers that mark the beginning of the runway and turns off halfway down the 7,000-foot strip. "Chart says the parking apron is cracked and sometimes has chunks of asphalt. I don't want to go any farther. And Tommy's seen us – there's the Humvee," Hokee announces.

Tommy and Niyol hop out of the Humvee to greet them and help load duffels into the vehicle. Hokee waits until they have driven away before turning the Beaver and taxiing to the runway. A scan of the sky, a radio call, and he turns left onto the runway. With his current load, he won't need more than 1,000 feet of the remaining 3,500 feet of runway. He runs up the 450 horsepower, 9-cylinder radial engine, checks the magnetos, and sets the gyrocompass to 360 degrees and cages it. He will release it on his rollout when the plane is aligned with the runway.

Below him, Tommy turns the Humvee northwest from the airport onto Utah Road 162.

"It will take us about thirty minutes to reach the Tonilih Chapter House. The Chapter President will meet us and will tell us why we are here," Dr. D says before tilting his Tilly hat over his eyes, and falling asleep.

The road runs through high desert – nearly 1500 meters elevation and barren except for scrubby trees and sagebrush. Houses are small. Many have a hogan nearby; it looks like all have at least one pickup truck parked on the dirt driveway or in the hardpan yard.

Forty percent of the Navajo do not have easy access to water. About halfway to Tonilih, a windmill and water tank mark a small trading post, a place where some of The People who don't have running water or wells can fill tanks and bottles. Graffiti – "No DAPL" – marks the eaves of the dun-colored building.

"What's that?" Spencer asks. "DAPL, I mean."

"Dakota Access Pipe Line," Niyol says. "Even here, feelings run strong about this attempt by the Bilagáana to desecrate the sacred lands of our brothers and sisters."

~~~~~

The Tonilih Chapter Government is one of 110 established under the Navajo Nation. Dr. Deschene's party is met by the Chapter President, the Council Delegate, and a nurse. After names are exchanged and coffee poured, the president defers to the nurse.

"I am Bertha Toon, Charge Nurse at the Tonilih Comprehensive Health Care Facility. For five years, we have seen more and more people with a wide and seemingly unrelated set of symptoms ranging from chronic, recurring headaches to muscle weakness and fatigue, to aching joints. Cirrhosis of the liver is on the rise, and there have been five miscarriages in the past fourteen months. All were among young and healthy women. A number of children have been treated for multiple broken bones. We suspected abuse, but there were no bruises and no other signs of abuse. There seems to be something wrong

29

with the bones' uptake of calcium. We have five children with acute lymphoblastic leukemia. That's twice what we would expect for the entire Nation in one year."

She pauses only long enough to catch her breath when Dr. Deschene asks, "Do you have any ideas of the etiology?"

Chuchip pokes Spencer in the ribs. Spencer whispers to him, "Etiology – cause of disease."

Nurse Toon responds to Dr. D's question. "We cannot conduct or afford all the tests that are indicated. The only tests we can do in-house are a Basic Metabolic Panel and Liver Function. The liver tests are almost always far outside of normal range, and, frankly, don't tell us anything we can't determine from other indications of alcoholism."

"Alcoholism," Dr. D says, and then asks, "Have you considered Fetal Alcohol Spectrum Disorder?"

Nurse Toon's face clouded. "That's something else we understand. And, yes, we see it, and there's some overlap between that and what we're finding in the youngest children. But there's something more, something we're not seeing.

"Our caseload has increased nearly fifty percent in the past eighteen months and the staff is overwhelmed. We don't know what to do."

"Very succinct, Nurse Toon," Dr. Deschene says. "There must be other symptoms documented in medical records. Has anyone listed, counted, and correlated them?"

"Yes and no, Doctor. There are other symptoms, but we do not have the resources to properly maintain the records, much less do any kind of analysis."

"That is where we shall begin. The Council said you would provide quarters?"

After the group discusses logistics, Nurse Toon takes the front passenger seat of the Humvee and directs Tommy to the Comprehensive Health Care Facility and a parking place marked

Police Only. "I understand Chief Joe is your uncle, and this is his vehicle. That makes you police. We have guest quarters – better than you would get at the Chapter House – and a cafeteria. An orderly will deliver your duffle bags while I take you to medical records."

~~~~~

Nurse Toon leads Dr. D and the others to a room crowded with file cabinets. Stacks of record folders cover the floor and every horizontal surface except for a table pushed against a bank of cabinets. "The folders which are not in file cabinets are the most recent," Dr. D guesses.

"Yes."

"Then, send someone for boxes, please … we passed a moving truck rental place in town. They sell boxes. Get the small ones. And some packing tape." He hands the nurse a credit card. "Council will pay."

Dr. D then sets ground rules for his assistants. "Each of you will take a stack of folders. Look in the records for all entries five years old or more recent. When you finish a folder, put it in a box. Label the folders and the boxes with your name. We'll help file them properly later. At least they won't be scattered.

"For each record folder, on a separate piece of paper, list name, age, sex, MRN – that would be Medical Record Number. Then list date, symptoms, test results, diagnosis, treatment, prognosis, any entry in the record. If there's a death certificate, record cause and manner of death and who signed it. If there's an autopsy report, give me the folder. Initial and date the folder and move on to the next folder. Sign and date the summary and pass it to Niyol.

"Niyol? You have your laptop. Everyone will give you their summaries. I want to be able to count symptoms, test results, diagnoses, and outcomes and do cross-correlations on every factor. If you don't understand what someone calls a symptom or diagnosis or outcome, ask them. Questions?

"What about location?" Spencer asks.

"What are you thinking?"

"You said we were looking for lymphoma, a cancer. What about cancer clusters?"

"Genetics, too," Chuchip says. "Some cancers have a genetic basis. At least, I remember that's what you said."

Dr. Deschene smiles at both young men. "Good thinking. And much faster than I was. Let's go to the cafeteria and talk about this over lunch. You have found something to help Niyol build his database. Maybe we will find more."

The cafeteria does not have as large a selection as the Navajo Western Regional Hospital, but the food is good and the room is quiet enough that Dr. D's team can hold a conversation.

Spencer begins. "The National Institutes of Health say cancer clusters are real but they haven't found much proof of environmental contributions."

"That's because they don't look very hard," Niyol says. "If the NIH admitted there was a cause of a cancer cluster, some big industry would get sued for cleanup and medical costs, and the industry would send lobbyists to the congress to cut funds for the NIH."

Chuchip snorts before saying, "That sounds like a conspiracy theory, brother."

"Conspiracy theories have to start somewhere, and somewhere at their root is something real," Niyol says.

Spencer tries to make peace between his kiva brothers. "The first cancer cluster wasn't geographic, but occupational. In the late 1700s a doctor found testicular cancer in chimney sweeps who were exposed to polycyclic aromatic hydrocarbons

– from burning coal. Of course, he didn't know what the chemicals were and just thought the cause was smoke and soot."

Niyol folds his arms and glares. "And what about mesothelioma, from asbestos? What about the ten-billion-dollar settlement fund for glyphosphate? They both are real and are happening right now! They prove my point."

Dr. D enters the discussion to restore harmony. "The point is that we should be looking at occupation and location and relatives. We'll add those to the list. The records should have the name of an emergency contact. Record that and the contact's phone number and address. We will have to do some field work to learn if relatives are in the database – or should be."

Five days later, the team looks over the Records Room. The folders which once were scattered on top of file cabinets and in stacks on the floor are now in labeled boxes. Niyol has entered data on more than two hundred patients into his laptop. "That was the easy part," Dr. D says. "Now, for some field work to fill in the blanks. Niyol has printed three lists with details – including name and address of the emergency contact person – and forms with blanks for the information we want. We can telephone many of them, but it would be better to visit. We will form three teams. Niyol and I will be with the Chapter President, Spencer and Chuchip with the Council Delegate, and Tommy and Nurse Toon will be the third team. The Chapter President and the Council Delegate will drive their own vehicles. Tommy will drive the Humvee."

Dr. D sets ground rules for contact, condolences, and data collection. "Not everyone has an address, but each team will have a local person who knows the territory."

"Yeah," Niyol says, "*Five miles from town on Road 2080, turn right at the cottonwood grove, it's two more miles on the left* isn't an address, which is how so many of us were disenfranchised in the last election. And that's not a conspiracy theory, it's a fact." His brow hoods his eyes in a way that dares anyone to contradict him.

~~~~~

Dr. D's first stop is a small settlement where the brother of one of the deceased lives. Cottonwood trees shade the two trailers. A few dozen meters away stands a windmill which turns slowly in the breeze and fills a stock tank to provide water for the sheep grazing nearby. The sheep are guarded and herded by two dogs which turn and bark at the truck before resuming their duty.

The Chapter President stops his truck about thirty meters from the trailers and taps the horn. A trailer door opens and a man steps out, signaling the truck might approach. When they are about ten meters from the trailer, they stop and then get out of the truck.

The Council President greets the man. "Ya´ateeh, Sani."

"Ya´ateeh, I know you," the man replies. "What brings you and strangers here?"

The Council President offers condolences on the death of the man's brother, introduces Dr. Deschene and Niyol, and explains their mission. Over coffee, the man talks about his brother while Niyol takes notes.

"This one went well," the Council President says as they drive away. "I've known Sani for years. Not all will be this easy."

~~~~~

The man at Spencer and Chuchip's first stop is wary until Spencer asks if he might fill his canteen at the horse trough kept filled by an Aermotor windmill. "It has been said, if you wait quietly enough for long enough the desert will speak to you, but

34

a person who does not listen to the desert will be dead in a few hours."

The man smiles at this obvious Bilagáana's understanding and his use of formal language to begin his statement. He gestures to a hand pump next to the hogan. "Fill your canteen from there. The water has not been fouled by horse spit."

Spencer laughs. "I've shared water with horses and more, but I thank you for your kindness."

~~~~~

The teams reassemble at the hospital that evening, and compare notes. They have completed fifteen data forms. Dr. D smiles when he speaks. "A good day's work. We started with those close in, and will have to drive farther tomorrow. If we continue at this rate, we should have at least forty-five visits completed before the end of the week."

"With the two hundred thirteen other forms, that's enough to run some statistical correlations," Niyol said. "Including getting correlation coefficients to tell us whether factors are related or just coincidence."

Five more days, and the work is complete. The Council President hosts a supper for Dr. D and his team. The boys avoid the pizza, and order Navajo Tacos, which they judge to be as good as those in Tuba City.

"I will tell the owner," Nurse Toon says. "He's my brother and will be very happy to hear your praise."

Tommy wakes everyone before dawn the next morning. "Chief Joe wants to know what you found and told me to bring you to Window Rock. It's about a two-hour drive. Then we will

35

drive to Folio." He turns to Dr. Deschene. "May we stop and visit Gaagii and Chatima?"

Dr. D agrees, and it is just after noon when they reach the trailer outside Kykotsmovi Village where Gaagii and Chatima live. After Gaagii pours coffee, Spencer speaks. "Chatima, you wrote me to say that you all agreed to change the name of the kiva from E´e´aahjigo to Ha´a´aahjigo, from 'westward' to 'eastward.' But you didn't tell me why. Will you tell me, now?"

"East is the white-shell direction, where *Jóhonaa´éí*, the Sunbearer wakes and begins his journey," Chatima says. "It symbolizes beginning, cleansing, and rebirth."

Gaagii adds to the story. "East symbolizes creativity, awareness, developing ideas, innovation. It is altogether right and proper for young men who desire to put aside the past."

"We first chose west because we were bitter when our relationships with the scouts, the church, and our parents ended and we were disfellowshipped," Chatima says. "We're all still good with the 'trustworthy, loyal, helpful,' part of it – but we draw the line at 'reverent' and the hard line of our troop leader and the Bishop."

Chapter 4 First Spirit Quest

The morning sun has barely breached the horizon when Gahtsoh struggles to step quietly through the ten-wide trailer. The trailer is the home of his *Shimá yázhi*, his only maternal aunt, and her common-law husband who Family Services assigned to be his guardians. Now, after locking Gahtsoh in the back bedroom, the two are passed out, drunk. The man slouches and snores in a tatty recliner while a television plays static. The woman lies on a broken-down couch surrounded by beer bottles. Gahtsoh still holds the slat from the Venetian blind he used to spring the lock and escape his prison. The slat is flimsy, but the edges are sharp and he is determined to use it to defend himself. He is spared that task when he stumbles and kicks a beer bottle against the wall, but the sleepers do not stir. Gahtsoh takes the keys to his grandfather's truck and works his way out the door and down the stack of cinderblocks that pass for steps. His only clothing is no-brand running shoes and a thin, cheap 'warm-up suit' from Family Services. They offer scarce protection from the chill.

His braces and crutches do not excuse him from going on Spirit Quest, a search for the totem animal who will guide his life. He should look for a place on one of the four sacred mountains. But, the sacred mountains no longer lie within Navajo territory, but are many miles away. Decades ago, the army of the Bilagáana pushed his people from the plains and mountains into a harsh desert which they called a reservation. The Bilagáana stripped the mountains of virgin timber and then plowed them for ski slopes where they make artificial snow from partly processed sewage water.

None of these places will suit Gahtsoh's Spirit Quest. He must find a different place of power where his spirit guide and his grandfather's spirit can find him. The truck has a quarter-tank of gas, and Gahtsoh has no money for more. He climbs into the driver's seat, unlocks his braces at the knees to fold his feet under the pedals, grabs the hand control Ton Yah installed, and points the truck to the east. He will drive until he finds a place that calls to him.

The gas gauge reads empty when Gahtsoh reaches the entrance of Chaco Canyon. He feels a pull from a rocky hill on his left, and drives towards the hill, across an arroyo and flat desert marked only by tumbleweeds. The engine dies from lack of fuel just as he reaches the foot of the hill. Leaving the now useless keys, he swings his legs onto the ground, locks his braces, and hooks the crutches around his arms. The duffle bag of sage Ton Yah was collecting when he was murdered is still in the truck. It will serve as fuel for Gahtsoh's fire. The weight of the bag threatens his balance as he lurches toward a hill isolated by aeons of erosion. The trail is stony; he makes no tracks for the Bilagáana Park Service to follow, and they are the only ones who might do so.

The boy carries only the bag of sage and his grandfather's smudge fan of three eagle feathers bound with a rawhide thong. They are all he needs for his quest and are more than most boys would have.

The higher he climbs, the stronger the Breath of Creator becomes. It whips his shirt and scours his face with sand. Is the wind a good sign or a bad one? Or is it neither? Gahtsoh's grandfather had been clear. "Not everything that happens, even during a ceremony, is a message from Creator. And it is never easy to understand what Creator says. Listen and learn, and remember what you see and hear, but more important, remember what you feel." With those words, Ton Yah had touched

Gahtsoh's breast. Even now, the boy feels that touch in his heart. *Perhaps this means I will see Grandfather's spirit,* he thinks.

Gahtsoh reaches a ledge and realizes he can go no further. The scant trail ends here. He drops the bag of sage.

After catching his breath, the boy begins his tasks. He removes his braces, but keeps them and the crutches close at hand. Using only his arms, he scuttles across the ledge and takes stones from the rubble to make a circle in which he will build his fire. Then, he sorts the sage, and selects the driest to start the fire. He shaves the thick, oily stem of one branch to serve as tinder and then takes flint and steel from his pocket. The wind dies. *That means the fire is important,* he thinks, before remembering his grandfather's caution. When the fire catches, Gahtsoh adds larger sticks. Slowly, carefully, he creates light to beat back the gathering darkness. He sits cross-legged and looks over the desert before him.

Gahtsoh feeds the fire, one bit of sage at a time. Night has fallen when Wolf approaches. Gahtsoh is both afraid and excited. Wolf is a powerful spirit, and an important totem. But the wolf only paces back and forth beyond the fire circle. The wolf stops his pacing, looks at Gahtsoh, and vanishes. Gahtsoh bends forward until his hair falls from his shoulders and touches the ground. *Wolf does not want to be the spirit guide of a crippled boy.*

Man Who Rotates, the stars the Bilagáana call the Big Dipper, has turned through a quarter of his circle when Raven appears. He flies around Gahtsoh and then perches for a moment on the limb of a Joshua tree. Raven cocks his head and looks at Gahtsoh through one eye before flying away.

Raven is a trickster, a thief, a joker, and sometimes a liar, but Raven can also see the truth in a person, can see into his heart, Gahtsoh thinks. *And Raven does not like what he sees in the heart of a crippled boy.*

He hears the yipping of a coyote on his left, followed by a howl. A moment later, he hears deeper barking on his right. A third voice behind him joins the chorus. Soon, coyotes are all around him. He knows there are not as many coyotes in this place as he hears, but this is a place for visions, spirits, and totem animals.

The sun turns the eastern sky pink when Eagle's cry replaces Coyote's voice. Gahtsoh knows Eagle is a powerful totem, and his heart fills with hope. But it is not to be. Eagle circles Gahtsoh's fire three times in a counter-clockwise direction before flying away. *Counter-clockwise, a sign of closing, of ending, of rejection.*

Gahtsoh slumps, thinking he has failed, but something calls to him, something like that which called him to kiva. It is not a voice, but a feeling that churns his stomach and makes his heart to beat more strongly. He pulls himself erect but bows his head to the rising sun. *Nothing says that spirit guides must appear at night. Perhaps, today.*

Gahtsoh watches and listens throughout the day as the sun rises to cross the sky and then set behind his back. Every bird he sees, every sound of an animal, even the scrabbling of desert mice in the rocks, becomes the voice of a spirit guide, but none appear. He has been on the ledge only one day, not long enough to give up hope. He sits upright, lips compressed, eyes wide, waiting.

Two more days pass this way. Gahtsoh is not sure he is in control of his body or mind when on the third morning Heron lands on the ledge. The bird has one wing raised and folded as if broken. Heron is an avatar of Earth Mother. An injured Heron is surely a sign something troubles her. A sour taste rises in Gahtsoh's throat.

Heron disappears, and Gahtsoh uses the last of his sage to rebuild the fire. He does not have *dził nát'oh*, the traditional mixture of plants called mountain smoke. The fire is little more than coals when Gahtsoh throws onto it the last of the sage. He smells the smoke which he hopes will speed his prayer to Creator. "Creator, let me help Earth Mother!"

~~~~~

Chief Joe intercepts Hokee on the way to morning roll call. "Neighbors of his aunt in White Rock reported Tsela – the boy they call Gahtsoh – is missing at least three days. His grandfather's truck is missing, too. The boy is thirteen and not licensed but neighbors say he drives the truck. We have alerted police and highway patrol in the four states."

Hokee, whose name means *Abandoned*, lost family and friends when he argued against the teachings of his church. After three years of abandonment, Hokee's *shidá'í* – a maternal uncle and retired senior noncommissioned officer in the Bilagáana Air Force – rescued him. The man ensured that Hokee reached his dream to become a pilot. Years before this, Hokee and Gahtsoh attended the same school, and Hokee knew Gahtsoh had been abandoned by his family except for the now-dead grandfather when polio struck the boy. *It's payback time*, Hokee thinks. "What can I do, Chief? Just say the word."

Chief Joe replies. "Everyone will be on the lookout for the truck, but I want you to check places people in patrol cars can't reach. Ravines and canyons, including Canyon de Chelly, Chaco, Monument Valley, and the Navajo National Monument. Use your judgment and don't limit your search to the reservation. Tommy will take you to the airport and go with you. Ahote and Niyol are already there. Keep in contact. Any questions?"

Hokee has none.

As Hokee arrives at the Window Rock Airport, Ahote snaps his cell phone shut. "Just talked to Gaagii. He and Chatima stood vigil with Gahtsoh after his grandfather's funeral. The boy is unfulfilled because he hasn't done a Spirit Quest. Best guess, that's where he's been or where he is going."

"Where would he go? One of the sacred mountains?"

"Too far away and he'd have to drive off the reservation and on state highways. His guardians' trailer is near White Rock. Closest place of power is Chaco Canyon. We should start there."

Hokee lays a transparent ruler on an aeronautical chart and then fiddles with a circular slide rule. "About 65 air miles to Chaco; 130 round-trip. Chief orders me to have a 30-minute fuel reserve. That'll give us … more than four hours' search time. Enough to cover Chaco."

Niyol helps Hokee pre-flight the aircraft and claims the right front seat as his reward. Tommy fills two jerry cans with water and secures them to the bulkhead behind the third seat. He and Ahote take the second-row seats.

Hokee warms the engine, runs checks, and taxis to the end of Runway 20. With 130 gallons of fuel, an elevation of 6,700 feet, a temperature near 90, and three passengers, he will take all the runway he can get. At the southwest end of the runway, he turns the plane, advances the throttle, and rolls for takeoff. As soon as the wheels are off the ground, he begins a slow turn toward the northeast. Niyol reports takeoff and destination to the police dispatcher.

Thirty minutes later, they reach Chaco Canyon and begin the search. Only five minutes pass when the intercom carries Niyol's voice to the others. "The truck is on the south side of Fajada Butte. It would be hidden from the road and the visitor center."

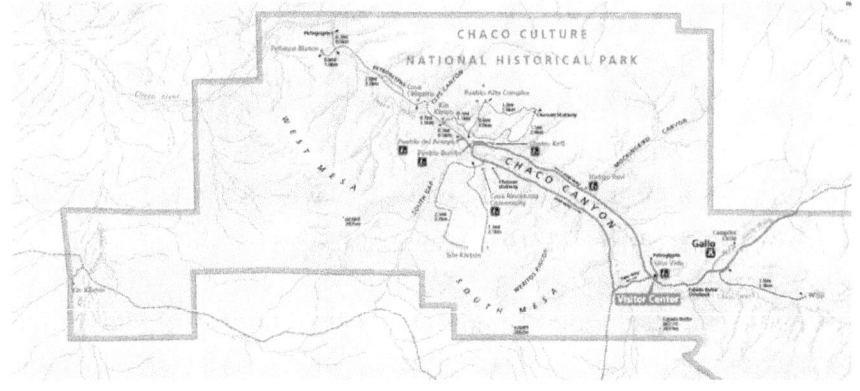

"How did he get there? He'd have to cross Chaco Wash."

"Anyone see him?" Hokee asks. "I'm dropping to five hundred feet AGL and will circle the butte."

Niyol's voice comes over the intercom. "Good boy," he says. "Gahtsoh, not you, Hokee. He's on the east side, facing the rising sun. He looks like – he is – he's bent over, not sitting up. He's not moving, but he must have heard the plane."

"I see him! He's collapsed! We've got to reach him."

"I can land west of the butte. Tell Chief Joe it's my call." Although Hokee is the youngest of the young men in the plane, he is the pilot-in-command. "Use your phone – not the radio – and tell him the kiva's been here. We know a safe way to reach Gahtsoh."

"I'll make the call," Tommy says. "Stay in line of sight of the repeater on the mesa."

"Uncle Joe," Tommy begins when the chief answers.

"Shiye´, Nephew, you call me on your own phone and you call me *uncle*. You are going to say something I do not want to hear."

"Yes, Uncle – Shizhé´é Yázhí. We found Tsela – Gahtsoh. He's on Fajada Butte in Chaco. Hokee will land and we will climb to reach him. He hasn't moved since we started circling the butte. We may lose touch part of the time when we can't hit the cellphone repeater. The kiva has been here before. We know a safe way to the top.

"Um, I think that's all."

Chief Joe gives his approval in a blessing. "May Creator watch over you and your friends, Shiye´."

Gahtsoh does not know he was reported missing to the Nations Police; he does not know they mounted a search for him. He has been on the ledge four days. Without food, his body breaks down stored fat, building up ketones in his blood. First, he feels nausea, then dizziness. His head aches; he is too tired to stand. His quest has failed. He will never have a spirit guide. Gahtsoh closes his eyes and prepares to die.

He does not hear the airplane that circles the butte before landing at its base, nor the rattle of rocks as four young men scramble up the path. He feels a hand behind his head, the touch of metal on his lips, and the softness of water dribbling into his parched mouth.

After a few sips, the canteen is taken away. Gahtsoh sees a figure wearing the khaki uniform of the Nation's Police kneeling beside him. Two other uniformed officers stand nearby, carrying a folded stretcher. A fourth young man in blue jeans and plaid shirt stands beside them.

His rescuers do not speak to Gahtsoh, but silently provide more water. Still silent, they strap the boy onto the stretcher and carry him down the butte.

Gahtsoh is delirious, but he realizes his rescuers know not to speak to him until he tells his dreams to an elder. *But who might that be?* He wonders. *Grandfather is dead. Who will listen to me? And why should they? I already know what my dream means – no one wants to be spirit guide to a crippled boy.*

Hokee, at one end of the stretcher, understands the custom, and knows they must take Tsela to Gaagii. He is the nearest to a Navajo Medicine Elder that remains.

When they reach the Beaver aircraft, Tommy gives Gahtsoh more water. The others reconfigure seats and strap down the stretcher. Hokee calls the dispatcher and reports.

"You must take him to the hospital in Farmington. It's closest," the dispatcher orders.

"No," Hokee says. "He is stable. We will take him to the Folio airport. Have an ambulance meet us there. Notify Dr. Deschene and ask him to have Gaagii or Chatima meet us at the hospital."

Tommy's cell phone buzzes; the call is from his uncle. Tommy speaks first.

"The boy has been on a spirit quest. We need to get him to a Medicine Elder. Gaagii is the closest thing to a Medicine Elder we know."

Police Chief Joseph White Eagle understands his nephew's words. "This is the correct action. Someone will meet you at the airport and deal with the plane so you all may go to the hospital with the boy."

~~~~~

Gaagii, whose name and spirit guide are *Raven*, sits beside Gahtsoh's bed as he has done for nearly a day since the boy reached the hospital. Gahtsoh's braces and crutches stand in a corner of the room. An intravenous line feeds saline and electrolytes into his arm. A Foley catheter removes urine.

Spencer explains the equipment to Gaagii – the infra-red sensor taped to Gahtsoh's finger measures blood oxygen; a machine monitors heartbeat and checks blood pressure every thirty minutes. "We change the urine bottle every hour and run tests. It showed evidence of dehydration, but that's being taken care of with the saline. Blood work showed a lot of imbalances." Spencer points to the second IV bag. "Electrolytes are correcting this.

"His pain from sitting cross-legged for days was terrible when he arrived. Dr. Deschene gave him morphine, but stopped

46

that early this morning. He is in natural sleep, now, and should wake by mid-morning. Give him a few ice chips to suck on. Make sure he knows his braces and crutches are close by – they will be important to him. Dr. D has told the staff no one except you or Chatima may talk to him until you allow it. But call Dr. D if you need help. He is an Elder."

Gaagii understands. Dr. Deschene is a new kind of Elder, but one who knows and honors the old ways.

Spencer's estimate is correct. Gaagii sees Gahtsoh's eyelids flutter and then open at 9:15 AM. When Gahtsoh looks at him, Gaagii greets him. "Ya´ateeh, Little Brother. I am happy to see you awake. Your braces and crutches are in the corner, there. Your friends will visit as soon as Dr. Deschene – he's your doctor – allows. Would you like some ice chips?"

Gahtsoh stares at Gaagii. His voice scratches from a parched throat. "Ya´ateeh; I know you. You are not old enough to be a Medicine Elder, but you know the songs. You sang them at my grandfather's vigil. Now you speak to me. What are you? Can you explain my dreams?"

"You look into my eyes when you speak," Gaagii says. "That is as it should be. Now, listen. The Bilagáana require our children to attend their schools. Some schools bring in elders to teach our language and traditions. But the Bilagáana do not understand K´é. They think it is only a chart of clan and family relationships and do not see behind it an important teaching, which is respect for all life on Earth and throughout the cosmos. More important, they do not understand hozho, *harmony, total harmony with others and with Earth Mother.* They do not understand the things that bring hozho – *Sa´ah naaghai bik´eh hozhoon* or the things that interfere with hozho.

"The Bilagáana do not understand that not every old person is an elder. They do not understand that an elder does not have to be old. Many of our youngest brothers and sisters do not hear. They are too impatient for play and lack the foundation for understanding."

Gaagii pauses for a sip of water before continuing. "My teacher revealed to me the principles of *bitsé siléí* – the foundational essence of the Navajo Way of Life – which must be passed from generation to generation verbally in stories that relate to the listener. He also insisted that because the *bitsé siléí* must relate to the listener, the true transfer of knowledge from elder to inquirer is one-on-one and requires the student be silent and keep eye contact." Gaagii stops speaking and gestures for Gahtsoh to speak.

"That is why you told me to look in your eyes, just as my grandfather did," Gahtsoh says. "I will listen and I will hear." He feels from Gaagii something he felt when his grandfather taught him. A confidence, a sureness of knowledge and belief, and a warm blessing.

Gaagii replenishes the ice chips several times before Gahtsoh finishes his story. "None of the totem animals wanted to be the spirit guide of a crippled boy. None of them spoke to me."

Gaagii presses a button to summon a nurse. "You told me your dream. I understand part of it, but I must think about it and talk to Chatima. You remember him from your grandfather's funeral vigil. I have called a nurse who will examine you, bring you food, and call Dr. Deschene. You may speak to her and to Dr. Deschene. He is an Elder, but a different kind. When he arrives, I will go outside to speak to Chatima. But I will return and speak more with you."

Mary Begay, RN, comes in at that moment and speaks to Gaagii. "Oh, good. I hoped the call meant he was awake. You have done what needed to be done?"

"Yes, ma'am. And after Dr. Deschene visits, I will return to talk privately again with Gahtsoh." He sees the nurse's confusion, and adds, "Tsela."

~~~~~

Dr. Deschene speaks sternly to Gahtsoh. "You risked a great deal for a Spirit Quest, and you are lucky the boys found you and knew what to do. You will stay here for a few days while we replace the fluids you lost, rebalance the chemicals in your blood, and put a little fat on your skinny bones." The doctor's smile and gentle poke in Gahtsoh's ribs take the sting from his words. The boy giggles and smiles.

"Next time you go mountain climbing, ask some of your friends to go with you."

The boy's smile disappears. "I have no friends," he says. "And my guardians are not likely to let me go anywhere, much less mountain climbing."

Dr. D cocks his head, stares at Gahtsoh, and smiles. "You have more friends than you know, and some will visit after Gaagii speaks to you again about your Spirit Quest. Other friends have already visited your guardians. They will tell you about that, too."

Gahtsoh does not understand everything Dr. D says, but feels truth and hope in the doctor's words.

Chapter 5 Peyote

Gaagii cranks up the head of the hospital bed and moves his chair so he and Gahtsoh can look into one another's eyes. "Chatima and I believe we know why none of the totem spirits spoke to you. Too many of our young people, Navajo, Hopi, and neighboring tribes – Ute, Apache, and others – have abandoned the old ways and replaced them with loud and discordant music and the schooling of the Bilagáana. Some have replaced Creator with the image of the Hispanglo god. While Creator has many aspects, the Hispanglo god is not one of them. Too many of our brothers and sisters have lost their connections to that which Creator gave us. They have forgotten *Sa'ah naaghai bik'eh hozhon*, 'that according to which harmony exists.' The totem animals either have lost the ability to speak or they refuse to do so.

"Chatima and I believe Creator sent Earth Mother to you as both a warning and a promise. We do not know what Creator's warning or promise might be, but we will, if you let us, help you search for the answer."

~~~~~

Nurse Begay insists Gaagii allow Gahtsoh to eat lunch and then nap. It is midafternoon when Gaagii escorts two members of the Nation's Police into the room. "Gahtsoh, these are two of your friends, Ahote and Niyol. They visited the trailer where you lived."

"*Ya'ateeh, Sitsili*, Greetings, Younger Brother," Niyol speaks. "I am Niyol of the Navajo. This is Ahote of the Hopi. We are friends of Gaagii, and we are your friends."

"*Ya'ateeh* … Friend and … *Shinaai,*" Gahtsoh replies, acknowledging Niyol as an elder brother, although with some hesitation.

"We visited your mother's sister to tell her we had found you and that you were in the hospital. Neither she nor her husband responded when we stopped our patrol car on the road and tapped the horn. They did not respond when we knocked on the door of their trailer. We looked in a window and saw them, but they did not move, even when we pounded on the door."

"We entered the trailer. They were passed out, drunk. There was no food in the kitchen except a box of cereal. We found a dead rat under the sink.

"We reported to Chief Joe who convinced Family Services to assign you a new guardian."

~~~~~

The buzz of his cell phone interrupts Dr. Deschene's breakfast. He looks at the screen; the call is from Chief Joe. "*Ya'ateeh,* Joseph. Something important, I'm sure."

"It is important, Nastas. Congratulations. You have a son."

Dr. D looks closely at Susan, who stands at the counter loading fruit into a blender. Her gravid belly is obvious under a loose blouse.

"Not funny, Joe. Susan still will not tell me the sex of our child."

"Not your and Susan's child, Nastas. I just received an emergency ruling from Family Services. You do remember signing up to be a foster parent, don't you?"

52

"That was only to prevent Spencer from being deported when the INS found his parents had disfellowshipped him and kicked him out of their home. It worked, too, didn't it?"

Both Chief Joe and Dr. Deschene chuckle. With the help of a mutual friend, Frank Falco, a US Attorney, and the Navajo court system, they had court orders floating back and forth long enough for Spencer to become a naturalized US citizen before he could be deported.

"Yes," Chief Joe interrupts their reminiscence, "but you're still on record. Tsela, also called Gahtsoh, has no living relatives other than the aunt. You are now his guardian. The head of Family Services signed the paperwork which is on your office fax machine." Chief Joe's chuckle fades as the cell phone system terminates the call.

"What is it, dear?" Susan asks. "Why would Chief Joe…?" Her question trails off.

"It seems, my love, I will have a child before you do." Dr. D laughs at Susan's obvious bemusement. "Joe has made me guardian of the boy, Gahtsoh."

~~~~~

Gahtsoh is wearing new clothes – blue jeans, plaid shirt, and white socks and trainers. They, and a Concho belt with real silver and turquoise are gifts from Dr. Deschene. The boy smiles when Gaagii and Chatima, two of his elder brothers, enter his hospital room followed by Dr. Deschene. Dr. D promised to discharge him today. His brother, Niyol, told him he would have new guardians. He wonders who this will be. Dr. D takes the chair and turns it to face Gahtsoh.

"Gahtsoh, Family Services assigned me to be your new guardian. I have agreed, but only so long as you and I can walk together in *hozho* – harmony. Do you know what that means?"

53

"Yes, Doctor, sort of. My grandfather told me about *Sa'ah Naagháí Bik'eh Hózhóón.* He called it 'the road to harmony,' but he said I would never learn all there was to know and would have to study it for all my life."

The boy's mature answer surprises Dr. D, but he does not show it. "Your father's father was a wise man. Gaagii and Chatima tell me he was teaching you to become a Medicine Elder. Therefore, although I will be your guardian, Gaagii and Chatima will teach you, and you will live with them most of the time. They will become more than your brothers, they will be the uncles you did not have before. You will obey them and learn from them. Do you find this harmonious and agreeable?"

Gahtsoh takes only seconds to assent.

"Then you may call me *shizhé'é* or Father or, if that is uncomfortable, you may call me, 'Dr. Deschene.' Your brothers tell me you prefer the name, Gahtsoh."

~~~~~

Gaagii and Chatima – and now Gahtsoh – live in a trailer in Kykotsmovi Village which is in an island of Hopi territory surrounded by the Navajo Nation. Seated among the sagebrush in the hardpan of the yard, the two students of tradition and magic teach simple songs to Gahtsoh. Late one afternoon, the buzz of Gahtsoh's cell phone interrupts the song Gaagii is teaching. Gahtsoh blushes, drops the sticks he is using to beat the rhythm of the song, fumbles with his phone, and looks at the screen. "It's Chief Joe."

He says only "Ya'ateeh," and then "Yes, sir" and "No, sir" several times before he takes the phone from his ear. "Chief Joe says a patrol saw lights around Grandfather's hogan last night. Whoever it was drove away before the police reached it.

He says it looks like someone trashed the hogan and he wants to know if you can take me there tomorrow."

"For Chief Joe, I'll overlook the interruption," Gaagii says "but next time, remember to turn off – not just silence, but turn off – your phone when we are studying. Even in practice, it is not a good thing to interrupt a medicine song."

Chatima is listening to their conversation. "It's a three-hour drive and one of the truck's headlights is out. It would be okay until we hit a state road where the Bilagáana police can stop us. We can't leave until daylight tomorrow – 6:30 maybe. Tell the chief we'll be there by 10."

~~~~~

The difference between
a medicine and a poison
is the dose thereof.
— Paracelsus (1493 – 1541 C.E.)
Earth Analogue III

Gahtsoh and Ahote stand in the doorway of the trashed hogan. Gaagii and Niyol are behind them, looking over their shoulders while Chatima scans the surrounding ground. Inside, broken pottery and glass, and spills of colored sand, corn pollen, dried flower petals, sage, and herbs – the tools of a Medicine Elder – mark the floor.

Ahote shines a tactical flashlight around the single room of the hogan "They stopped looking before breaking every pot and container. They found what they were looking for," he says.

Gahtsoh points to the wall from which hangs a headpiece of eagle feathers. His voice whistles through a throat constricted by emotion. "They didn't take his medicine bonnet. The eagle feathers are the most valuable thing he owned – the only valuable thing."

"Not valuable to an enrolled Navajo, but to Bilagáana collectors who cannot legally get or own the feathers," Niyol says. "The people who raided the hogan are neither Navajo nor Bilagáana, but something else."

Gaagii understands Niyol's mistrust of anyone not Navajo, and tries to defuse the situation. "The people who trashed the hogan were after something more valuable – to them, at least," he says, and points. "Chatima, shine your light there."

Chatima has completed his survey of the ground around the hogan and stands beside Gaagii. He unclips his flashlight. "Peyote button," he says. "The eagle feathers might be legal, but peyote is not."

"Ton Yah didn't have peyote by accident. Peyote is not native to this area, but to Mexico and parts of south Texas."

"And if he had more of it – or someone believed he did – that could be motive for burglary."

"Or murder."

"Sitsilí," Niyol says. "Your grandfather was not a member of the Native American Church, was he? Did he collect peyote?"

Sitsilí, little brother, Gahtsoh thinks. *He calls me 'little brother' to remind me he has the right to question me, to teach me, and to punish me.* It takes only a moment for him to digest this thought and defend his grandfather. "Yes. He collected it, brewed it into tea, and gave it to people who were in pain and those who were dying. It was his right and duty as a Medicine Elder."

After a whispered talk with Niyol, Chatima turns on the lights, kneels, and begins scooping up dried plants. "What are those?" Ahote asks.

Chatima hesitates and looks at Gaagii, who nods approval.

"These are ingredients of *dził nát'oh* – mountain smoke. Most people call it 'tobacco,' but it contains no commercial tobacco. It is an important tool of the Medicine Elders, and it is what we throw on the fire to make smoke to carry prayers to the *Dinyiin Diné* – Holy People – and to Creator. It is not something we speak of widely."

Ahote breaks the silence which follows with a practical question. "What does a snake mean? It's on this bottle."

Gahtsoh has reached a shelf of undisturbed jars. Beads of four colors are visible through the glass. He puts the jars carefully into a bag. At Ahote's question, he looks up. "The snake marks poison and the other symbol is a yew tree. That bottle holds tea brewed from yew bark. Too much is a poison, but a little helps people with liver disease."

The thought of poison triggers Gahtsoh's memory. "There's something else you should see." At Gahtsoh's direction, Ahote pushes aside a workbench made of scraps of lumber and plywood and then lifts a board from the floor. In the cavity beneath the board are twelve glass pint canning jars with metal rings holding their lids. Ahote lifts the jars one at a time. Each label includes a snake for poison and Navajo letters that do not spell any words the boys recognize.

"What are these?" Chatima asks.

Gahtsoh lowers his head. "I do not know, but they are not medicine."

Gahtsoh carefully folds and packs the medicine bonnet, even though he knows there is no longer anyone eligible to wear it. The police officers are careful to pack the dozen jars discovered under the floorboards. Gahtsoh holds a bag with beads of the four sacred colors and then closes the curtain that is the only door to the hogan. There is nothing left for him, here. He turns his back and gets into the police car that will take him to Window Rock.

≈≈≈≈≈

Chatima, Gaagii, and Gahtsoh wait in the break room of the police station while Ahote and Niyol report to Chief Joe. "We found one peyote button and a jar of peyote tea. It is likely Ton Yah knew where it grew and collected it. Gahtsoh said his grandfather used peyote in healing."

"I will ask Dr. Deschene to autopsy one of Ton Yah's patients," Chief Joe says. "That will tell us what we need to know."

"There are also a dozen jars like this, hidden under a workbench. They are all marked with a snake, which Gahtsoh says is Ton Yah's symbol for poison. They all have Navajo characters, but none of them makes sense."

Chief Joe sits quietly for a moment. "Photograph the labels and then take the jars to Dr. Deschene and ask him to analyze them."

Chapter 6 Red Marks Death

Two days later, at mid-morning, the Waffle Palace Restaurant in Folio is empty except for Chief Joe, Dr. Deschene, and Niyol who sit at one table, and the younger folks, Hokee, Chuchip, Spencer, and Ahote, who sit across the room.

"Niyol is not happy with the results of his analysis of the data gathered at Tonilih." Chief Joe says. "He believes there are too many variables."

"What have you done so far?" Dr. D asks Niyol.

"Chuchip and Spencer helped me group patients based on symptoms the same way we might do triage patients.

"Red is deaths. Orange, for urgent, are people with life-threatening problems. Yellow are people with problems that could become life-threatening. Green are people with symptoms that are easy to treat – people who complained of nausea, diarrhea, and stomach cramps.

"The Yellow Group had what Dr. Deschene calls peripheral neuropathy – numbness and tingling of hands and feet – and cardiac dysrhythmia. Somewhat debilitating, but not immediately fatal. The children with broken or warped bones went into this group because we didn't find any evidence of abuse. Some of these also had Green Group symptoms.

"Orange Group had high liver numbers or kidney damage, convulsions or loss of muscle coordination, or symptoms resembling stroke. Some had dementia that was not consistent with their age. Dr. Deschene looked at death certificates and found ten people who died of lymphoma and eight from other symptoms. We put them in the Red Group, along with the miscarriages without a known cause. Some people in the Red and Orange Groups also had Yellow and Green symptoms. I'm running statistical software looking for links among variables like age, sex, and location. I'm finding some, but the correlation coefficients are too close to zero – the variables are not nearly related."

"Does that mean there are multiple causes?" Chief Joe asks.

"Multiple causes, yes, sir. But some causes may have multiple effects, and sometimes it takes two causes to produce one effect. And sometimes it takes time for a cause to produce an effect. If that makes sense. That's why this is so hard. There may be multiple genetic factors, multiple diet factors, multiple geographic factors, and multiple unknown environmental factors.

"None of the dead were autopsied, and many of the DCs – death certificates – list manner and cause of death as *natural* and *unknown*. Since these people all died in hospital, the DCs were signed by attending physicians – sometimes physicians' assistants or nurse-practitioners – not pathologists."

Dr. D describes the next step. "The Tonilih Hospital has a morgue and rudimentary pathology laboratory, but no pathologist. I have asked them to put all cadavers in refrigerated drawers until I can get there. I'll conduct autopsies no more than seven days after death, before too many post-mortem changes occur. We will bring evidence bags and sample containers when we visit. Looks like Chuchip and Spencer and I will be doing a lot of traveling."

"I'll keep working on the data," Niyol promises.

～～～～

Spencer kicks off the discussion at the other table. "Dr. D said you found peyote in Gahtsoh's grandfather's hogan."

"One button, but Gahtsoh admitted his grandfather used peyote and showed him where the peyote patch is – took him there more than once," Hokee says. "Niyol and Ahote know this and they had to tell Chief Joe."

"What will the chief do?" Spencer asks.

"First thing – Dr. D. has ordered an autopsy of one of Ton Yah's patients, if we can identify one."

"Why an autopsy?" Chuchip asks.

"To find out if they drank the peyote Ton Yah brewed."

"Why?"

"I don't know, but the chief will probably tell us."

~~~~~

The next morning, Chuchip drives the coroner's truck to visit Chatima, Gaagii, and Gahtsoh at Kykotsmovi Village. After Gaagii pours coffee, Chuchip hands Gahtsoh a printout of the names of people recently autopsied at the hospital.

Gahtsoh stares at the page, runs his index finger down the list, and stops at the third name. "This one."

"He lived in Sheep Springs. How did he end up in the hospital at Folio?

"Next of kin is a brother in Lechee, a few miles south of the hospital.

"Do you remember why he saw your grandfather?"

"He had diarrhea and kept throwing up. He was in great pain. Grandfather made a tea with herbs and a peyote button."

"Do you remember the herbs?"

"Only some of them." Gahtsoh lists several ingredients familiar to Chuchip but also one not found in the desert.

"Where did your grandfather find goldenseal?"

Gahtsoh laughs. He does not do that often. "At a Bilagáana natural food store in Gallup."

"Did it help?"

Gahtsoh's laughter dies. His eyebrows droop to hood his eyes. "This man was not in pain when he died."

"I remember the autopsy," Chuchip says. "We have tissue samples in formalin. We may not have to do another autopsy for Chief Joe. I will tell Dr. D. Do you want to come back to the hospital with me for a few days? There's plenty of room in the truck, and Spencer and I have awesome rooms at the community college."

~~~~~

Gahtsoh, Chuchip, Chatima, Gaagii, and Spencer crowd Dr. Deschene's office when he invites Chief Joe to a teleconference. The chief sits at his desk. Behind him is his crime map of the Navajo Nation and surrounding Bilagáana states. Colored map pins mark different kinds of crime. Red are violent deaths; green are assaults; blue are crimes against property. Yellow now represents deaths from unusual diseases; purple, as always, marks drug crimes. The chief uses India ink to put a white dot on the top of red and green pins to represent drug involvement, including deaths from overdose. Computers can display the same information more rapidly and precisely, but Chief Joe used his map for years before computers, and likes the breadth of its display.

"That was fast work," Chief Joe says. "Do you have someone to autopsy already? The judge wants names of next-of-kin before he will issue an order for exhumation."

"That may not be necessary," Dr. Deschene says. "One of Ton Yah's patients was a recent autopsy. We routinely preserve tissue samples. He died in the hospital the day after he arrived complaining of weakness, nausea, and dizziness following diarrhea and vomiting. The autopsy was clinical – not

64

forensic – but it was also a teaching moment for Chuchip. With the brother's permission, we opened the skull and removed the brain. We have the entire brain preserved in formalin where it has hardened. We can slice and examine it at any time. Cause of death was hyponatremia – a sodium deficiency – caused by extreme dehydration from vomiting and diarrhea. We may get the information you need from the samples, including the brain, without exhumation."

Spencer looks troubled. "If we don't know all the herbs and stuff Ton Yah used, we won't know what to look for in the tox exam."

"Do the best you can," Dr. D says. "The most important thing to look for is peyote. Its characteristic pattern is in the mass spectrometer's database."

~~~~~

Spencer leads the effort to sample bits of tissue and brain, and he and Chuchip keep the microtome, microscope, and mass spectrometer busy. After a week, they report to Dr. Deschene. "The brain and liver test positive for trimethoxyphenethylamine – mescaline, found in peyote. It usually takes up to ten days to eliminate mescaline from the body. It can be detected in hair follicles for up to ninety days, but we didn't have any hair to work with.

"There are also some chemicals the mass spec cannot identify. They're not in its database."

Dr. D looks over the printouts from the mass spec. "Very good work. Perhaps the Denver lab can identify the other chemicals. I'll contact Chief Joe."

"*As I understand it,*" Spencer begins with a formal statement which denies any claim to sure knowledge, "we must not implicate Gahtsoh." His voice is soft, but firm. "He's only thirteen, crippled by polio, and nearly alone except for kiva members. He can't be put in juvie just because he knew about this. He's an accessory-after-the-fact, and—"

Dr. D's chuckle interrupts Spencer and brings puzzlement to the young man's face. "Shiye´, nephew, you have been watching too much Bilagáana television. Their law does not extend here except where we allow it, and not always then. Gahtsoh is an accessory only if included in my report or Chief Joe's. He will not be."

~~~~~

Chuchip unzips the bag holding the body and freezes. Spencer sees his brother's hesitation. "What?"

"I know him."

Chuchip's voice breaks when his throat constricts. "He was in my grade in school. We played intermural footy together. He was always – always alive, fast, hustling, smiling when he stole the ball but cheering when anyone, even on the other team, made a good move.

"*Atsa*, brother, I cannot do this." Chuchip turns away and walks from the laboratory, leaving Spencer standing by the gurney with a young man's body.

Dr. Deschene walks in moments later, finding one assistant when he expects two. Spencer anticipates his question.

"Dr. D, Chuchip knows this boy. I will do his tasks and when he is ready, I will ask him any necessary questions."

"*T'áá'áko*, it is right. We should never have to—"

"I'm ready, sir." Spencer interrupts his mentor. He doesn't want to think about what he will do.

"Then begin." While Spencer does the external examination, Dr. D pulls down the microphone and speaks for the recording.

"We have the body of a seventeen-year-old Navajo boy who was found dead in the toilet of the Folio Diner. Identification was provided by the Nation's Police." Dr. Deschene continues through the formalities – height, weight, apparent ethnicity, and other obvious markers while Spencer minutely examines the body.

"There are blue tattoos on his hand," Spencer says, examining the skin between the thumb and forefinger. Dots that look like the 'five' on a domino."

"Borstal tattoos—" Dr. D interrupts himself. "The Borstals were reformatories – boarding schools – for youthful offenders. The British created them and imposed them on the First Peoples in the east and north during colonial days. The custom spread west with the Bilagáana. The boys made the tattoos. That pattern represents the four corners of a cell with the prisoner inside."

"He was in a reformatory?" Spencer asks.

"The Borstals were abolished by the US government in 1982. I suspect some gang has resurrected this ancient tradition – to their own ends."

Spencer glances at Dr. D and then removes a rhinoscope from the instrument tray and uses it to spread and examine each of the boy's nostrils. "Inflammation of both nostrils and — light, please?"

Dr. D doesn't hesitate, but puts an LED penlight in Spencer's outstretched hand.

"Is this a hole in the septum between the nostrils?" Spencer asks.

"In the drug cabinet, phenylephrine – labeled Neo-Synephrine – please."

The doctor sprays the drug into both nostrils. "In a few moments—"

"But he's dead? I mean … he's dead." Spencer is clearly confused.

"The drug is a chemical which will act even on non-living tissue if not too much time has passed. Look, now."

"There is a ragged hole – about half-a-centimeter across and well inside the nose – in the cartilage that separates the nostrils. That's strange, Dr. D. Have you seen this before?"

"Only in photographs, but I know what it indicates. A perforated septum suggests significant use of cocaine or methamphetamine. These drugs reduce blood flow, destroy tissue, and numb the inside of the nose so the damage is not noticed. He was a serious drug user. We'll get more from the tox screen. I will leave a book for you. It will be your homework for tonight."

"I'm not sure how to tell Chuchip. I don't think the boy was a close friend, but still—"

"Tell him the truth," Dr. D interrupts. "This boy was addicted to cocaine or methamphetamine. It is likely he died of an overdose or organ failure. We will leave the death certificate as *pending* until the tox screen results are returned. Tell Chuchip the police will do what they can to find whoever sold him the drugs. Comfort him; give him your support and then move on. We are a small but essential part of this war."

~~~~~

A Hopi police car surprises Gaagii, Chatima, and Gahtsoh when it arrives at the trailer where they live. The driver stops about thirty meters away and taps the horn. Chatima looks out the window and then moves to the door. "Hopi police."

Chatima leaves the door of the trailer open when he steps onto the hardpan of the yard. His appearance at the open door signals the police someone is home and visitors are welcome. The car rolls slowly down the dirt track and stops about ten meters from Chatima.

"Ha'u'" the policeman says as he leaves the car. Chatima replies with the same Hopi *Hello*.

"I have a visitor from the Navajo Nation," the policeman says, and Chief Joe steps from the passenger door. His greeting in Hopi surprises Chatima who replies in that language, "You are welcome Chief Joseph of the Navajo. Will you both take coffee with us?"

The Hopi policeman begs off, but says he will return. Chief Joe, although not a member of the Eastward Kiva, is uncle to their brother, Tommy, and honorary uncle to them all.

"What can I do for my uncle?" Chatima asks, after the Hopi policeman has left.

"Coffee sounds good."

Chapter 7 Peyote Patch

The trailer belonged to Chatima's teacher before his death. The interior is clean and well organized. Shelves hold ceramic and glass jars of herbs and tinctures. A workbench runs along one wall of the front room and holds a mortar and pestle, scales, and glass distillation apparatus. A small drum hangs on the wall opposite the workbench.

Gaagii has brewed coffee, and pours for everyone. Chief Joseph sits at a table with two young men and one boy – Gahtsoh.

The chief speaks to Gahtsoh. "I must ask this. Will you tell me where your grandfather grew peyote?"

Gahtsoh's face pales. He wraps his arms around his chest, looks at the floor, and withdraws into himself. He does not speak.

Gaagii touches the boy's shoulder. "Gahtsoh, brother who is also named Tsela, *Stars Lying Down*, I am your brother and Chief Joseph is my uncle, therefore he is your uncle. Gahtsoh does not have to answer this question, but as Tsela you must answer since it is your uncle who asks."

"They will take me to juvie or back to that woman and her husband."

"No, Shiye´," Chief Joe says. "That will not happen."

The boy unfolds when he hears this. He understands that by calling him *nephew*, the chief seals his promise. Gahtsoh's words are slow and measured. "I cannot tell you, only show you. It is south of Road 59, west of Many Farms. Even knowing that, you could not find it."

"Thank you, Tsela, I—"

71

"Call me Gahtsoh," the boy interrupts Chief Joe. "It is my name, even though Rabbit did not appear to me." He squeezes his eyes shut and turns his head away so the others will not see his pain.

Chief Joe addresses the two members of the Eastward Kiva and Gahtsoh. "Tommy will arrive early tomorrow in the Humvee. Will you show him the way to the peyote? A brother will harvest it for the Native American Church."

The Hopi police car returns, as if the driver knows it is time for Chief Joe to depart.

~~~~~

The Humvee is Chief Joe's personal vehicle. It does not carry the markings of the Nation's Police, but has blue and red lights hidden behind the grill and a forest of antennas on the roof. In midmorning, Tommy drives to the trailer and gives a quick blast on the siren. Without waiting for the customary welcome of an open door, Tommy, Ahote, and a third young man jump from the vehicle. Gaagii is first out of the trailer.

Ahote introduces the third person who wears the uniform of the Hopi police. "This is Hawiovi of the Hopi. He is a member of the Native American Church and a Police Officer. He will take custody of the peyote," Ahote says. "Chief Joe also thought you should have some adult supervision."

Gaagii punches Ahote's shoulder just hard enough to count coup. "Then he shouldn't have sent you. Come in for coffee."

Ahote scoffs, frowns, and then grins. He and Gaagii started counting coup years ago, but have long since lost the count.

The team of peyote-pickers approaches Jeddito, on the eastern border of Hopi territory, when an ocean of white blocks the road. Sheep, shorn earlier in the spring, are already sporting their new wool. Tommy slows the Humvee, yielding right of way to the sheep. An old man on a pinto raises his arm and whistles to two dogs. Guided by the dogs, the sheep part for the Humvee like the waters of a lake parting for a canoe. Tommy waves to the old man and slowly pushes through the sheep.

After a two-hour drive, Gahtsoh directs Tommy to turn off Navajo Route 59 south into the desert. "Go slow – there's a wash just ahead."

The wash is both marked and hidden from view by the water-seeking scrub that grows along it. Tommy turns west for a dozen meters to find a break in the scrub, then takes the Humvee straight across the wash. Gahtsoh points to a copse of Piñon trees and directs Tommy toward them. Just before reaching the trees, Gahtsoh calls, "Stop. There, on the left."

"You should allow me to harvest the buds, and then destroy the cactus," Hawiovi says. "It would not do for you to be found holding peyote."

"We won't tell if you won't tell," Gaagii says. "I will help you gather while the others destroy the roots. If we save some of the plants, perhaps you can replant them?"

"I thought I was the adult supervision," Ahote says. "Don't I get to say who does what?"

"Not this time, *Sitsili* – little brother." Gaagii says, and then laughs.

The crew collects peyote buttons and digs up and destroys most roots, but saves a dozen plants in plastic bags for replanting.

73

Gaagii points to marks in the dust. "Someone else has been here. Someone driving a dually. See? Parallel tire marks from the four rear wheels. I don't suppose anyone brought a crime scene kit with plaster."

"Couldn't get anything here," Tommy says. "Too faint. Let's look when we cross the wash."

Tommy is correct. The damp and softer soil in the wash preserved perfect impressions of all four rear wheels of the dually, and the chief's Humvee does have a crime scene kit. Ahote and Tommy inject the binary chemicals into the depression. The others are becoming antsy when Ahote declares the casting to be firm enough to lift. "Nothing jumps out as being unique except maybe that mark. Still, it's more than we had before."

Hawiovi thanks the others for their help. "It's almost two o'clock. We've missed lunch, and there's a pizza place in Many Farms. Anyone hungry? My treat as a thank-you gift."

"I'm not sure we should stop with a load of peyote," Gaagii says.

"Did you forget I'm a cop?" Ahote asks and strikes coup on Gaagii's shoulder. The two young men grin at one another.

The pizza place is not crowded and the buffet is over when they arrive at 2:30. Gahtsoh is unsure what to order. "I never had pizza. Grandfather couldn't afford it."

Ahote pretends to be in shock before he speaks. "Then you are in for something truly wonderful, Little Brother."

"Pizza is good, but not as good as a Navajo Taco," Gaagii says.

"I've never had one of those, either," Gahtsoh answers.

74

"What's it like? I mean, using the peyote," Gaagii asks Hawiovi.

Hawiovi is slow to answer. When he does, his voice is almost a whisper. "A little bit opens the mind to what we say are visions but others call 'hallucinations.' More can cause nausea and vomiting, create feelings of anxiety and fear, and elevate blood pressure, heart rate, and respiration. Too much can be fatal. I cannot say more about the visions. My church is very careful with the peyote. We don't use it every day or every week, not even every month."

"I think I'll stick with coffee," Gaagii says. "No offense."

"None taken," Hawiovi says, and then chuckles. "My father imports coffee, roasts it, and sells it to restaurants, chain grocery stores, and the little convenience stores all over the reservations – Hopi, Navajo, Zuni, Apache, and Ute. With all the Mormons who don't drink coffee, I'm glad to know some cops who do."

He does not see the looks exchanged as Gaagii turns his eyes to his brothers. These boys were among the first to be disfellowshipped before their church dissolved its relationship with the scouts.

After they reach the trailer, Gaagii watches Hawiovi ride away with a member of his church. "Tommy, Ahote, you will stay with us tonight. You have done enough driving today."

Ahote agrees. "Chief Joe will want to hear how things went, but there will be no written report. Officially, I was off duty the whole day, and Tommy is a civilian."

Tommy and Ahote return to Window Rock the next day. Ahote takes Niyol to the Evidence Room and shows him the cast of the tire tracks made yesterday. "This looks like the one made where Ton Yah was murdered – see where there's a cut in one tire."

Niyol squints at the mark made by the defect. "Are you sure of chain of custody?"

"You'd better believe it, especially after I mislabeled that vomit from the school gym. Who would have thought vomit was important!" Ahote says.

"The chief didn't say anything, though."

"Chief Joe only frowned at me, but it was a million-kilowatt frown. I never felt so bad in my life. The history of these samples is clean, but they don't tell us anything."

"Actually, they do." Niyol points to the two casts. "They both show the same flaw in an outboard tire. It's likely the same truck made the tracks where Ton Yah was murdered and at his peyote patch."

"But we don't have the truck. All this can do is exclude trucks until – and if – we find the right one – or he buys a new tire."

"But it is one more bit of data to support a hypothesis I have," Niyol says. "The person who killed Ton Yah and the person who visited his peyote patch are the same person. This person learned, somehow, about the peyote patch and he killed Ton Yah. I believe the killer is from a drug gang."

Ahote agrees. "That makes sense. The killer wanted the peyote. You are right. Killing Ton Yah was part of a drug war. Someone thought he was undercutting their peyote market and killed him to keep his peyote patch for themselves."

~~~~~

Chief Joe is more interested in the tire tracks than the disposition of the peyote. He tells them to label the impression taken at the wash and enter it into evidence. "It is unlikely we will find a truck with that tire before wear erases the uniqueness."

"I think it answers a question, though" Niyol says. "Even though Ton Yah was using peyote only as a medicine, someone thought otherwise and killed him to eliminate competition."

"*Ha'tchi* – you have spoken well."

~~~~~

The drive from Folio to Tonilih will take Dr. Deschene and his two assistants two-and-a-half hours. They leave the hospital at false dawn with Dr. D asleep in the back seat of the crew-cab truck and arrive at the Tonilih Comprehensive Health Care Facility in time for a late breakfast.

Spencer and Chuchip have gone through the cafeteria line and sit waiting for Dr. D.

"I've figured him out," Spencer says. Chuchip knows his brother means Dr. Deschene.

"Sleep when you can; eat when you can. And make opportunities for both. That's probably something he learned in Afghanistan." Spencer ducks his head toward his own tray when he sees Dr. D walking toward the table.

After they put their trays and empty dishes on the conveyor, Dr. Deschene leads the young men toward the pathology lab. "We have four autopsies. Nurse Toon arranged a medical secretary to transcribe notes, and a photographer. We will do all the work. Think you're up to it?"

"Are you buying supper?" Chuchip grins.

Dr. D snorts, but before he can answer, a woman turns a corner in front of them. She is first to overcome her surprise.

77

"Hello, Nastas. Somehow, after what Bertha told me, I'm not surprised to see you here."

"This is a friend from Washington, Doli Tabaaha," Dr. Deschene tells his assistants, pronouncing her first name, *dough-lee*. "She is a lawyer." Turning to Doli, he asks, "Does the hospital administration know you are wandering around without a guard? Should they worry?"

Doli laughs as she shakes hands with Chuchip and Spencer, and hugs Dr. D. "Bertha Toon and I are old friends," she says. "When I heard about children with leukemia, multiple broken bones, and developmental delays in hearing and speech, I had to see for myself. Nastas, you are a long way from your hospital. What is going on?"

"That is exactly what we are trying to find out. We have four autopsies to perform, so we'll be staying at least one night. Can you meet us for supper? Nurse Toon's brother makes the best Navajo Tacos on the eastern half of the reservation."

Nurse Toon appears behind Doli and shakes her head at Dr. D's words. "Please don't let him hear you say that. He's already hard to live with!"

~~~~~

Dr. Deschene looks at the label on the refrigerated locker. "You've never autopsied a child."

Chuchip and Spencer hear a slight catch in his voice, a rough pace to his speech. "No, sir. But we'll get over it, sir." Spencer speaks for himself and his brother.

"My nephews. I hope you never get over it. I have not."

Chapter 8 Child's Autopsy

Dr. Deschene reminded Chuchip and Spencer they are brothers in kiva and that Dr. D is the elder. The young men understand. "*Ahéhee'*, brother – thank you. Give us your strength," Chuchip speaks for them both.

Dr. D nods and opens the locker. Chuchip rolls a tray onto the gurney. The body bag is white and about half the size of the usual steel-gray bag.

Spencer waves away Dr. D's hand, unzips the bag, and lifts the child's body from the gurney onto the autopsy table.

Dr. D turns on the microphone and hands a record folder to Chuchip, who recites the child's name, his mother's and father's clans, and his date of birth. Still reading, Chuchip adds, "The body is a male child, six years of age confirmed by hospital records. The boy died after suffering from lymphoblastic leukemia for thirteen months. He is emaciated, which is common following leukemia. There are no marks on his body except from intravenous infusions – all documented. X-rays show multiple broken bones over many years." Chuchip directs the photographer to capture images where he points.

Then, before Dr. Deschene can move, Spencer picks up a scalpel and places the blade on the boy's right acromion. He looks to Dr. D, who nods. Spencer makes the first of the incisions that will splay the boy's body and lay him bare to the autopsy.

~~~~~

After two more autopsies, Dr. D, Chuchip, and Spencer exchange blood-spattered white scrubs, aprons, and rubber boots for their regular clothes.

"Dr. D? Something about the first autopsy bothers me."

Dr. D stands patiently, waiting for Chuchip to say more.

"It's not that he is a child. But you're right. I don't think I'll ever forget this. It is his bones."

Dr. D knows what Chuchip means. "Shorter than normal for his age, and with many healed breaks."

"Remodeling of the bones – a lot of it. That's one of the syndromes we found in the records earlier," Spencer says.

"Yes. I would like to have examined the bones more closely, but we didn't have permission from the family to do more than the law requires. We did that. But we have X-rays, photographs, and measurements. And maybe, we can use these as justification for a closer examination the next time we see this."

~~~~~

The restaurant is crowded, but Bertha's brother held a table in a quiet corner for them. Chuchip is an adult by the laws of both the Navajo and Hopi nations. However, he is a seventeen-year-old boy who is overwhelmed to be seated across the table from Doli. Her skin and liquid black hair glow in the light of the votive candle in the center of the table. She realizes Chuchip is staring at her, smiles, and winks. Chuchip's skin and the room are dark enough she doesn't see him blush, but she knows he does. "Chuchip, I have known Dr. Deschene for many years. For someone as young as you to be working with him speaks a great deal about you and your abilities."

Dr. D suppresses his chuckle. *A polite and masterful speech to break Chuchip's infatuation. I suspect over the years she has had practice.* "Chuchip has been my lead technician since the community college began its fall quarter last year, and I lost the students who had been my interns. This summer, he is taking a light course load at the college, which allows him to work full time with me. I hope, like Spencer, he will find the practical work to be as important as the academic. So far, that is working – for both of them."

Doli turns the conversation to Susan, and Dr. D brings her up to date on Susan's pregnancy. "She is fortunate not to have had morning sickness. So far, everything is on track for a delivery in mid-September."

"Boy or girl?" Nurse Toon asks.

"She won't tell me," Dr. D says. "She's had an ultrasound that would have told her, but she swore the technician and her obstetrician to secrecy." He puts down his fork. "Doli? Would you ask her and tell me?"

Doli laughs, and then says, "Nastas, it would cost my friendship with Susan to reveal her secret."

Dr. D picks up his fork. "I know, and I knew that would be your answer. But I had to ask. She's busy working with some of the boys – Niyol, Chatima, and Gaagii – on a series of children's books with our People's legends and histories."

"So very different from the investigative reporting she did before," Doli says.

"I'm not so sure of that. Many of our legends have been lost – or corrupted – by history. She does a lot of research."

They fill the rest of the meal with talk about diseases, symptoms, and syndromes that appeared at Tonilih. Chuchip stutters at first, but soon is confidently describing what he saw at autopsies – the child with leukemia, the multiple broken bones.

It takes Doli only moments to assess the facts and create a hypothesis. "Heavy metals. Heavy metal poisoning. Cadmium, for example, weakens the bones – it interferes with the uptake of calcium," Doli says.

"*T'áá'áko* – you are right," Dr. D says. "But there are other symptoms and syndromes not associated with heavy metals. There's something we're missing."

Doli shakes her head, a mare shaking off a bothersome fly with a whip of her tail. "The most likely source is the water. The water around Tonilih may be contaminated." She picks up, and then puts down, the glass from which she has been drinking.

In the restaurant, banter and laughter fall silent and the lights dim as a tattered rag of darkness passes through the room. The candles in the centers of the tables fade before settling to points of light, then flare. Forks which had paused between plate and mouth, move. The sound of the diners resumes.

Few people notice the silence. Those who do, attribute it to the odd, random phenomenon that occurs at parties and gatherings when everyone falls silent at the same moment. Dr. D understands that something important has happened and calls his dinner companions back to reality. "I forgot, Doli, your undergraduate degree is pre-med with a lot of chemistry, and that's a likely hypothesis."

"My undergraduate work was at the University of New Mexico. People there have been studying for years the physiological effects of uranium, lead, and other heavy metals. Nastas, if you agree, I will make some calls and put people in touch with you."

"*Ahéhee'*, thank you, Doli."

~~~~~

The next morning, Dr. Deschene and his assistants complete the last autopsy. This one is of an adult who died after suffering early-onset dementia. Spencer uses a scalpel to make

82

a U-shaped cut across the top of the man's skull from just behind one ear to the other. Then, he carefully peels the scalp forward over the eyes and backward toward the neck until he reveals the entire skull.

"Gives a new meaning to scalping, Paleface," Chuchip says and ignores Spencer's snort before turning on a vibrating saw and cutting a circle around the top of the head. Dr. D watches closely as Chuchip pulls the skullcap away from the brain.

"I will take it from here." Dr. D sticks his fingers under the brow, hooks the frontal lobes, and pulls out the brain while Spencer cuts nerves and blood vessels. The last step is to cut the spinal cord, completely freeing the brain.

"Nothing obvious from external examination," Spencer says. He holds a large jar of formalin into which Dr. D carefully places the brain.

"It will be firm enough to section in a couple of days," Spencer says.

"There is something we must do before we return home," Dr. D says. "We will need ten sterile sample bottles, masks, and a box of exam gloves. Nurse Toon will accompany us to collect water samples from wells around Tonilih – wells at the homes of people we interviewed on our last visit."

"And the trading post," Spencer says. "The one with DAPL graffiti. A lot of people get their water, there."

~~~~~

It is late Friday night before Dr. D, Chuchip, and Spencer reach Folio and the hospital. "There are three autopsies for us to do, and we need to clean up our notes from Tonilih," Dr. D said. "But, tomorrow is a day off. You will not, under any

83

circumstances, think about autopsies, chemicals, or Doli Tabaaha. Monday is soon enough."

Chuchip grins at Dr. D's teasing, but is too tired to do more than drive to the dormitory where he and Spencer live.

Chapter 9 Second Spirit Quest

Gahtsoh and Chatima face one another across a small fire circle in the hardpan yard of the trailer. Chatima looks into Gahtsoh's eyes and sings the Creation Story of the Hopi. The words are in the Hopi language, but he stops after each verse to tell the story in the Navajo language.

"Creator formed my people to live in the underworld. Our existence was spiritual and immortal and in harmony with Earth, Sky, and all people. We lived there until Creator opened a hole in the top of the cave and let down a ladder. It was time to leave that world and enter another. We entered this world at the Place of Emergence, which we call *Kuhmin A'lakkwenne*, a place the Bilagáana have named *Grand Canyon*. Earth Mother charged those early Puebloans with a quest to find the Center Place, telling them they would receive a sign when they found it.

"Bands of Hopi traveled in four of the sacred directions – north, south, east, and west. They walked in spiraling paths and left records of their travels – petroglyphs of spirals and circles – in the rocks of two continents.

"They discovered the Center Place in Chaco Canyon, which we call *Yupköyvi*, on the spot where they built Pueblo Bonito, the largest of the great houses in Chaco, between about 900 CE and 1150 CE according to the Bilagáana archeologists. All this sounds a lot better in Hopi, by the way."

"Why do you use the Bilagáana dates?" Gahtsoh asks.

"Ha! Because the Hopi do not reckon time as do the Bilagáana or the Navajo. How the Hopi move through time is something you will learn much later."

Gaagii has remained silent until this point. "As I understand it, the Navajo also believe Chaco is a sacred place, but we abandoned it long ago. After serving its purpose, it returns to Earth Mother. The Hopi emerged into this world at the Grand Canyon. The ancestors of the Navajo entered this world from Xajiinai, in what the Hispanglos named the La Platta Mountains."

Gaagii then asks, "Did your grandfather teach you the Navajo creation story?"

Gahtsoh surprises Gaagii and Chatima by singing the story. He tells how Creator made the Basket Makers who made *Átsé Hastiin* and *Átsé 'Asdzáán – Fi*rst Man and First Woman – from yellow corn and white corn. "First Man and First Woman lived in the First World, which was dark. Their only food was insects; their only company was bats. They and their children and their children's children lived in First World until a flood forced them to another world."

Gahtsoh continues to sing, telling how many gods created other worlds as the Diné emerged from one after another of the black, blue, yellow, and white worlds, driven by wars, floods, and rivers filled with salt, until they reached *Nihalgai*, the Glittering World in which they now live. "The Holy People put all this world in *hozho*, or harmony, and taught us how to live in harmony with Earth Mother, Father Sky, and other people, animals, plants, and insects. By the time we reached this world, we were more than just the Navajo. There were also A'shiwi, Ute, and Acoma, as well as Toltec, Apache, Algonquin, Cherokee, and others of our kin. From Xajiinai where they entered this world, they moved away in all directions. Later,

86

some returned to this place to become the guardians of the mysteries."

"*Kót'é*, it is so," Chatima says to Gahtsoh in Navajo. "We Hopi still consider Chaco sacred. Archeologists have opened and excavated some of the rock shelters – *tsebida 't'ini'ani* – behind the Chetro Ketl Great House. They are high places, sacred places, and there is a safe path to one of them. Gaagii and I will take you there and then wait below."

Gahtsoh understands what Chatima says. Chatima and Gaagii mean for him to make another Spirit Quest. Perhaps this time he will succeed. "*Aho*, yes, I agree."

"*T'áá'áko* – it is right," Gaagii says. "I will tell Dr. Deschene and Chief Joe our plans. Eat well tonight. We will leave tomorrow morning and reach Chaco by mid-afternoon. We have a loincloth, leggings, vest, and moccasins for you. There is no fuel for your fire at Chaco, so we will take a bundle from here. Nothing in either Hopi or Navajo traditions says you cannot have help before you begin your quest."

"*Ahéhee'* – Thank you."

~~~~~

Gaagii and Chatima walk behind Gahtsoh to the rock shelter and help the boy collect stones for his fire circle. He carries a bundle of twigs and small branches on his back. Flint and steel are in a pocket of his vest. A fan of eagle feathers that belonged to his grandfather and a medicine bag with a bundle of sage and *mountain smoke* – the dried plants called 'tobacco' – hang from his neck. The mountain smoke is a gift from Gaagii, who each season travels through the Navajo territory and among the four sacred mountains to harvest the traditional plants. Gahtsoh ducks his head, enters the rock shelter, and turns to face the southwest where Gaagii and Chatima stand. "I will see the sun set beyond the canyon before I step onto the ledge in front of the shelter and start the fire."

Gaagii and Chatima's footsteps fade. Gahtsoh unhooks the braces from his legs and places them and his crutches near enough to touch. On the ledge in front of the shelter, he builds his fire circle and lays small sticks. He uses his arms to arrange his legs and opens his spirit to Earth Mother, hoping to feel her. The sun crosses the meridian. It shines hot on his face. *Nilch'i,* a spirit wind, drifts past the ledge and cools him. He feels content and believes the wind tells him he is in the place he belongs.

As the wind touches him, he begins a song Gaagii taught, a Song of Summoning, a song to call his spirit guide.

The sun sets behind the canyon wall, but the sky remains bright. Gahtsoh watches the sky darken to a heavy purple and then black. The voices of the first stars tell him to light his fire. The flames catch and Gahtsoh throws onto the fire Gaagii's gift of mountain smoke to carry his prayers to Creator, and then corn meal as an offering to Earth Mother. *Perhaps I will see Heron, again. Perhaps her wing will not be broken.* The boy continues the Song of Summoning while stars wheel across the sky and sink in the west.

The time for dawn approaches, but the sky is still bright with stars when Gahtsoh hears whispers. He stops his song and sits, silent and still, as the whispers become loud enough to understand. The words are unfamiliar, more a conversation than a chant. Gahtsoh tries to memorize the words and their cadence, but they are too complex. He understands these words are the voices of spirits, and he knows not to interrupt. The voices tell of the Athabascan people before the Spanish Conquistadores. Catholic missionaries. The Bilagáana Army. The Bureau of Indian Affairs. Protestant evangelical churches.

Before the sun rises, the whispers stop, and a shadow passes between Gahtsoh and the stars. The shadow speaks.

"Who are you, *Ashkii* – Boy, and what do you seek?" The words are Navajo, but they are only in Gahtsoh's mind, not his ears.

The boy answers without hesitation or fear. "I seek my totem animal, my spirit guide. I also want to speak to my grandfather's spirit. He is a Medicine Elder. I want to know why Earth Mother appeared to me as an injured Heron. I want to know if Creator has a task for me. Why are you here, *Naatáanii?*" The boy calls the shadow, *Great Teacher.*

"I felt you when I came to greet the dawn. As I approached, I heard the Song of Summoning, but it is wrong."

"How is the song wrong?"

The man steps onto the ledge and sits across the fire from Gahtsoh. The fire is not bright enough for Gahtsoh to see more than a shadow and a few sparks of firelight reflected on beads of sacred colors in the man's necklace. "Listen carefully," the man says and begins the Song of Summoning. It is enough like the one Gaagii taught that it takes only a few repetitions before Gahtsoh is singing with the man. *This is right,* Gahtsoh thinks. *I feel its rightness in my heart and in my mind.*

When the song ends, the man stands. "*T'áá'áko,* very good. The dawn comes and I must return to my home."

"Will you visit me again? I need to know so much…"

"Tomorrow when the stars appear. If you have had a vision, I will interpret it for you." The man moves away. The stars fade into the cerulean blue that slowly becomes nearly white as the rising sun heats the sky.

Gahtsoh allows his fire to die. He wonders why *Naatáanii's* Song of Summoning is different from what Gaagii taught him. *Gaagii said he and Chatima had merged Hopi and Navajo magic. Maybe they changed the song, too.*

Gaagii and Chatima come to the ledge and help Gahtsoh down the path. When they reach the place where Gaagii and Chatima have camped, Gahtsoh tells them about the old man and

89

the song. When his teacher-uncles assure him it would not be wrong, Gahtsoh sings the Song of Summoning into Chatima's memo recorder. As Gahtsoh sings the new song, Gaagii's face lights up. "The words are unfamiliar and their pronunciation is strange, but I feel the power of the song. Your friend is indeed wise."

Then, after a breakfast of fry bread and beans, Gahtsoh naps.

Before dusk, Gahtsoh returns to the ledge and strikes flint and steel to restart his fire. The fire catches and the old man appears. Tonight, the light from the fire is enough for Gahtsoh to see him clearly. *He is the giant who sprinkled corn pollen on grandfather, who spoke to me, who said Creator had a task for me.*

"Ya´ateeh, Achaii." Gahtsoh uses a polite and nonspecific word for *Grandfather*.

"Ya´ateeh, Hatsói ashkiígíí – Grandson," the man says, acknowledging not only Gahtsoh but also a bond between them. "Are you ready to learn?"

"Yes, Grandfather. Will you tell me why Heron appeared to me with a broken wing? Does it mean something troubles Earth Mother?"

"Tell me what you saw."

Gahtsoh tells of his first Spirit Quest and the totem animals who appeared and rejected him – Wolf, Raven, Coyote, and Eagle – and he tells of Heron's appearance with a broken wing. "Gaagii, a Medicine Elder, believes the totem animals are disappointed with the children of humankind and refuse to talk to us. I think they do not want to be the spirit guide of a crippled boy. He says Earth Mother sent Heron as a warning and a promise."

The old man closes his eyes and sings a song unfamiliar to Gahtsoh. Gahtsoh tries to memorize it, but like the voices of the spirits, it is too complex. When the old man opens his eyes, he speaks softly. "I feel your spirit. It is wounded like your body. I feel your desire to find a spirit guide. I feel your wish to help Earth Mother."

The man stands and then speaks. *"It has been revealed to me* that something troubles Earth Mother, but it has also been revealed that you will help her. Your Spirit Quest is not ended, but must continue. For now, go to your home; rest, eat and drink, and return to this place on the first day of the new moon, and begin your quest anew. You will find your totem animal, your spirit guide. He will answer your questions.

"That is all I may say."

The man stands, turns away, and disappears into the night.

My quest is over? But it's dark, and I dare not walk the path at night. And he did not answer all my questions! As Gahtsoh thinks these things, he hears footsteps and Gaagii's voice calling. The beam of a flashlight switches back and forth along the trail.

"Gahtsoh? Are you all right? We heard – we think we heard – a voice and felt you calling to us. What happened? Did you—"

"I did not see my spirit guide, but something strange happened. Will you wait with me for the dawn when it will be safe to go down the path?"

~~~~~

Gahtsoh does not speak until the three reach the trailer on the Hopi Reservation. "When will you be ready to resume your spirit quest? Will the old man visit you, again?" Gaagii asks.

"He did not tell me if I would see him," Gahtsoh replies, "but he said I would meet my spirit guide on the day of the new moon."

Chapter 10 She Rains

Spencer and Chuchip run through rain into the hospital. Their first stop is the changing room outside the pathology lab where they put on dry scrubs and carry their wet garments to a drying cabinet usually reserved for victims' clothes.

Chuchip twists his head back and forth. Water droplets from his hair sparkle like stars in the bright lights. "The She Rains have been very heavy – and they've lasted longer this year."

"I left my umbrella in Boston," Spencer says. "Never thought I would need it in the desert during summer. What are 'she rains,' anyway?"

"That's what my *shimásání* – mother's mother – calls the spring rains. She says they have come back to us."

When they reach the lab, Dr. Deschene has two bits of news for them. "James Holomon University sent a report on the lymph nodes of the woman we autopsied. The lymph nodes show significant and positive signs of metastatic lymphoma. They examined the samples using a 3-Tesla MRI with a SIPO tracer – superparamagnetic iron oxide particles. Looking that up is your assignment for tonight. They were, of course, unable to determine the cause of the cancer. That will involve some very basic research, which will be up to us.

"No, Spencer. I see the look in your eyes. When you think *3-T MRI*, think *three million dollars*. We are not going to buy a 3-T MRI." Dr. D smiles, but only to himself. The company that manufactures 3-Tesla machines called him just the day before to say the device would reach Denver on a cargo plane from Germany and be delivered by truck in five days. *Just in time for Spencer's birthday,* Dr. D thinks. *And courtesy of a Bilagáana plutocrat who is willing to play golf with a Navajo.*

Dr. D surprises the boys with his next question. "Have you read the *Four Corners Tattler* this morning?"

Spencer is first to answer. "I've seen that … in the checkout line at the grocery store. The headlines are enough to keep me away."

Chuchip agrees. "I've seen it, but have never bought—"

"That headline—" Chuchip interrupts himself when he sees the headline on the paper Dr. Deschene waves. "Skinwalkers?"

"They are a myth," Spencer says. "I mean, *aren't they a myth?*"

Dr. D tosses the newspaper into a wastebasket. "Myth or real, somehow the *Tattler* found a story. The *Tattler* prints some amazing things, but they've never actually said something untrue. They simply take what they hear and make it sound supernatural or scurrilous. They create imaginary links that defy both cause-and-effect and logic. They claim to quote experts, then refuse to name their sources, citing the First Amendment to the Bilagáana constitution. Since their offices are off the reservation and no crime has been committed, it's hard to challenge that."

Spencer fishes the newspaper from the wastebasket and looks closely at the story. "With all the things that happen around here, there's no need to make anything up. But this isn't just imaginary, it's wrong! A Skinwalker is a Medicine Elder who is usually evil. It's not the ghost of an evil person – that's a *chįįdii*. And it's certainly not the spirit of a totem animal. Heck, I'm a Bilagáana and know better than that. Is this a Navajo newspaper?"

"The question is not who publishes the newspaper. What *is* the question?" Dr. D brings his assistant's attention back to ground using what they know as his *teaching voice.*

"The question," Spencer says, "is not what we believe, but what do the readers of this paper believe? The *Tattler* is playing on the traditional Navajo fear of the dead."

"Think, *respect for the dead* rather than *fear*," Chuchip says. "And, the bigger question is what is behind this story?".

Dr. D nods. "*Aho,* I agree. This is why we will drive to Window Rock, tomorrow, to meet with Chief Joe."

~~~~~

The eastern sky is still dark when Dr. Deschene falls asleep in the back of the boxy ambulance that serves as the primary coroner's vehicle, leaving Chuchip and Spencer in the driver's compartment. "At least he went to sleep in the box," Spencer says. "We can talk without waking him."

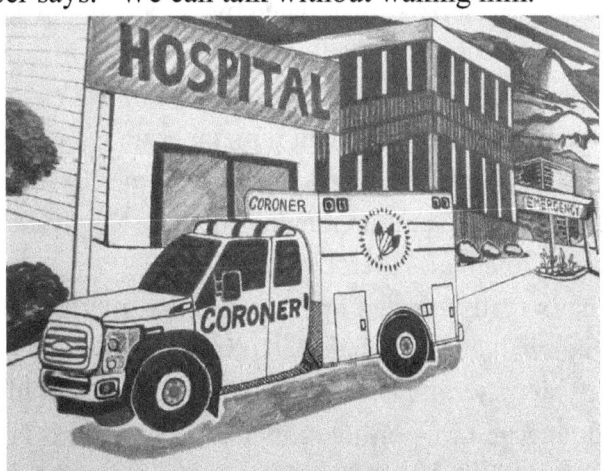

Chuchip steers the oversized vehicle through the narrow streets of Folio. "I think Dr. D wants us to talk about the article in the *Tattler*," he says.

Spencer agrees. "The newspaper ties together a lot of public information with gossip and things they ferret out. They have confused Skinwalkers with ghosts, which is not part of our traditions. They tied the murder of the Medicine Elder Ton Yah, Gahtsoh's grandfather, to Skinwalkers. There are still too many questions about Gahtsoh's grandfather.

"I saw the autopsy photos you took and read your file," Spencer adds. "Would a ghost use a sniper rifle? It's ridiculous! Anyone reading that should consider the entire article ridiculous. *Falsus in uno, falsus in omnibus.* Latin for 'If someone lies about one thing, you should suspect everything he or she says.' It's an aphorism, not a natural law, but it may hold a kernel of truth and it may be a place to start an investigation."

"Do you not remember the Navajo Creation Story Gaagii told?" Chuchip asks. "'*Átsé Hastiin* and *'Átsé 'Asdzáán* – First Man and First Woman – were shape-shifters who could transform into birds and animals to hunt game for their children. Their abilities were seized and twisted by evil people to do more evil. I do not believe Skinwalkers are real, but my father's brothers and my father – my *shizé'é yázhí* and *shizhé'é* – told me stories of them from the first I can remember until I was fifteen and disfellowshipped and forced from my home. By then they weren't telling stories, but threatening me with Skinwalkers if I would not obey them and their church."

"That's really messed up," Spencer says. "How do they reconcile Skinwalkers with their belief in the Hispanglo god?"

Chuchip snorts and shakes his head. Rain hits the windshield, and he turns on the wipers. "What's with the rain, anyway. Did you bring it all from Boston?"

"Global climate change," Spencer replies. "Changes in weather patterns world-wide. We've discovered recently that ENSO – the El Niño–Southern Oscillation – has more effect on North American weather patterns than anyone knew. The Four

Corners region is getting a lot of the rain that's skipping California."

~~~~~

By the time they reach Window Rock, the rain weakens to a light drizzle. Chief Joe had instructed them to go to the Council building rather than the police station. They find a parking space reserved for police vehicles.

"You know since Dr. D is the coroner he can arrest people, right? That means we're police, too, right?" Chuchip asks. Without waiting for Spencer to answer, he pulls into the spot.

~~~~~

The Navajo Nation's Council Chamber is in a building made of red sandstone. Wooden timbers extend from eight towers to support the roof. They serve a similar purpose to the flying buttresses on a medieval cathedral. The eight-sided chamber evokes the design of a traditional hogan. The eight clerestory windows echo the holes in kivas that admit the sun on certain dates. The heavy wooden beams anchor the building to Earth while lifting it to Sky. The main entrance faces east in affirmation of Navajo tradition.

A man who waits just inside greets them. "*Ya'ateeh*, how may I help you?"

"*Ya'ateeh*. I am Dr. Deschene. Chief Joseph of the Nation's Police asked us to meet him here."

"You are expected, Doctor. The young men?"

"They will go with me."

The man leads them to a conference room in the rear of the building. It holds a table and chairs for twenty people. The walls are covered with maps of *Dinétah*, the traditional homeland of the Navajo People. Some maps are of the area's underlying geology, some have contour lines showing elevations, some are soil maps, some are spotted with trailers, hogans, and buildings. Spencer recognizes these as aerial photographs, stitched together. Some maps have highway numbers and the logo of a Bilagáana automobile club. Their guide offers coffee, and then leaves the three in the otherwise empty room. Spencer studies the soil map that shows the sand and gravel aquifer underlying most of the reservation before Dr. D's voice pulls him away.

"Spencer, Chuchip. You may not discuss what you learn today except with the people you meet here." Before he can say more, Chief Joe enters with his nephew, Tommy and two police officers – Niyol and Ahote – their brothers in the kiva society. Chief Joe introduces the man who follows them as the Speaker of the Nation's Council – the council of delegates who represent the one hundred ten units of local Navajo government.

After everyone has coffee, the Council Speaker begins the discussion. "First, I understand you all have read the latest edition of the *Tattler*. They write about the weird and fascinating, but what they report as fact has always been true. They reported that someone masquerades as Skinwalkers and attempts to terrorize our people. Second, the San Juan River runs yellow. Not the entire river, but in many places, there is yellow scum. I spoke at length with Dr. Deschene, who thinks these things are related."

Dr. D responds. "I have only a hypothesis.

"You all know of the Gold King Mine spill in 2015 when a contractor for the Bilagáana EPA – their so-called Environmental Protection Agency – released three million gallons of wastewater containing 875,000 pounds of arsenic, cadmium, lead, and other heavy metals into the Animas River. The river ran yellow for weeks."

"And did it again the next year," Niyol adds. He speaks less stridently than usual, respecting the place and people present.

Dr. D uses a laser pointer to show on one of the maps the location of the mine, east of US Highway 550 and north of Silverton, Colorado. Then, he runs the pointer's red spot along the Animas River which merges with the San Juan River at Farmington. The San Juan enters the reservation at Farmington and dips to the town of Shiprock before turning north and west to form the northern border of Navajo territory until the San Juan meets the Colorado River at Lake Powell.

"There is something else that may be relevant. For several years, the hospital at Tonilih has experienced a suite of symptoms and syndromes that may be associated with water contaminated by heavy metals. One of my assistants is best qualified to describe this."

Spencer's blush is amplified by his pale skin. However, he speaks with confidence. "We took ten samples of water from around Tonilih, at homes where people with some of the symptoms lived, including people who had died. Seven of the Tonilih water samples, including the one from the Trading Post, have traces of mercury, arsenic, and cadmium and a bunch of molecules our mass spectrometer can't identify. I don't know enough chemistry to figure them out, but they can't be good. Those wells are contaminated."

Dr. D continues the briefing. "One of the chemicals is alpha-mercuri-acetaldehide." The man's lips are tight when he turns to the Council Speaker. "In the 1950s and '60s, there was a major mercury poisoning event in Japan. Hundreds died from the immediate effects; thousands experienced neurological damage – chronic numbness and birth defects. It was all thought to be methylmercury. It was only recently they were able to identify alpha-mercuri-acetaldehyde from tissues preserved years ago. Oddly, the tissue was a cat's brain. But, from where is this *new* mercury coming? And these other chemicals? Not the abandoned mines, I don't think.

"Spencer's question was why our mass spectrometer couldn't identify some of the chemicals. My first thought is they are too new to be in the database; my second is they are proprietary to some industrial process, and are kept secret. We need more than just names; we need details of composition and the degree of concentration. We have sent samples to the lab at James Holomon University. They will be able to identify the new chemicals and determine concentration better than we can."

Dr. D pauses to let this information sink in before continuing. "The San Juan River runs with yellow scum. I believe it is polluted from old mining operations like the spill from the Gold King Mine. I believe that pollution has found its way into the wells around Tonilih. People in the Four Corners area report seeing Skinwalkers. I believe this is not coincidence."

Spencer immediately makes the connection. "The Skinwalkers are trying to frighten people away from the source of the contamination."

Chuchip remembers what Spencer said about the rain and what his grandmother said about the She Rains. "The She Rains are flooding old mines and washing pollution into the river."

"Very good, Chuchip. You have identified the most likely proximate cause of the pollution," Dr. D says. Chuchip blushes at his teacher's affirmation.

"Why Skinwalkers?" Spencer asks. "Is Chuchip's hypothesis correct, or are there other explanations? Who are these people and what is their motive – and does it have anything to do with the river and pollution, or is it something else?"

"I have to limit my questions to the law," Chief Joe says. "Is something illegal going on? If so, what? It's not against the law to dress up as a Skinwalker. Further, many of the reports are north and east of Four Corners, in the Ute Mountain Reservation, and outside my jurisdiction."

The Speaker steps to a photo-map which shows hundreds of circles that cluster east and west of Route 371 south of NAPI – the Navajo Agricultural Products Industry town. "The problem may be greater. These are fields watered by center-pivot irrigation systems. They draw water from an aquifer that underlies much of the reservation. Seventy-three thousand acres of crops including alfalfa, corn, and pinto beans grow in these fields. Over three hundred people depend on NAPI for their jobs. The aquifer is fed largely from the San Juan and Animas Rivers.

"Our geologists tell us water moves through the aquifer about one foot per day. The nearest irrigated fields are less than two miles from the river. Is this aquifer being polluted? It would take years for polluted water from the rivers to reach the aquifer, but it could also take years for the aquifer to clean itself after the source of pollution was removed."

Then, the Council Speaker summarizes the discussion. "If you are all correct – and I believe you are – then old mines are being flooded, spreading old poison. However, add the Skinwalkers, and perhaps there's something else going on – something more than heavy rainfall, perhaps something illegal."

Spencer stands. "The San Juan river practically surrounds the Tonilih Chapter," he says. "We have reason to believe the water in some wells there is contaminated. The most important thing – the most immediate need – is to provide clean water. Only the Council can do this." He folds his arms across his chest. Dr. D and Chief Joe understand his body language. Spencer has taken a stand, and will not be moved by anything less than complete agreement. It is a weakness, but it has paid off in the past.

The Council Speaker breaks the brittle silence that follows. He looks Spencer in the eye before speaking. "Young man, I would learn from you. Tell me what I should know."

Spencer sits down and summarizes his findings. "We believe the water in some wells around Tonilih is contaminated with heavy metals – mercury, cadmium, and lead. We believe there are other chemicals, but we don't know what they are or where they come from. We don't even know if they are natural or artificial. We have seen many unusual medical conditions at Tonilih. While correlation does not prove causation, some of those conditions are known to be caused by heavy metals.

"Chemicals in the water can be toxic even at low concentrations if they are not expelled from the body but accumulate over time. The processes to clean the water – distillation and reverse osmosis – are expensive. And, they leave concentrated toxic waste that has to be disposed of."

The Council Speaker's eyes follow Spencer as he stands and walks to one of the maps on the wall of the room. "And, sir? The sand and gravel of the aquifer trap most of the mercury, lead, and cadmium in the water. The water is quite pure before it reaches the NAPI fields. But, there's too high a concentration and not enough distance to clean the water that reaches Tonilih. The immediate need is to provide a source of clean water and truck it to every home in Tonilih. After that, we can explore other problems."

The Council Speaker grasps what Spencer has left unsaid. "The river is the source of contamination at Tonilih, then?"

Spencer looks at his hands, resting on the table. He glances at Dr. D and sees confidence and understanding. He looks at his other brothers-in-kiva, Chuchip, Niyol, Tommy, and

Ahote and feels their approval and support. "As Chuchip said, the She Rains are washing pollution from old mines and that is the proximate cause of the pollution – and likely cause of some of the diseases we see at Tonilih."

"The hospital at Tonilih has begun chelation therapy for some patients," Dr. D says. "They are injecting chemicals to bind the poisons in the blood and flush it out. But that is not always successful. It is very expensive and risky."

Niyol glares at the others at the table, and then speaks. "The Bilagáana have agreed since a treaty in 1908 – more than a hundred years ago – that we have priority water rights over the rivers that run through our land. However, the states surrounding us have negotiated water rights with one another, without leaving anything for us. Every year some state challenges our access to water, and we must litigate in the Bilagáana courts to decide just how much water we are entitled to. And now? Now that we are winning some of those legal actions, we find the water to which we are entitled is polluted?

"What is that phrase you use, Dr. D? 'Time to pay the piper?' No, Teacher. It's time the piper presents the bill to the Bilagáana."

Before Dr. D can answer, Chief Joe seizes Niyol's thoughts and says what others cannot say. "Niyol is correct. So are Chuchip and Spencer. However, the Council's resources are stretched. Further, there is not a consensus among the Council Delegates about how to address the situation. Some fear the stories in the *Tattler* will jeopardize tourism or the reputation of NAPI produce. Some believe it is a hoax. All are ultimately concerned in one way or another for the welfare of our people but all see the cause and the solution differently. The Speaker and I hope Dr. Deschene might act where the Council cannot.

"A Skinwalker is more than Tempura paint from a Dollar Store, white clay from a streambed, a few bells and rattles, and a loincloth. Keep our beliefs and their power, rely on them for strength; but make damn sure no one uses them to fool you."

Chief Joe fixes his eyes first on Niyol, then on Dr. D, then on each of the doctor's assistants. "Ton Yah was killed. Where murder is concerned, I don't believe in coincidence. Be careful."

Chapter 11 The Hunter

Buzzards kettle a few miles south of a cottonwood grove. The sun has passed the zenith, and the ancient weathered volcanic pipe the Bilagáana named *Shiprock* and the Navajo call *Tsé Bit'a'í* – Rock with Wings – shades two boys who watch buzzards circle and dive toward the ground in the center of their vortex.

"They smell something dead," the elder says. "Mercaptan, the science teacher told us. Could be a sheep. Let's ride."

His younger brother is reluctant. "*Jeeshóó* – buzzard – is a troublemaker, a bully, and a cheater. Besides, even if it is one of our sheep, it's too late."

"Come on, *Sitsilí*. We have to know." The older boy touches heels to his horse's flanks and rides toward the avian vortex; his brother reluctantly follows.

The older boy fires his scattergun into the air. To lighten themselves as they struggle to fly, the buzzards regurgitate what they had stripped from the corpse and eaten.

"It's a person. A man. He's dead." The younger boy stutters.

They stand beside what had been a shallow grave. The older boy points to runnels in the sand. "Rain from a thunderstorm sent by *Tó Neinilii* uncovered him – see where flowing water has washed across the grave?"

"A bearskin," the younger says. "He was wrapped in a bearskin. This honors him as a hunter.

"They buried him with his weapons," the older boy says. "Someone who knows the old ways buried him here. But they didn't count on the thunderstorm."

The older boy's cell phone picks up a signal. He reports to the Nation's Police and then turns to his brother. "They took our position from the phone's GPS. Someone from the Shiprock Police Station will be here in about an hour. They want us to protect the body from predators until they get here."

"As long as *Shash* doesn't come looking," the younger boy mutters. He fixes his eyes on the bearskin and wonders if *Shash*, the Bear, would be offended to see it there.

The volcanic field that surrounds *Tsé Bit'a'í* is much too rough for even a four-wheel-drive vehicle. The police tow a horse trailer southwest on Service Route 13 and then travel on horseback to meet the boys.

~~~~~

A body bag from the Shiprock Police Post arrives the next morning at the pathology laboratory of the Navajo Western Regional Hospital. It holds the man wrapped in a bearskin and the things found with him including a bow made of ash laminated with wood from the Osage orange – named by early French trappers, *bois d'arc*, bow wood – and arrows, a traditional spear with flint point, and a modern tomahawk with steel blade. Putrefaction of the body has nearly destroyed his beaded deerskin clothing.

Now, he lies on one of Dr. Deschene's autopsy tables.

Alerted by Chief Joe to the man's unique burial, Dr. D summons Gaagii and Chatima. They and Gahtsoh arrive after dark and spend the night around a small fire in Dr. D's back yard. Early the next morning, they gather with Dr. D and his assistants, Spencer and Chuchip, in the pathology laboratory.

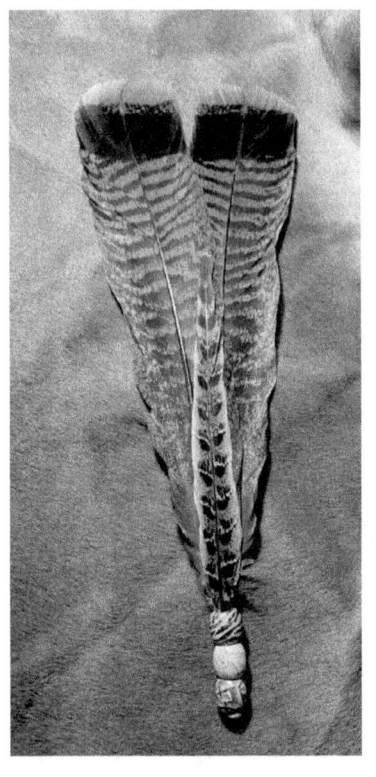

Gaagii stands apart from the others and tells them what will happen next. "I have sage, gathered with suitable ritual and prayer, and dried. I will ignite the sage and then, using this fan..." he lifts two feathers tied with a leather thong. "...I will wash the body of this hunter with the smoke. I will wash the others present. Last, I will wash myself before quenching the sage. The smoke from the sage will cleanse the hunter of negative energy and remind the rest of us of our connection to this man and to all life. Does anyone have questions?"

"What about the smoke detectors?" Spencer asks.

"Good question," Dr. D replies. "Just before Gaagii lights the sage, I will turn on an exhaust fan. It makes Gaagii's task more difficult, but it also keeps the ceremony from being interrupted."

All the others, except Gahtsoh, have seen Gaagii smudge the gatherings of the kiva. Gahtsoh watched his grandfather use sage smoke in healing. No one offers any more questions, and Gaagii begins.

He gently squeezes together a handful of sage twigs and leaves, puts them in a small pan, and lights the bundle with a kitchen match. The flames catch, but quickly burn out, leaving most of the sage to smolder slowly and release its pungent smoke. "Never blow it out," Chatima whispers to the others. "That blows away the spirit of the sage."

Gaagii sings as he walks around the autopsy table and then those standing by it – Dr. D, Spencer, and Chuchip. After washing Chatima and Gahtsoh in the smoke, he uses the fan to wash himself. When he completes the ceremony, he covers the pan. "*Hágoónee'*. It is done."

"What was the song?" Gahtsoh asks.

"Two songs," Gaagii says. "One says we are going to undertake something necessary but unclean – the autopsy – and asks Creator's understanding. The other asks Creator to guide the spirit of Hunter through the mist."

Gaagii sees puzzled looks on several faces. "Lacking a name to put in the songs, I called him *Hunter*."

Gaagii, Chatima, and Gahtsoh leave the lab, and Dr. D begins the autopsy. "Time of death is going to be very much a guess because of the condition of the body. Anywhere from a week ago to a month ago. Spencer, what was his age at death?"

"I use the 3-T MRI and a CT scanner before radiology opened this morning. One of the radiology techs came in early to help. A high-resolution scan of the trabecular bone at the head of the humerus suggests an age greater than 60 years. Given the putrefaction and damage by the birds, that's probably the best we're going to get."

"What about autolysis?" Chuchip asked.

"Normally," Dr. D says "measuring individual organ breakdown would be an appropriate method to estimate TOD. But, putrefaction is too far advanced. It would be difficult to figure out the differences in time for individual organs. That's a good technique otherwise. Collect and record the data from each organ and we will discuss your results."

"What about radiocarbon dating? The University of Arizona did a study back in 2012," Spencer asks.

"If he's 60 or less, he was born after the 1950s. With all the nuclear testing then, radiocarbon and other radioactive elements in the fallout flooded the global atmosphere. Someone born after the 1950s can't be accurately carbon dated. The university lab might find date of death to within perhaps three years using soft tissues. That would be more accurate than any guess we might make, but it's also much more expensive. Only if we cannot identify him or if identification shows a significantly different age.

"We used radiocarbon dating on wooden beams in Chaco. That helped date some of the bones there. It's a good technique, Spencer. Don't lose it."

"No, sir," Spencer says and thinks, what Dr. D means is *don't forget it*. He bombards us with new information every day, and he is trying to make sure even though we sometimes get smothered, we don't forget something important.

Chuchip brings Spencer's attention back to the autopsy table by pointing to places where flesh has fallen away from bones. "There is a green stain on the left temporal bone and on the left trapezium – here, just below the thumb."

"After exhumations, medical examiners have seen a green stain associated with copper hardware in cheap caskets, but someone buried this man in a bearskin. What else might it indicate?" Dr. D asks.

Chuchip and Spencer throw ideas at their teacher.

"Copper in the soil where he was buried."

"Killed with a copper weapon, but there's no fracturing or cut marks on either bone."

"Buried with a copper weapon the police didn't find."

"It's not copper, but something else."

"Ha´tchi – *You have spoken well*," Dr. D says, pleased with his students' responses. "First, be sure it's copper. Spencer, take samples and run them through your mass spec."

Spencer blushes. "It's not really my mass spec, you know. It's like Hokee's airplane. He's the only qualified pilot, so everyone treats it as his airplane. You and I are the only ones qualified to use the mass spec, and you don't like to, so it's kind of mine. But Chuchip is getting very good at using it."

Dr. D chuckles before proceeding. "In addition to the two green bones, what do we need to collect for analysis?"

"There were a lot of maggots when we first opened the body," Spencer replies. "They boiled out of his chest when we took him from the bag. We captured half a liter or so. They would have ingested any recent poisons or drugs. We can run them through the blender and then the mass spec. It's too late to get urine samples. The vitreous humor in the eyes is gone. We may get some coagulated cardiac blood."

"And pleural effusion – if the membrane around the lungs is intact," Chuchip adds. "The liver and bone marrow might tell us something."

"Kidneys, bile from the gallbladder, and the brain," Spencer concludes the list.

"All very good," Dr. D says. "Add head hair to your list. Remember, some drugs don't remain in the organs but may be preserved in hair. His hair is about thirty centimeters long. Cut strands in one-centimeter lengths and analyze them individually. Hair grows at a rate of about one centimeter per month, so that should give you a two-and-a-half-year history of any drug use. All set?"

Spencer nods and picks up a scalpel. Because of the condition of the body, the normal Y-incision is neither possible nor necessary.

~~~~~

"Cause of death, lacking any contrary indicators and given his probable age, is likely organ failure from old age. But we will wait for the results of tox screens," Dr. Deschene assures his assistants. "I don't like to leave any case open. As someone said, 'There are no unexplained deaths, only lazy pathologists.' However, we will wait for the experts."

Dr. D and his assistants clean up after the autopsy and sit in the hospital cafeteria with coffee and, for Chuchip and Spencer, high-sugar pastries.

"We collected a lot of samples for testing," Spencer says. "But you said he probably died of old age."

"Is there a question there?" Dr. D asks.

"Yes, sir. I guess. Why all the samples?"

"I think I know," Chuchip interrupts whatever Dr. D was going to say. "I've watched you figure out cause of death. Sometimes, you look for the cause; sometimes, you eliminate causes until there's only one left. We took the samples to eliminate causes, like was he a drug user."

"That is correct. Now, we wait for the tox screens from the Denver lab. Meanwhile, you two can report on what you find under the microscope and on Spencer's mass spectrometer."

~~~~~

The gas chromatographic mass spectrometer shows copper sulphate pentahydrate, cadmium, and mercury absorbed by the bones.

"And what is the common link between the chemicals?" Dr. D asks.

Chuchip takes the question. "They all are used in gold mining – copper and mercury to extract gold from low-grade ore. Could he have been a miner? Most of the mines were closed forty years ago, but he's old enough to have worked them."

Spencer summarizes the mass spec results and relates them to the body's condition. "Both bones where we found the green deposits are normally thinly covered with flesh. If he were a miner, an injury, even just a scrape, could result in contact with chemicals. A mining accident could have caused the discoloration."

"Good work, both of you."

~~~~~

Three weeks later, an overnight envelope from the Denver lab arrives. Dr. Deschene hands it to Spencer and asks him to compare it with what he and Chuchip had found.

"The Denver lab confirms what we and the Holomon lab found. Traces of heavy metal including copper, cadmium, and mercury in the samples we took from Hunter." Spencer studies the three-page report. "And throughout his hair. That means it's recent, not just maybe an accident when he was younger."

"And what is the question?" Dr. D asks.

"Are the heavy metals in the water coming from the old mine tailings, washed by the rain, or is someone working the mines now?" Spencer replies. "Was he working an old mine?"

"And are the *yee naaldlooshi*, the Skinwalkers, trying to keep people away from the mines?" Chuchip adds.

"Those are the questions. Send a summary of the analyses to Chief Joe."

~~~~~

There is no need to send samples from Hunter to the university for dating. Two families in Farmington identify and claim him. One clan is traditional; the other is Mormon. They had argued over earth burial or sky burial. They had compromised with an earth burial near the sacred icon of *Tsé Bit'a'í* – Shiprock. The families gave his age as sixty-two years, confirming what Spencer had seen in the scans. The families also confirmed the man had been a miner in his youth. They claimed not to know if he was working an old mine.

"I'm not happy about this," Spencer says after the body is taken away. "We don't know if the chemicals we found were from mining or the water. And they will rebury him in a Bilagáana cemetery. They and their religion have corrupted our traditions."

Dr. Deschene does not miss Spencer's implicit declaration of adherence to Navajo traditions. "You are correct, *Shiye'*, but long ago he journeyed through the mist and is now with Creator. What these people do with his remains has no effect on that." Dr. D continues the thought in his mind. *Rain sent by Tó Neinilii uncovered him, but Tó Neiniliiis a joker who laughs at cloudbursts. Jeeshóó – buzzard – who pointed the way for two boys to find him, is also a trickster and one who profits from the misery of others. Did Creator give us these clues to his death? Is Creator showing something we should see? What is Creator placing before us?*

Chapter 12
Gahtsoh Meets Gahtsoh

Gahtsoh unrolls a blanket among the sagebrush that surrounds the trailer. He lies on his back, folds his hands behind his head, and watches the stars wheel around the *Igniter of the Revolving Ones*, the star the Bilagáana named the North Star. He presses his palms against the caliche and sand beneath him and feels the beat of Earth Mother's heart before sleep takes him to a place where he dreams.

The dream is about his grandfather. Ton Yah walks through the mist. Gahtsoh's grandfather wears knee-length moccasins, a loincloth of wool woven in traditional patterns and colors, beaded doeskin vest, and his medicine bonnet with the double tails of eagle feathers. He carries a calumet from which

 smoke rises. He does not wander as if lost, but as someone who finds it comfortable to walk in the mist and is confident of his destination. Gahtsoh finds himself in the mist with his grandfather. Ton Yah steps toward Gahtsoh until another figure, a man, enters the dream and stands between Ton Yah and Gahtsoh.

The figure is unclear, but Gahtsoh fears him.

The dream fades, but another begins. Light rises around him until Gahtsoh sees he is walking across the desert toward a ridge of rock. He looks along the ridge and sees that it is the remains of one of the wings – one of the magma dikes created by the ancient volcano whose central pipe is known as Shiprock. He knows he must climb the ridge, but he also knows he cannot. His legs are in braces that extend from hip to toe. Crutches clamp onto both arms. Gahtsoh is helpless without both braces and crutches. What does it matter what might lie beyond the ridge? What does it matter what he might see from the top? He cannot know the answer because he cannot go farther than the base of the volcanic wing. A figure stands atop the wing. The figure's laughter crackles through the air. The mist swirls to obscures his vision, and Gahtsoh cannot see who the figure is, but he knows it stands between him and his grandfather.

Gahtsoh puts a hand on the rock ridge and pushes. He realizes he is dreaming, and he decides if he cannot climb the rock, perhaps he can walk through it. With that thought, his hand sinks into the rock and Gahtsoh falls. His crutches push into the sand as Gahtsoh struggles to stand. He is once again in the mist, but he has passed through the rock. Now, he sees the figure clearly as a man from earlier visions. The man drops to his hands and knees and transforms into Coyote. Gahtsoh's braces disappear; he is no longer crippled, but still holds his crutches. He runs toward Coyote and strikes him with a crutch. Coyote vanishes. Gahtsoh's grandfather, the Medicine Elder Ton Yah, appears to the boy and speaks. *Take beads of the four sacred colors you rescued from my hogan and put them into your medicine bag.*

Coyote is protean, able to change often and easily. At this moment, he morphs into human form and steps through the mist between Gahtsoh and Ton Yah. He seizes Gahtsoh's arms and holds the struggling boy. Gahtsoh swings his arms, striking Coyote with a crutch and freeing himself. He sees his grandfather wave the smoke from his calumet toward him in blessing and then disappear. Gahtsoh wakes, knowing it is through his own strong spirit he escaped to this world, but he still fears Coyote.

There is no moon on this night, and high, thin clouds now obscure the stars. Gahtsoh blinks in the darkness, but after his battle in the mist he no longer has any fear of the dark. He waits quietly for the eastern sky to light with the dawn. He does not see behind him the western sky fill with clouds which brighten with pink, salmon, and red. Even here in the desert, pollution from coal-fired power plants creates an unholy beauty.

Chatima steps from the open door of the trailer and calls to Gahtsoh. "Coffee is ready, Little Brother. I feel your troubled heart. Will you tell Gaagii and me why?"

"*Aho*, for I need your help."

~~~~~

"All dreams fall from the same sky." After breakfast, Chatima quotes from ancient wisdom. "Will you tell us your dream?"

Gahtsoh looks into Chatima's eyes and relates his dream, including the fear and the triumph.

Chatima and Gaagii sit silently for several minutes before Chatima speaks. "Your dream tells of the knowledge you will need. It also tells of challenges you will face."

Gaagii agrees, and says, "You must complete your spirit quest. When you first went on quest, you were poorly prepared. Now you have more understanding. Last night, you learned you have an enemy in the mist – Coyote, who is a powerful totem figure. You have faced him and overcome him. You learned you do not have to fear him."

"The totem animals approached you at first," Chatima says. "They did not speak to you. The elder taught you a new Song of Summoning. With that song, you may call your spirit guide to you. The elder said to continue your quest at the new moon."

Two days later, when the first sliver of the new moon appears in the morning sky, Chatima and Gaagii take Gahtsoh to Chaco Canyon and wait below while Gahtsoh walks the trail to the rock shelter above Chetro Ketl, the Great House. Gahtsoh softly sings the Song of Summoning as he walks. The trail has not started to climb when Gahtsoh senses danger and sees Bear, who is called *Shash*. Gahtsoh remembers teaching stories from his grandfather. The stories told him how to greet *Shash*. The boy respectfully drops his eyes and stares at his own feet, trembling and no longer singing. He feels the bear's curiosity. He hears the bear's voice. *You are named Gahtsoh. But you do not know what your name means. You seek your spirit guide. I am not he. You seek meaning. You seek that which links you to life and to Earth Mother; therefore, you may pass.* The bear huffs, and then crashes through the brush on Gahtsoh's left. When the boy looks up, the bear is gone and the path is clear.

A gust of wind blows sand into Gahtsoh's eyes. He blinks and wipes away tears. When his eyes clear, the familiar trail has vanished, but Gahtsoh smells woodsmoke and something more. He follows his nose and the smell of cooking mutton and onion leads him to a small fire. A young man sits beside the fire and stirs a pot set upon the coals. He wears blue jeans, moccasins, a doeskin vest, and a necklace of beads. The necklace catches the light of the fire and reflects the four sacred colors: turquoise, yellow, black, and white.

Gahsoh takes beads from his medicine bag, the beads of the sacred colors he rescued from his grandfather's hogan. The young man ignores him while the boy carefully places beads around the fire to match their ancient positions. He puts the white shell beads representing dawn at the east and the turquoise beads of high sun at the south. The yellow beads of evening twilight he places at the west; the obsidian beads of night, at the north.

"I do not have all the beads of my clans," the boy says to the young man. "I give you what I have.

"*Ahéhee´* – thank you," the young man says and sprinkles herbs into the pot. Some herbs fall onto the fire and smoke rises. Gahtsoh smells cardamom and sage.

When the smoke clears, Gahtsoh speaks politely, but he does not hesitate to say his nickname. "I am Gahtsoh. Who are you?"

"Who did you expect to see?" the young man asks. He continues to stir the pot. Gahtsoh is hungry. His mouth fills with saliva. He swallows.

The man fills a bowl from the pot, and hands it to Gahtsoh. "Have you not borne my name since you were nine summers? Did you hope to find a powerful spirit guide such as *Atsa*, the Eagle? Perhaps *Mą́ííłitsxoo´í*, known as Fox, or *Mą́´ii*, Coyote?"

Gahtsoh is puzzled. I have borne his name? Tsela? Surely, he doesn't mean Gahtsoh.

"You look for your spirit guide and think of Coyote. Coyote is a powerful spirit guide, but he is a troublemaker who cannot be trusted. We also know him as Anger.

"Sit in silence while you eat and hear of Coyote's encounter with Rabbit."

Gahtsoh dips his fingers in the bowl and eats while the young man tells the story.

≈≈≈≈

Coyote prowls *Tséyi´* – what the Bilagáana call Canyon de Chelly – looking for a way to cause mischief, when he sees Rabbit.

Coyote chases Rabbit, who runs until he finds a hole in the ground. He jumps into the hole.

"I'll get you out of that hole!" Coyote says and sits down to think.

"I know," Coyote says. "I'll get weeds and stuff them in your hole and set fire to them. Then you will come out of your hole."

"No, Cousin Coyote," Rabbit says. "I like weeds and I will eat them before you can set them on fire."

"Do you eat milkweed? I will get milkweed."

"Yes, I like milkweed. I will eat the milkweed."

"Do you eat foxtail grass? I will get foxtail grass."

"Yes," Rabbit says. "I like foxtail grass and will eat it all."

"Do you eat rabbitbrush? I will get rabbitbrush."

"Yes, Cousin Coyote, I like rabbitbrush most of all."

"I know, I'll get pitch of the Piñyon pine. And burn it. That will make you come from your hole."

"Then you will kill me because I do not eat Piñyon pitch."

Coyote runs from Piñyon tree to Piñyon tree, gathering pinecones sticky with pitch. He stuffs the cones into Rabbit's hole and sets them on fire. He bends low and blows on the fire.

"Please," says Rabbit. "Do not come closer, do not blow so hard!"

Coyote comes closer and blows harder.

"I am nearly dead," says Rabbit. "Come no closer. Blow no harder."

Coyote bends down and blows as hard as he can.

Rabbit turns and kicks, hard. The fire flies into Coyote's face. He turns his head and scrubs the burning Piñyon pitch with his paws.

Rabbit laughs very hard and runs away.

~~~~~

The young man takes for himself a bowl of stew from the pot and eats. "There are many stories of how Rabbit tricks Coyote or turns one of Coyote's tricks back on him," he says.

"I am Gahtsoh," the boy says. "Despite my withered legs, I climbed the trail to be here."

The young man refills Gahtsoh's bowl. They sit quietly, eating, until the man says, "I am Rabbit, your spirit guide. You must learn the ways of a Medicine Elder. You have met one teacher and you will return here at full moon to learn more from him. I, too, am your teacher, but like Life and Death, I do not follow a schedule or a pattern, but I always know how to find you. Do you understand?"

"No, I do not understand, but I will do as you say. *Ahéhee´*." Gahtsoh's 'thank you' echoes from a suddenly familiar ledge holding only himself and a failing fire. Even the pot and the bowls are gone. Has this been a dream? A vision? The beads he placed around the fire have also disappeared. Gahtsoh understands this could not have been a dream.

When the sun rises, Gahtsoh walks the trail to the place Gaagii and Chatima have set up a camp behind the ruins of the great house. His story satisfies their curiosity about his return. Gahtsoh has completed his Spirit Quest and is now an adult, although he is still crippled and still very young. However, in the eyes of Creator and his peers – and in his own eyes – he is now a man.

Chapter 13 Burn Victim

The voice of Joseph White Eagle, Chief of the Nation's Police, crackles through the telephone. "People living in Sweetwater reported seeing a fire north of the settlement early this morning. Sweetwater is three miles west of Red Mesa on County Road 36. Officers on site found a burned-out pickup truck with a body in the driver's seat. These officers are not trained or equipped as crime scene investigators, but they know not to disturb the scene and to protect it. Will you take charge of the investigation?"

Dr. Deschene walks from his office to the cafeteria where Chuchip and Spencer see the astringent smile on his face and grab cardboard to-go boxes and cups for their barely begun breakfasts. They follow Dr. D to the coroner's boxy ambulance. "You two finish your breakfast. I'll drive."

"Hail Mary, full—"

"Knock it off, Spencer," Chuchip interrupts. "You're not Mormon anymore – and you never were Catholic!" As he speaks, Chuchip strikes Spencer's shoulder just hard enough to count coup, and both boys laugh.

~~~~~

Sweetwater is a small settlement with a garage and fuel station, a few houses, several trailers, pens for sheep, and a larger-than-usual hogan. When Dr. D pulls into the settlement and taps the horn, children boil from one of the buildings and surround the boxy ambulance. Mothers follow more sedately and try to shoo the children back. Men follow the women and children and greet Dr. Deschene. The men look askance at Spencer's blinding white hair and pale skin. Dr. D sees their faces and the looks the men exchange, but doesn't address their concerns except to say, "I am Dr. Nastas Deschene, the Navajo Nation's coroner." He gestures to one of his assistants, then the other. "These are Chuchip and Atsa, my assistants. I understand you have something for us to see."

Calling Spencer by his Navajo name, *Atsa*, meaning Eagle, should have reassured the men, but they remain silent. A child speaks where his elders did not. "If you're Eagle, why is your hair white?"

Before Spencer can think how to answer, other children ask, "How does a paleface have a Navajo name?" and "Chuchip – are you Hopi?" "Can we ride in the ambulance?" "Will you turn on the siren?"

A man who looks to be the eldest speaks to the women. "Take the children back to the school. Dr. Deschene, you will join us in the hogan. The boys must wait outside."

Dr. D demurs. "Atsa and Chuchip are not boys; they are adults, and, they are my brothers. I will not go where they may not. We are here at the request of the Nation's police chief. Who will take us to the place of the fire?"

The man who has taken charge points to another and seems happy when Dr. D and his assistants leave.

Chuchip follows a pickup truck through the settlement and northwest on a dirt road. The road disappears after a half-mile, but the desert floor is smooth. After another mile, they approach a pickup truck with an integrated light bar and several antennas, and a second pickup truck – a dually.

A hole in the windshield of the dually shows where the glass has melted. Scorch marks rise above the hole and from the side windows, which are open or had also melted. "Hot fire," Spencer says.

"How hot?" Dr. Deschene asks.

Spencer jumps from the coroner's vehicle. "Two thousand degrees Fahrenheit to melt the windshield."

"Centigrade, please," Chuchip demands.

"Uh, almost eleven hundred."

Two policemen greet them and point to the burned truck.

"Body in the front seat. Fire was reported at 0500. We got here at 0710. One of the men from Sweetwater had driven here, but he said the fire was out when he got here at 0515. He saw the body and called dispatch. He says no one was seen last night or this morning and he didn't touch anything. Saw the body when he was still a ways away and didn't come any closer. Crime scene is probably undisturbed."

The hard caliche of the desert floor does not show prints as Dr. D and his two technicians walk to the truck. The body is upright in the driver's seat. Dr. D offers a preliminary description. "The seat may have protected his back, buttocks, and bottoms of his thighs from the flames. Most of the burns elsewhere appear to be second and third degree. Third and fourth degree on the skull where the skin is thin. See? Scorched temporal and zygomatic bones and missing ear and lips. Large skull, prominent brow ridges, and behind the ears, large mastoid processes. Likely male. We'll know more when we can move the body."

"The skull is shattered and some pieces are missing. Could this be the cause of death?" Spencer asks.

Dr. D looks where Spencer is pointing. "Could have been broken when the brain burst through from the heat of the fire. Look very carefully for the missing pieces."

The body's arms are curled across the chest and its hands are closed into fists as if the victim were trying to defend himself.

"Pugilistic pose," Chuchip says. "I remember reading about that. Muscles contract in the heat. Flexor muscles like the biceps are stronger than the extensor muscles like the triceps, so the hands curl up and the arms draw up toward the chest."

"Exactly correct." Chuchip beams in Dr. D's praise.

"The human body is about eighty percent water," Dr. D says. "It's like a sopping wet sponge, so it is hard to burn. This one isn't so badly burned that major joints will separate when we handle it, but the hands and head are fragile. After you get pictures, bag the hands and head."

Multiple flashes from Chuchip's camera illuminate the grisly scene. Then, Spencer slides plastic bags over the body's hands and head and secures them. Their purpose is to collect anything that might fall off; protecting the hands and head from post-mortem artifact damage is secondary. While Dr. D supports the body's head and torso, Spencer puts his gloved hands under the thighs and buttocks. "It's going to be tight," Dr. D says. "Spencer, lift slowly."

Dr. D's assessment that the truck's seat protected buttocks, bottoms of thighs, and back from the flames is correct. He and Spencer remove the body and put it on a plastic sheet. "We don't have a body bag big enough to accommodate the pugilistic pose and his bent knees, and I don't want to break adhesion at the joints just yet. Spencer, please tape up the plastic and put him in the van. Strap him down. We'll do the autopsy as soon as we get back."

Dr. D and Chuchip are examining the burned truck and filling evidence bags with bottles, a syringe, the melted remains of a cheap butane lighter, and a tin that once held throat lozenges. Spencer reports what he saw while strapping the corpse into the coroner's van. "Lividity on the right side of the back and on the right buttock and thigh, but none on his left side. He lay on his right side for several hours after he died and before he was put in the truck. I got pictures including pictures of what look like two knife wounds in his back. What's in the bottles?"

"Labels are burned, but the cretins who make and sell this stuff are right proud of it. The brand name is molded into the glass bottles. Everpure," Dr. D names one of the grain neutral spirits sold in stores around the reservation.

Chuchip whistles his astonishment. "That's nearly two-hundred proof."

"Would it burn hot enough to do this?" Spencer waves at the truck.

"I don't think I've ever seen information on how hot and for how long a bottle of Everpure burns," Dr. D said. "Since we're going to do the autopsy tonight, finding that information will be your homework for tomorrow night.

"Anything else?" Dr. D asks.

"It's a dually," Spencer says. "Remember what was found at Ton Yah's murder and the peyote patch? We should check the outboard tires for a nick."

"There's a heavy-duty trailer hitch," Chuchip says. "Wonder what he hauled."

Chuchip and Spencer squat, stoop, and crawl to examine the tires, but do not find a nick. "We need to look at the bottom of the tires," Chuchip says. "We can't roll the truck, though – it's way, way too big."

"The solution just arrived," Spencer says and points to an approaching flatbed wrecker. They watch as the wrecker driver hooks the burned pickup to a cable, tilts the bed of the wrecker, and gradually tightens the cable. He pauses at Chuchip's signal. Dr. D's two assistants check the partly rotated tires, and then shake their heads.

"It was a long shot," Chuchip grumbles. "I kind of hoped we'd find a match."

<p style="text-align:center">~~~~~</p>

The trio returns to Dr. D's pathology lab at the hospital and X-rays the body. Now, it lies on one of the autopsy tables. Dr. D adopts his teaching voice and begins. "Many murderers think a fire is a sure and certain way of hiding identity and cause of death. They are wrong. This autopsy will be an important lesson for you both. Spencer, what can you see to help determine time of death?"

"He's not wearing a watch and liver temperature isn't going to be useful after a fire – even though I did check it when I strapped him into the van. Lividity is fixed when the blood cells autolyze and block the capillaries. This takes about six hours. His lividity is on the right side of his back and legs. He was lying on his right side for at least six hours before being put upright in the driver's seat. The police say the fire was reported at 5:00 AM. Subtract six hours and say TOD is at least before 11:00 PM, yesterday."

"Chuchip, what clues might you get from rigor mortis?"

"None, sir. His arms are in the pugilistic pose which comes from muscles contracting, shrinking from the heat. I would not use rigor to determine time of death."

"Anything else, Chuchip?"

"I would make slides of the lungs, heart, liver, and pancreas and look for autolytic alteration. There's a table in one of your books that shows rate of autolysis in these organs. We might get TOD from that, but I don't know how the fire might have affected it."

"Excellent." Dr. D says. "And you are correct. The heat of the fire would have speeded up autolysis. You will collect samples, and we will look at them. Once we know more about the fire, we will reconsider this."

Dr. D sets ground rules for the autopsy.

"The condition of the body means the autopsy will be more butchery than surgery. We will break the elbow and shoulder joints in order to position the arms to open the torso and to examine the back, especially those two marks that look like stab wounds. The fire may have heated the internal organs – cooked them to some extent – but we will remove, weigh, and take samples, as usual. And, as usual, this includes extra samples for your training. Get two vials of cardiac blood and run a carboxyhemoglobin – COHb – test on one. That will help confirm something we already assume – he was dead before the fire started and didn't breathe carbon monoxide. The second sample is for a tox screen at the Denver lab. The syringe, spoon and lighter suggest he was using drugs. If so, I'd like to know what kind. Also, sample lymph nodes. Now, if you two will brace the body, I will break the arms."

The first crisis of confidence comes midway in the autopsy.

"Spencer asked at the scene if the damage to the skull could be the cause of death. Chuchip, you will clean and reconstruct the skull to address that question."

Chuchip grimaces. "Dr. D, I've never done this. I don't even know where to start."

"What you will do is called *thermal maceration,*" Dr. D explains. "The low temperature of the cooker will separate the remaining flesh from the skull without damaging it. You know, don't you, that besides the drawing-up of muscles, heat can make the long bones shrink and fracture? The skull will shrink, too, but only a little. It's unlikely the skull bones will shrink in the cooker, but we don't want to do further damage to them. Once the skull is cleaned, it's a simple process – like a three-dimensional jigsaw puzzle, and an anatomy book will tell you where the pieces go."

Dr. D stands back, but watches closely while Chuchip puts on wire-mesh gloves resembling very fine chain-mail armor and covers them with heavy rubber gloves. The combination will protect his hands from bone shards and sharp objects while he scoops out the remaining brain matter. Next, Chuchip carries the skull to a large slow-cooker in which water with a few drops of detergent is heating. He places the skull, including mandible, and the two pieces of bone found in the truck, into the water.

After the bones have been in the slow-cooker for a few hours, Chuchip uses a toothbrush to remove the remaining flesh, and dries the bones with a hair dryer. With Spencer holding pieces of bone while the glue dries, Chuchip puts together the entire skull, including the two bone segments found on the floor of the truck, pieces that had separated in the slow-cooker, and several teeth which had fallen out and been recovered.

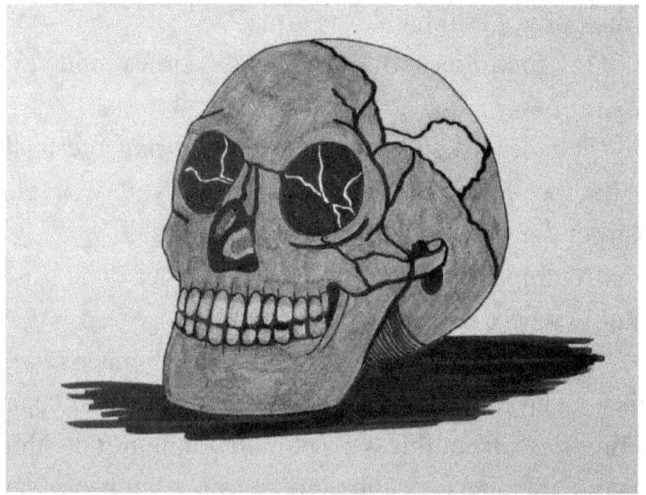

Dr. D holds up the glued-together skull. "What do you observe?"

"It's all there," Spencer says. "And it doesn't look like he was killed by a blow to the head."

"Or a bullet in the brain," Chuchip adds.

"What else? Perhaps something you don't usually look for or expect to see."

After waiting, Dr. D answers his own question. "The two pieces that fell out are brown, the ones that stayed on are darker, nearly black. Different burn pattern."

Spencer puts pictures from the crime scene on the HDTV, and scans through them, looking for the images of the pieces that had fallen out.

"We found the two that fell on the floor beside the seat, including the one which fell on the ground when we opened the door. The side of the seat didn't burn." He flips through more pictures. "The fire was limited to the body, the bench seat near him, and the floor at his feet. Someone applied accelerant carefully and didn't just splash everywhere."

"Another reason to believe he was dead when the fire started," Dr. D agrees.

~~~~~

Hours later, the three gather in Dr. D's office to discuss their findings. Dr. D encourages Spencer and Chuchip to speak. "What is the most likely cause of death? Was he dead before the fire?"

Spencer starts. "Either of the two stab wounds could have been fatal in a few hours, but not immediately. The pattern of lividity suggests he was dead several hours before the fire. He was stabbed, and then held, likely restrained, on his right side, for several hours. The stab wounds could have been cause-of-death."

"There was no soot in his lungs," Chuchip says. "That suggests he was dead before the fire. If his internal organs were pink, that would have suggested he breathed carbon monoxide,

131

but they weren't pink. I think neither his lungs nor his heart were working during the fire."

"Or the fire burned clean and didn't create CO," Spencer says.

"A good thought," Dr. D says. "Don't lose it. Everpure and open windows of the truck may have resulted in a clean burn. For now, we will keep time of death as sometime earlier than 11:00 last night; cause of death, undetermined; manner of death, undetermined – although almost certainly homicide. We'll wait for tox screens before making the final report."

~~~~~

The next day, after transcribing the autopsy notes, Spencer and Chuchip stay to use laptops in the pathology lab. After two hours, Spencer logs off. "The answer's not there. Nobody has published time or temperature of an Everpure fire. We will have to do our own test – like that TV show."

"The one where they blow things up? That's a joke; this is serious," Chuchip says.

Spencer grins. "I am serious. And here's what we'll do."

Dr. D listens to the proposal the next morning. "Whose truck do you plan to destroy?"

"Neighbor of Chatima who has a wrecking yard. He has a truck that's similar enough, but doesn't have an engine. The neighbor will tow it wherever we want as long as he gets to watch."

"Where do you plan to do this?

"On the fire department training range. They agreed to provide a safety crew, fully suited and with foam extinguishers."

"Who is going to bring the Everpure onto the reservation? It's very illegal, you know."

"Tommy has agreed to talk his Uncle Joe into doing it. And into lending Tommy a couple of police video cameras. Actually, I bet the chief will want to see this, too."

"How will you measure temperatures?"

Spencer hands Dr. D a printout from a website that sells high school science lab supplies, including thermocouples. "A dozen of these and a multi-strand cable plugged into a laptop. They're designed to burn up, but not until about 2500 degrees C, and they're designed to be hooked to a laptop. Everything we need is less than a hundred dollars."

Dr. D still has questions. "When we were discussing the fire during the autopsy, Spencer suggested the fire burned clean and didn't produce carbon monoxide. How will you test that?"

"That's going to cost a little more, 'cause we couldn't find any cheap CO detectors," Chuchip says. "But it should only take two and some more wires." He shows Dr. D a page from a home-fixit store website. "These home CO detectors are designed for remote reading."

"It may be sufficient. The autopsy did not suggest CO poisoning, but it would be nice to confirm that. How will you start the fire?" Dr. D asks the last question which has a chance of stumping the two boys.

Spencer hands the doctor another printout from the science supply company. "Igniters for model rockets on the end of another cable, and a nine-volt battery."

"And you're sure there's nothing on the internet?"

The boys nod.

"You will publish a full report of your test – after it goes through review at the community college."

~~~~~~~~

133

Less than an hour later, Dr. D's phone rings and shows a call from Chief Joe.

"Ya´ateeh, Joe. After what Spencer and Chuchip told me, I expected your call. I am surprised it took this long."

"Ya´ateeh Nastas. Tommy got their call when he was exercising the horses and couldn't get to me right away. What's this about?"

"Joe, I have some questions of my own about the truck fire, but I don't want to tell Spencer and Chuchip what the questions are or how to go about finding answers. This test is more a lark than I expected, but there's some real science behind it. Besides, they and their friends, including Tommy and your deputies, all of whom want to be present, have been working very hard this summer. They deserve a little fun."

Chief Joe chuckles. "In that case, I won't charge you for the Everpure."

~~~~~

Spencer and Chuchip lay the web of sensors around the cab of the pickup truck. A firefighter, wearing a suit covered with vacuum-deposited aluminized materials pours two bottles of Everpure over a crash dummy in the driver's seat.

Chuchip insists on doing the countdown. His voice echoes from the concrete tower of the fire department's training range. "Test in five … four … three … two … one … ignition we have ignition!" Spencer clicks a stopwatch to time the burn.

The fire burns for five minutes and eight seconds. The fire marshal and Dr. D examine the data and the dummy and agree that five minutes would not be long enough or an Everpure fire hot enough to do the damage the body or the truck received in the original fire.

"This means there was extra fuel," the fire marshal suggests.

Dr. D agrees. "Spencer and Chuchip will use the mass spec on the samples from the original truck. We have pieces of dashboard, seat cover and cushion, floor mats, headliner, and the victim's clothes."

~~~~~

Two days later, Dr. D announces the results during a video conference. "There was more fuel than the Everpure. Spencer?"

"Diesel fuel," Spencer says. "Which burns at over two thousand degrees Centigrade. Chuchip and I found not only that but also the red dye that marks off-road fuel used in farm equipment. And we've identified the body. Hashkem Naabah."

"You might as well continue with cause of death," Dr. D says.

Spencer adds details. "The liver is like a filter, trying to get rid of toxins. The fire wasn't hot enough for long enough to destroy it. Preliminary tox screen showed massive amounts of heroin and fentanyl in his body. Whoever did this tried too hard to kill him. Gave him an overdose of drugs, stabbed him, and set fire to him."

"Ha´tchi, you have spoken well, nephew." Police Chief Joseph White Eagle says. "You surely gave us sight into a murky picture."

135

Chapter 14 Murder

Chief Joe opens a video conference with Dr. Deschene, Spencer, and Chuchip, and introduces a man seated beside him as an agent of the Drug Enforcement Administration. "Agent Brooks assures me your work at the crime scene and autopsy of the burn victim was useful to his case. He and I want your continued help. This is an ongoing investigation, and you must not discuss it with anyone not part of the investigation. Will you agree to this, and to provide any new information you learn?"

After he receives everyone's agreement, Agent Brooks answers several questions. The burn victim, Hashkem Naabah, operated a food truck. He towed a trailer from place to place where he prepared and sold fry bread, hot dogs, and funnel cake at farmers' markets, festivals, and the Four Corners Monument.

"The DEA is interested," Agent Brooks says, "because we know he also sold Everpure and heroin laced with fentanyl. Of course, he didn't advertise that, but word got around both the Navajo and Ute Reservations. The Ute Nation Police found his trailer in a ravine in the Canyon of the Ancients. The DEA speculates, but cannot prove, that he visited one or more of the drilling sites there and that persons unknown killed him for his drug supply, dumped the trailer, and set the fire to cover their theft and his murder. We have no leads, and since Chief Joseph's officers and technicians and Dr. Deschene's assistants have been involved, I decided we would all benefit if we shared information. Chief Joseph agreed."

When Agent Brooks pauses, Dr. D speaks. "We send to Chief Joe all our crime scene investigation reports and forensic autopsy reports in criminal cases and all drug overdoses. I am not sure what else we can contribute except open eyes and minds."

After Agent Brooks assures Dr. D both would be helpful, Chief Joe terminates the conference. He takes a bottle of white ink from his desk and adds a dot to the red pin near Sweetwater where Naabah's truck and body had been found. The dot means "drug involvement."

~~~~~

The intake air filters of the diesel engines powering the pumps at the SAREMCO drilling site haven't been cleaned in weeks. Pollen, mostly from pine trees, clogs the filters. The engines burn dirty and push black smoke into the air from the unmuffled exhaust stacks. This pollution is not the worst, however. The pumps forced a brew of chemicals deep into the ground, fracturing rock and releasing methane, the main component of natural gas. Some chemicals flow back to the surface, where they are separated from the methane and pumped into settling ponds. By law, the ponds must be lined with plastic sheeting that is impervious to the chemicals. They must also be covered with more plastic to prevent evaporation until the contents can be properly treated. Here, in the depths of the Canyon of the Ancients National Monument, those laws are enforced with a wink and a nod by low-paid inspectors from the Bilagáana government.

"Who's the new guy – the ginsel?" one roustabout asks another. They are straining to move a six-foot monkey wrench attached to a bolt on a cover plate.

"Local talent. Navajo," the second grunts as the frozen bolt lets go.

"Next time, put him on the end of the monkey wrench, not me!"

138

The two men stopped work for lunch and are sitting at a table in the shade of a pine tree. "Where's the ginsel," one asks.

"I dunno. Took his lunch box in that direction, there. Communing with nature or whatever those people do."

"It's hotter'n hell, and there ain't any shade. Just the flowback pool."

The two roustabouts exchange glances. The nature and makeup of the chemicals is a trade secret of the Saramco corporation, their employer. "Come on," the first says.

~~~~~

"What do you think you're doin'?" one roustabout calls to the new guy.

It is obvious what the new guy is doing. The men watched him dip his thermos into the flowback pool and cap it. He is taking a sample of the chemical soup in the pool.

"Uh ... nothin'."

"Who you workin' for?"

"Uh ... nobody."

"Get him, Tom!" The two men grab the ginsel's arms and force him to drop the thermos into the pool of chemicals."

"Who you workin' for?"

The ginsel sets his lips in a line and shakes his head.

The two roustabouts tug on his arms and shove his head into the pool of flowback. He gasps and chokes when they let him up. He might have answered them, but he cannot.

The men push his head under the liquid again and again until the ginsel's struggles grow weaker.

"Come'on. That's enough," one man says.

"More than enough. He's dead."

"What we gonna do?"

"Take him to the decon station, and wash this crap off'n him and us. We'll throw him in your truck, drive him to the Navajo reservation, and dump him."

~~~~~

In contrast to the Saramco drilling site, the pathology laboratory at the Navajo Western Regional Hospital is clean. Bright lights shine on polished stainless-steel surfaces and make the crisp, white scrubs of the autopsy technicians glow. "Our first autopsy today is an eighth grader at the Tonilih School, Richard Yazzie. Do either of you know him?" Dr. Deschene asks Spencer and Chuchip, who have pushed a gurney holding a body bag into the pathology laboratory. The two assistants shake their heads.

"Good. Both of you are strong; I do not want to test that strength by asking you to autopsy a friend."

The autopsy technicians add plastic aprons, face shields, gloves, and a pair of white Wellington boots before taking the boy from the body bag and moving him to the table. Dr. D activates the microphone which hangs over the table and states the boy's name and age.

Spencer reads additional data from the hospital records. Dr. D watches Chuchip conduct the external examination. "Thin for his recorded age and height. Sallow complexion. He was not well—"

"A good assumption," Dr. D interrupts. "It will help us know where to look further, but for the record, we will say the complexion may indicate an underlying condition."

Chuchip nods, acknowledging the lesson. "Yes, sir. His right hand is clenched in cadaveric spasm. I am prying it open … he is holding a clear plastic packet with a press-seal, which seems to have survived the on-site examination and the

140

movement of the body to the pathology lab. I am removing the packet."

Chuchip holds the packet to the light. "Empty, but the inside is dusted with a white powder." He looks at Dr. D. "Could it be cocaine?"

"Another assumption, but a reasonable one. We know those packets are how *carteles* package cocaine for distribution to—"

"Children," Spencer spits. "Enough for a single snort, priced low enough they can afford it. Just enough to get them hooked. I want to put his heart under the microscope!"

"We will know more after the tox screens," Dr. D says. "Spencer? You will analyze the powder in the plastic packet. This completes the external examination. Chuchip?"

Spencer types notes on the computer terminal while Chuchip makes the Y-incision. Spencer turns in time to see Chuchip fold the upper triangle of flesh over the boy's face and cut the lateral flesh from the ribs. Spencer picks up a pair of garden shears and cuts the ribs and removes them and the sternum.

"I want the heart," Spencer says. "I will make microscope slides although I know what I will find."

"Of course, Spencer. You and Chuchip will examine the slides and write reports. You will work independently, but your reports will not become part of the official record until I have reviewed them. I know what you think you will find. I will give you a journal article on contraction-band necrosis – CBN – but do not allow what you read to prejudice your findings. Several conditions and treatments besides cocaine use can cause CBN."

<center>~~~~~</center>

In their suite that night, Chuchip challenges Spencer. "You opened a can of scorpions! I thought if I worked for Dr. D during the summer, I wouldn't have much homework. You really messed up that plan."

"Chewey, I'm sorry. I sort of lied to Dr. D when he asked if we knew the victim. About four years ago, we were in the same school. He was younger than me, but after I saw him being picked on, I tried to protect him. At least, to let the bullies know he had a friend. I sat with him at lunch. I talked to him. I didn't get past that, but I thought, maybe, I had made some kind of difference. I didn't really get to know him, and haven't seen or spoken to him in more than three years, so I wasn't quite lying."

Chuchip sits quietly at the table. He folds his hands and looks into Spencer's eyes. "You did lie, and because of the lie you were not objective at the autopsy."

Chuchip knows this accusation angers Spencer. He tries to defuse the situation. "Besides, you got us more homework! If you hadn't wanted to examine the heart, Dr. D would have relied on the tox screen. You want more of that pizza? And don't call me Chewey! I'm not a Wookie. And what's contraction band necrosis, anyway?"

Chuchip's words and manner unwind Spencer's anger.

"Damage to the heart muscles. It can only be seen through the microscope, and it's common in cocaine-related deaths. It can also be caused by prolonged torture. That's probably why Dr. D knows about it. You know he did pathology for the US Government in Afghanistan."

"He was in the Army?"

"Yes, but he doesn't talk about it. And I think a lot of what he did was actually for the CIA. But he doesn't talk about that, either."

"How do you know this?"

"Last year, when his office was burgled and trashed? I helped clean up and saw his medals and some citations. I asked him. He told me. He didn't say it was secret, but I've never felt comfortable asking him about it."

The microscope slides show what Spencer suspects. They also show no myocardial fibrosis, which supports Spencer's diagnosis of cocaine use rather than natural causes. He and Chuchip present their reports to Dr. D.

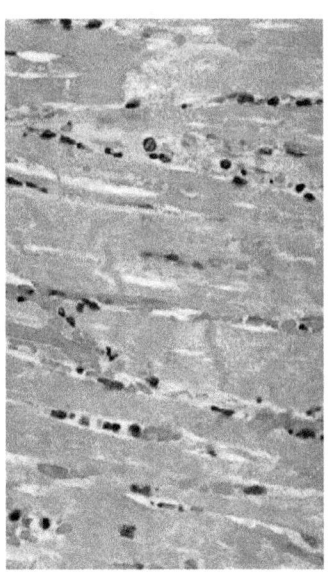

The doctor reads the reports and then looks at a page in a book on his desk. "Well done, and correct. We will wait for the tox screen results from Denver to confirm that.

"Yes, Spencer?"

Spencer admits to having run his own tests using the lab's mass spectrometer, and that they showed cocaine.

"As you suspected," Dr. D says. "Denver's confirmation will overcome any concern about objectivity. Chuchip, when we receive Denver's results, you will dictate the final report."

This is the first time Dr. D has asked Chuchip to take responsibility for a final autopsy report. His voice shakes a little when he dictates the report. "The autopsy did not find a disease or physical injury with an extent or severity consistent with death. The only indications point to a history of cocaine use. Cause of death – drug intoxication. Manner of death – accidental."

Dr. D switches off the microphone. "Very good, both of you."

Chapter 15 Death on the Powerline

The operators at the Nation's Emergency Dispatch Center are trained to keep their voices low and to stay calm. The room is dark, lit only by the operators' computer screens and three red "EXIT" signs. A large screen at the front of the room is dark. It is used only for situations needing a greater-than-normal response, so every operator looks up when it illuminates.

<<Operator 7 – navajo utility authority
powerline inspector reports body near
powerline appx 10 miles north red mesa
foam on mouth and nose inspector
suspects anthrax inspector still on phone
will remain on site>>

The senior operator issues orders. "Operator One, roll a crime scene team and notify the coroner. Tell the team to protect the scene and not move the body until the coroner arrives. Operator Two, notify the chief. Tell him we have sent a crime team and will notify the coroner. Operator Seven, ask where the crime team and coroner can get on the powerline access road and radio that to them. We may get some overtime today. I'll make coffee … and order donuts."

The operators respond with whispered cheers.

Four miles east of Red Mesa, a crew-cab pickup truck carrying the crime scene team turns north onto the powerline access road. The road is little more than a dirt track that runs along the 765,000-volt high tension powerline. Ten bumpy, lurching miles later, the team spots the inspector's truck.

After donning clean-suits and masks, the crime scene team walks to the body. It is lying on its back. Foam covers the man's nose and mouth. The team leader tries to rotate the man's head, then to lift an arm and a leg. "Rigor throughout. Been dead anywhere from a day to two days. Who has the liver thermometer? Get a body temp. We have an air temperature of 33 degrees Celsius. Who's taking notes?"

The thermometer used to check liver temperature looks like a kitchen meat thermometer – a circular dial with a sharp, metal probe that extends twenty-five centimeters. A technician pulls the man's shirt from his pants and jabs the thermometer into the liver. "Sir, this doesn't match the time of death from rigor. It's reading 35 degrees which puts TOD just a couple of hours ago – but he's been in the sun and heat, so the temperature reading is no good."

"Record it. The coroner will have to decide what to believe. And somebody get a sample of that foam. Treat it like a biohazard. The rest of you, start checking all around the body. Ground's too hard for tracks, but maybe somebody left a cigarette butt."

Almost three hours later, Dr. Deschene and Chuchip step from the coroner's vehicle and are greeted by the crime team leader. "*Ya'ateeh*, I know you, Dr. Deschene. This is a strange one. You heard the man who discovered the body thought anthrax. I thought a drug overdose or seizure. We collected foam from his nose and mouth. And he's in full rigor mortis."

Dr. D kneels and looks closely at the body. Resistance when he tries to lift one arm confirms that the body is in rigor.

He gestures to Chuchip. "Unbutton the shirt and help me roll him over. Now, lift the shirt so I can examine his back."

"The back of the shirt is damp," Chuchip observes. "And the seat of his blue jeans is, too. No lividity anywhere. His skin is dark, but—"

Dr. Deschene stands and strips off his gloves. "This is more strange than either rabies or anthrax, neither of which it is. The most likely cause of death is drowning."

The crime scene team leader does not snort or scoff, but his words make his disbelief clear. "In the middle of the desert? Come on, Doctor. The closest water is the San Juan River, and it's at least twenty miles away."

"Look at his finger tips," Dr. D says. "Whitish flesh, wrinkled and swollen – often called *washerwoman's skin*. The damp clothes and the foam suggest this body has been in water recently. I'll know more after the autopsy. You have photos and the foam sample for me?"

~~~~~

Dr. D and Chuchip reach the pathology lab at 5:00 PM. Spencer and an orderly are waiting, and help load the body bag onto a gurney. "Put him in a cooler – not a freezer," Dr. D orders. "And don't open the bag. We may have a biohazard. Lock the cooler. Autopsy first thing tomorrow morning. Full protective suits including the helmets."

Chuchip's face lights up. "Spacesuits, tomorrow?" For him, wearing the protective suit is a perk of the job, and gives his imagination a place to play.

"Yes, spacesuits tomorrow." Dr. D returns Chuchip's smile. "It's late, so please just text Chief Joe and tell him I think the COD is drowning. That will get his attention. If he wants to

147

attend the autopsy, let him know we'll wait until he gets here. Please tell me what he says."

~~~~~

Chief Joe, who is nursing a large cup of coffee, yawns broadly. "You really need to move to the hospital at Window Rock."

"Not until someone puts in a decent golf course closer than Gallup," Dr. D says. "And you convince the Hospital Administrator here to move all of Spencer's expensive toys to Window Rock."

"Isn't going to happen," Spencer says. When the chief frowns, Spencer adds, "It's not me saying that – it's the administrator. It took a lot of kissing up to get him to buy these things, but now, he's pretty proud of his forensic pathology lab."

"Enough chatter. Everyone not in spacesuits needs to go to the observation room. That would be you, Chief."

In the observation room, the chief turns on the HDTV, sets it to receive signals from the isolation room, and relaxes. He sees two people wheel a gurney holding a body bag with a wide strip of yellow warning tape across it. The helmets of the protective suits obscure faces. He recognizes Dr. D by his height, but Spencer and Chuchip are indistinguishable.

Dr. D begins the autopsy. "We have the body of a man of Athabascan ancestry who matches a missing person report for Martin Begay, last seen by his family in Kayenta three days ago. The body was in full rigor when found and remains in rigor. The body temperature when found was 35 degrees; however, air temperature was 33 degrees. Liver temperature is not useful to determine time of death.

"There was a firm and tenacious pink foam at the mouth and nostrils.

"Some maceration – whitish flesh, wrinkled and swollen – was visible in the finger tips at the scene, but has since vanished. Spencer, make sure the scene photographs of his hands get in the report.

"The back of his clothing was damp where it had been protected from the air. It has since dried."

While Dr. D speaks, Spencer and Chuchip remove the man's clothes. Spencer puts them in a washing machine whose drain hose leads to a catch basin where the water passes through five filters of decreasing absolute ratings. The setup will extract and trap particles and pollen in the cloth. Meanwhile, Chuchip begins the external examination. "Bruises on the upper back, shoulders, arms, and upper chest suggest violence ante-mortem."

Dr. D turns off the microphone. "Why do you say the bruises are ante-mortem?"

"Because bruises will form only if the heart is still beating. These bruises look like hand prints, sir. Watch." Chuchip puts his gloved hands over the bruises on the man's left arm. "It looks like someone standing behind him held him and gripped hard."

Spencer looks at the bruises and the position of Chuchip's hands. There is a second set of bruises on the right arm and shoulder, which Spencer's hands are not big enough to cover. "Two people were involved," Spencer concludes.

Dr. D turns on the recorder and summarizes their thoughts, adding, "No lividity was visible at the scene, although his dark skin may have obscured it. The body rested on its back from the scene – what time did we leave? – at 1500 yesterday until now, 0900, eighteen hours. Lividity is now visible on the back, buttocks, and back of the legs."

He takes a syringe from the instrument tray, pulls back an eyelid, and plunges the needle of the syringe into the right eyeball. After drawing fluid from both eyeballs, he hands the syringe to Chuchip. "Please put this in a tube with preservative. We'll get a tox screen on this and, if we can, on some urine. Spencer? How would you draw urine from the body?"

"I would try with a catheter, first. Second choice would be to wait until the bladder is exposed after the body is opened. Last choice, a suprapubic puncture – a long needle through the skin, but I'm not sure how to find the bladder."

"*Aho*, a good answer. But today is for learning. You will do the catheter for the autopsy. If that works, you both will do the puncture for learning."

After the external examination and sample collection are complete, Dr. D hands Chuchip the scalpel.

Chuchip makes the Y-incision and folds the top flap over the man's head. He uses a large kitchen knife to cut skin and muscles away from the centerline and reveal the membranes over the pleural, pericardial, and abdominal cavities. Dr. D cuts away the membranes, exposing the lungs, heart, trachea, esophagus, thymus gland, intestines, and stomach. Spencer uses pruning shears to cut away the ribs and sternum, then lifts them into a stainless-steel pan.

While he watches his assistants work, Dr. D continues to teach. "There is no singular autopsy finding that is absolutely characteristic of drowning." Spencer cuts away the lungs and puts them, one at a time, in stainless-steel bowls on the scales.

Dr. D pokes the lungs. "Heavy. The froth at the mouth, the over-inflated and heavy lungs, the crepitant rales – crackling sounds – when I prod the lungs, and the maceration of his fingers all point to drowning, whether found in the desert or the middle of the ocean."

He turns off the recorder but leaves the sound feed to the observation room where Chief Joe is watching. "Assume drowning. Spencer? What was the TOD?"

Spencer doesn't hurry. He knows Dr. D has given him all the clues he needs to find the answer. "Rigor mortis is caused by the depletion of adenosine triphosphate and glycogen in the muscles, post-mortem. He was in full rigor when found. Normally, that would take up to two days. I cannot assume that. A drowning victim may use up these chemicals while struggling, so rigor often starts early in drowning victims, except that cold water delays onset of rigor. I don't know the temperature of the water in which he drowned, so I can't use that. Maceration of the fingertips may take as few as 20 minutes to develop, and it goes away fairly slowly, but faster in the dry air of the desert. There was no lividity visible at the scene, although because of his dark skin, it might take several hours to become visible. It is visible now."

"You could have sat up with him last night," Chuchip says. Spencer snorts before continuing. Had they been somewhere else, Chuchip would have accompanied his words with a coup strike. but Dr. D's rules prohibit that in the laboratory – the danger presented by sharp instruments is too great. However, Chuchip and Spencer will settle up after work.

Spencer completes his estimate. "I suspect the body was dumped only minutes before it was discovered. I set TOD between 10:00 and 12:00 AM, yesterday. Had we gotten there an hour later, there might have been no maceration for us to see and the clothes might have been completely dry."

"Very good." Dr. D turns on the microphone and records Spencer's estimate and how he arrived at it. "Now, please check stomach contents."

Spencer cuts away the stomach and drains it into a four-quart plastic bucket that once held ice cream. Dr. D uses a kitchen spatula to prod the bucket's contents. "Barely digested food – looks like mutton and perhaps fry bread. He had eaten recently. Check it under the microscope, please. Chuchip –

151

preserve a sample, please. There's a lot of liquid and a smell of alcohol."

"He had been drinking?" Chuchip asks.

"Maybe. However, alcohol can form in the body after death, and it's difficult to assess blood-alcohol concentration in a body that's been in water. The vitreous from the eyes and the urine may tell us more. I think we know enough to record the cause of death as drowning and manner of death to be homicide. I'm convinced those bruises were from people holding him under water, perhaps in a stock tank. There are no other signs of violence or trauma, and no indication of disease. We will list both cause and manner of death as *pending* until the tox screen is complete.

"Chuchip, send the usual samples to the lab at Denver for a tox screen. Then, prepare samples of organs and stomach and lung contents and send them to the lab at James Holomon University. Spencer? You will do everything you can on lung and stomach contents. Every test you can imagine."

~~~~~

Spencer analyzes the contents of the man's stomach and the liquid in his lungs and reports to Dr. Deschene. "The samples from his lungs match the mass spectrometer readings of the samples from Tonilih except there's no mercury, cadmium, or lead. I still don't know what the other chemicals are. Maybe when we get the results from the Holomon lab.

"The lab tech at Holomon asked us to list her as a principal co-researcher when this is published. I told her if we published it would be through a community college, and I'd have to ask you. She's an intern, but sharp."

"Ask for her CV and ask if her boss will be willing to referee the paper," Dr. D says. "No, just ask for her boss's name.

152

I'll call. Holomon University has helped us in the past, and it may be time to pay the piper."

"Dr. D? Pay the piper? What does that mean?" Chuchip asks.

"Do you remember what Spencer said the first night he was home? About diseases in small, insular populations? Holomon helps us with analysis and reconstruction; we provide data for their studies. One hand washes the other."

Two weeks later, the Denver lab sends tox screen results showing no drugs. Dr. D declares cause of death to be drowning and manner of death to be homicide, and Chief Joe puts a red pin on his map.

Chapter 16 Gahtsoh and Hatałii

Half the month passes and the night of the full moon arrives. Gaagii and Chatima set up camp in the ruins of Chaco and then watch as Gahtsoh climbs to the rock shelter above the Great House of Chetro Ketl where thirteen days ago he met his spirit guide. Tonight, he hopes to see the old man. He carries wood for his fire, corn pollen, water, food, and *mountain smoke*. He also carries an eagle feather from his grandfather's medicine bonnet, a gift for Hatałii – for Gahtsoh believes the old man is a Medicine Elder, even though Gaagii says there are no more Medicine Elders.

Gahtsoh sits on the ledge at the front of the rock shelter. Darkness falls; he lights the fire and throws mountain smoke onto the flames. Again, he asks Creator to help him help Earth Mother. After the smoke drifts away, the old man steps onto the ledge. He sits across the fire from Gahtsoh.

"*Ya'ateeh, Achaii, Hatałii,*" Gahtsoh says, and then holds his breath, wondering if the old man will accept the title of *Medicine Elder*.

The man replies as he did before. "*Ya'ateeh, Hatsói ashkiigíí* – greeting to you, grandson. Are you ready to learn?"

Gahtsoh nods. In the light of the fire, he looks into Hatałii's eyes as his grandfather taught him.

"Listen to me and learn." Hatałii sings a Song of Healing. Like the Song of Summoning, it is different from what Gaagii and Chatima taught, but Gahtsoh feels its power.

Gahtsoh and Hatałii sing the Song of Healing until nearly dawn. As the western sky brightens, the old man stands. Before he speaks, Gahtsoh offers the eagle feather from his grandfather's bonnet. The old man accepts it. "Thank you, grandson. My time tonight is done. I will return with the stars," he says, before vanishing from Gahtsoh's sight.

Gahtsoh unfolds his legs, straps on his braces, and descends from the rock shelter. Gaagii and Chatima are waiting with food, water, and questions.

"He is a Medicine Elder," Gahtsoh says. "At least, he didn't object when I called him *Hatałii*, and he taught a new Song of Healing."

At their urging, Gahtsoh sings the song for Chatima's memo recorder before napping.

Gahtsoh wakes in mid-afternoon. Chatima is ready with food and water – and a question. "The one you call *Hatałii* must pass Gaagii and me to reach the trail that leads to the ledge where you build your fire. But we do not see him. How can that be?"

"I do not know," Gahtsoh says. "I do not see him until he is on the ledge. I don't even know from what direction he comes. Are you sure you do not see him?"

"The trail you take is the only path from Chetro Ketl to the ledge," Gaagii says. "He must pass us, but he does not. How is that?"

Neither Gahtsoh nor Chatima can answer.

~~~~~

Gahtsoh takes another bundle of sticks to the ledge and lays the fire. He fidgets while he waits for night. When the last light fades in the west and the firsts star blink on, the old man's silhouette crosses between Gahtsoh and the night sky. "*Ya'ateeh, Hatsóí ashkiigíí*. Are you ready to learn?"

The song this night is a Song of Thanks to Creator – the first medicine song his grandfather taught Gahtsoh. This time, the words are the same as what Ton Yah taught, although they sound different in Gahtsoh's ears and mind. Gahtsoh dutifully memorizes the new sounds.

"You will be a powerful Medicine Elder, and something more." As dawn approaches, the old man stands. "I see the beginning, but I cannot see the end." He turns and leaves.

Three more days and nights pass as the moon wanes. Each morning, Gahtsoh naps until Gaagii and Chatima wake him and feed him. Carrying a bundle of sticks on his back, he climbs to the ledge. Each night, the old man teaches Gahtsoh new songs. On the last night, the teacher has nothing new, and Gahtsoh braves a question. "You and Rabbit say I am to be a Medicine Elder. How do you know these things?"

The old man hesitates. It is the first time Gahtsoh has seen him do so.

"I am troubled by what I have seen in the times we spend together," the old man speaks. "I see strangers in black robes coming to the *nava hu* – the fields of corn, beans, and squash tended by The People. I see them gathering our children into something the black-robes call *reductions*, but which are prisons. I see them threatening our children with a horrible fate that is not part of our beliefs. I see them conquering us with unstoppable weapons. I see our people herded into lands our enemies call *reservations*. I see things brought onto these reservations that poison our brothers, including the children. I see death and destruction. But I also see spots of light, such as you are becoming; however, the points of light grow fewer as the years pass."

Gahtsoh is quick to understand. This man has seen what happened to the Navajo during the past hundreds of years – the incursions of the Hispanic Catholic missionaries, the wars with the Hispanglo army that forced The People onto reservations, the sellers of alcohol and drugs that surround and infect the reservation, the abject poverty in which so many of the Navajo

157

have been forced to live. Gahtsoh wonders if this can be reversed.

"I know what you have seen, Grandfather. It is indeed as you say. Our people were forced into *reductions* and now, onto *reservations*. These are places where with difficulty we scratch out a living. These are places the Bilagáana police have sway, and places where the Bilagáana use their power to seize control of mineral deposits, from coal to oil to uranium. Places they mine for gold, even on the territories they have sworn are ours by treaty.

"Grandfather, I hear you say these things as if they have not yet happened. How can that be?" Gahtsoh holds his breath while he waits for an answer.

"Grandson, I have lived in a hogan in Chaco for many years. I was here when the Chetro Ketl Great House was built. I was here when the builders abandoned this place of power. I was here when the Hopi discarded Chaco for other, more powerful places. I was here when you climbed what is now called Fajada Butte, and I thought perhaps the power of this place would be renewed.

"Alas, that is not to be. The Hopi know this."

"With the dawn, you will go to your home. You will return here at the next full moon." The old man stands, raises his hand, and recites a blessing. Then he vanishes from Gahtsoh's sight.

Gaagii is waiting behind Chetro Ketl when Gahtsoh descends. "Breakfast is corn mush with honey, but we will have mutton stew when we get home." When Gahtsoh raises his eyebrows in question, Chatima pats his cell phone. "Niyol kind of, uh, hacked the Bilagáana Park Service cell phone system. We don't have to worry about them listening to us."

158

Chatima explains how they knew Gahtsoh would return home, today. "The old man is in your mind. That does not mean he is not real. The old man waxes and wanes with the moon. You will be here to greet him at the next full moon."

~~~~~

After mutton stew and a nap at the trailer, Gahtsoh speaks to his uncles, Gaagii and Chatima. "We sang the Song of Healing all night. The old man is a powerful Medicine Elder – I could feel his power. Why was I not healed?"

Gaagii and Chatima exchange looks that pierce each other's hearts before Gaagii answers Gahtsoh's question. "There is more to healing than a song. It requires ceremonies, herbs, sand paintings." He does not say, *dancing*, because he knows Gahtsoh can never again do that.

"The song is the beginning of understanding," Chatima offers.

Gaagii's understanding is different. "Healing requires hozho – balance and harmony. No, that's not right. Healing is one face of hozho."

Gaagii is afraid to say the rest, but as one of Gahtsoh's teacher-uncles, he must not hide truth from the boy. "Chatima and I have heard the power in your singing. I believe Creator gave you the song and the power in exchange for your legs. That is the balance."

When Gaagii stops speaking, Gahtsoh sits frozen. The small drum is within reach. He takes it into his lap. Beating time with his fingers, he looks into Gaagii's eyes and sings the Song of Thanks. "I sing this to you, my teachers, because you told me what was hard for you to say. You told me something I must understand and accept."

Gaagii watches and hears the boy, and thinks, *He is becoming something, but I do not know what.* "Dr. Deschene knows that healing is more effective when it is possible to combine both traditional ceremonies and contemporary medicine. He has been present for many ceremonies, including the Blessing Way. If we invite him to visit, will you sing the Song of Healing for him?"

~~~~~

Gahtsoh agrees to Gaagii's request, and three days later, Gaagii prepares a fire circle in the hardpan yard outside the trailer while Chatima gathers twigs and limbs for a fire. They exchange silent greetings – handclasps – when Dr. D, Spencer, and Chuchip arrive and join them around the fire. Gaagii signals to Gahtsoh, who takes up the small drum and a padded mallet and beats the rhythm. No one smiles when his voice cracks on the third phrase, and he begins the song anew. When the boy finishes the song, Gahtsoh looks to Dr. D, hopeful, seeking approval.

"I have heard that song many times," Dr. D says. "Often enough that I have memorized it. But I have not heard it sung so well, and never in a boy's first voice. There is something else different about it. The words are correct, but their sound is different. Would you sing the first few words, again?"

"Gaagii said not to interrupt a song … I shouldn't," Gahtsoh says.

"Do not beat the drum, do not sing, but only say the first words," Gaagii says. "It will be okay; Creator will understand."

Gahtsoh recites the first phrase of the song. At the same time, Dr. D whispers the words.

"It's as if your tongue has moved to the back of your throat," Dr. D says. "When I say the words, my tongue is in the

160

front of my mouth. I think we need help with this. There is a Professor of Linguistics at the community college who has been studying the Navajo language for years. Would you sing for him?"

Chatima speaks before Gahtsoh can answer. "I have recordings of all the songs Gahtsoh learned. I will give you the tapes for this professor to copy if he knows how to treat them properly?"

Dr. D assures them the professor is Navajo and will treat the songs with respect. "Now, do you by chance have any coffee?"

"Not by chance, Brother," Gaagii says. "We still have some of Hawiovi's father's gift of thanks for helping harvest the peyote."

~~~~~

Gahtsoh drives a wooden peg into the hardpan dirt outside the trailer where he lives with Gaagii and Chatima. He ties two meters of heavy twine, carefully measured, to the peg. On the free end of the twine, he ties a pointed stick. He pulls himself along the ground with his arms, keeping the twine tight and pressing the stick into the ground. The result is a circle scratched into the dirt. In the center of the circle, he creates a smaller circle of stones in which he builds a fire. When the fire catches, he sprinkles mountain smoke on the flames in the tradition of the Navajo.

He sits with his braces unlocked and his legs crossed and sings the Song of Seeking. On the ground at his feet is the small drum. Gahtsoh beats out the complex rhythm as he sings. Chatima steps into the circle and sits across the fire from Gahtsoh. He sprinkles corn pollen on the fire in the Hopi tradition.

Chatima feels Gahtsoh's discomfort and then his confidence, but in the darkness, neither of the boys sees Heron light on the roof of the trailer, watch them, and then fly away.

Chapter 17 Laughing Boy

It is nearly midnight when the video call wakens Dr. Deschene. He stares at Chief Joe's face on the monitor. The chief's eyes are hooded. When he is not speaking, he presses his lips into a hard, narrow line. When the chief does speak, Dr. D hears both weariness and anger in his voice. The words come out slowly, and the chief bites off each one as he might spit out a bite of spoiled apple. "There is a dead child at the Four Corners Chapter House. The child was in custody of Family Services there. The FS representative on duty says the boy 'just died.' The body was stiff with rigor when the Emergency Medical Technicians arrived. They called dispatch and reported they had to physically restrain a Family Services employee who demanded to move the body. The EMTs are still there and will wait for a crime team."

Dr. D understands the chief's agony. "Under the circumstances, I will lead the crime scene team. Chuchip and Spencer will accompany me."

Chief Joe signals agreement. "May Creator watch over you."

The Family Services employee who meets Dr. D at the entrance to the Chapter House snarls, "What do you want? It's three o'clock in the morning and we don't do intakes until office hours, which start at nine AM."

Dr. D removes a leather folder from his pocket and opens it to show an identification card and a badge. "Ya'ateeh. I usually find it easy to get along with people and I will give you an opportunity to cooperate. I am Dr. Nastas Deschene, Coroner for the Navajo Nation. I am here to investigate the death of a child in your custody. Our law requires this."

He closes the folder and returns it to his pocket. "I am always surprised when I remember I have arrest powers. I don't like surprises; they disturb harmony. Please take me to the child."

Perhaps it is the way he speaks casually of arrest. Perhaps it is his physical appearance – several inches taller than average. Perhaps it is the two young men who stand behind him carrying aluminum suitcases containing their crime scene kits. Whatever the reason, the Family Services employee grumbles what might have been *follow me* before turning and walking away. Dr. D lifts his own metal suitcase and follows.

Dr. D and his assistants recognize the older of the two EMTs who stand by the bed. Johnny Highrock had been an autopsy technician working for Dr. D until a year ago, when he earned his Emergency Medical Technician Certification and took a job in Four Corners.

"Ya´ateeh, Dr. Deschene, Chuchip, Spencer. I know you," Johnny says.

Dr. D replies, "Ya´ateeh, Johnny Highrock; we know you and are glad you are here. Who is with you?"

"Dispatch said things weren't busy tonight," Johnny says. "And Chief Joe asked us to stay." He gestures to the second EMT. "This is Frank Falcon."

Dr. D greets Frank, while Johnny turns to the bed where a small, sheet-covered form lies. He pulls back the sheet to reveal a boy-child who appears to be about eight years old. "Family Services here lists his name in their records as *Ashkii* – 'Boy,' with no last name or clans. Not very much imagination. In our report he's officially 'Unidentified male child,' but we call him *Ashkii Anashdloh* – Laughing Boy. It's better than *Ashkii*, and better than *Ashkii Hokee*, Abandoned Boy, although

164

it seems he was. Someone found him wandering down State Road 162 south of Tonilih on Monday and dropped him off at the Four Corners police post. The police weren't able to record who the someone was."

The second EMT hands Dr. D papers clipped together. "We made a copy for you. The only thing we'll add is that you arrived at 0310 and took charge of the scene, and the time when we leave."

Dr. D thanks the young man and scans the report. "Dispatch received the call at 10:45 PM; you arrived at 11:00 – that was quick."

Johnny explains. "The fire station where we hang out is only forty meters down the road, and we were awake. We could have walked forty meters in less than fifteen minutes."

Dr. D nods and continues reading. "You found the child on the bed and declared him dead at 11:15 PM. What was the basis? I know it's in the report, but I want to hear it from you."

"I realized the body was in full rigor when I tried to raise an arm to take a pulse. There was no radial artery or carotid artery pulse. No heartbeat or breathing detected with a stethoscope. Frank checked and found no blood pressure. His eyes were open; pupils uneven and not responsive to light; corneas completely clouded – probably from post-mortem autolysis. And like I said. Full rigor. I felt like I was hurting him when I tried—" Johnny falls silent. Dr. D waits.

Johnny Highrock's breath catches in his throat. "I've never, even during the years I worked for you ... a child ... so young ..." He breathes deeply several times before his voice once again reflects his professional calm. "His skin is dark, but lividity is present and fixed, and shows he's been lying on his back since death. I estimate at least twelve hours.

Dr. D takes the child's left hand. "His spirit is on its way to Creator; this will not hurt." He lifts the arm against the

165

resistance of the rigor mortis. The forearm is bowed; the upper arm is oddly twisted. "Likely bones were broken but not reset properly, then grew back in unusual ways. The rigor is too advanced to know how much mobility might have been lost because of this. His legs are similarly warped and twisted. Chuchip, are you taking notes?"

Chuchip looks up from his video camera. "Recording, sir."

Dr. D turns to Johnny. "Was he naked when you found him?"

"Yes, sir."

"Right. Spencer, close his eyes, comb his hair – be sure to collect anything dislodged when you do so – and take a picture, a head shot. Send it to Chief Joe right away and tell him we have an unidentified child. We want to know who he is and who brought him to the Four Corners police post. Ask the chief to approve a full forensic autopsy. Then, take this release to the Family Services representative and ask him to sign. Tell him only it is routine. Be polite and thank him. We will want his cooperation, later."

Chuchip takes a series of photographs, and then, with the help of the two EMTs, re-wraps the child in the sheet and transfers him to a small, white body bag in which they will carry him to the coroner's van. A quick survey of the room does not find the boy's clothes or any personal possessions. The grumpy Family Services representative is unhelpful. Although he signs the form for the autopsy, he claims he hadn't been on duty when the client – as he insists on calling the boy – came in. He says the boy's clothes would have been put in the trash, which is collected every day and there is no record of any personal possessions.

When Spencer returns, he reports that the FS representative, whom he calls 'Mr. Grumpy,' seemed anxious

166

for them to remove the body. "And didn't you say he tried to do that earlier, but Johnny wouldn't let him?"

Dr. D gestures for Johnny to speak.

"Many Navajo fear the dead—"

"More a respect than fear, Chuchip told me," Spencer interrupts.

"*Aho*, that is correct," Johnny says. "But traditional fear of the dead lingers among some of The People. It has been said the evil a person has done during his or her lifetime is released at death to become a *ch'įįdii* – an evil spirit – and that this evil remains wherever the person died until a Medicine Elder removes it. This belief is so strong in some, mostly the oldest ones, they will abandon a house or hogan in which someone dies."

"I suspect 'Mr. Grumpy' is more concerned about other people's beliefs that the Chapter House might host the *ch'įįdii* of Laughing Boy," Spencer says. "Although as young as he is, I doubt he had time to do much evil."

"Not just evil he might have done, but evil done to him and his hatred for that," Dr. D says. "If Family Services or the Chapter officers are concerned, they can hire a singer to conduct the proper ceremony. Even though Ton Yah was the last Medicine Elder of The People, there are some who know the ceremonies well enough to be believed."

Frank Falcon helps Chuchip and Spencer move the gurney holding the body bag, leaving Dr. D and Johnny Highrock in the Chapter House. Dr. D accepts a cup of coffee. "Johnny Highrock, you know that I saw your gang tattoos long ago."

The young man freezes and then relaxes. He knows that although Dr. D follows the old ways, Johnny's modern tattoos are an open book to this Elder.

167

"Yes, Naatáanii." Johnny calls Dr. Deschene, *Great Teacher*.

Dr. D knows it is important to disabuse Johnny and explains what he understands the salutation to mean. "There is no one person to whom the title of Great Teacher applies. Think back on the stories of your childhood. Naatáanii exists in those who believe his teachings. This includes you. You are strong, having endured many trials. Strong enough to face this man from Family Services."

Johnny does not answer at once. When he does, his voice is firm. "Yes. I can face him and surely count coup on him."

"That is good. Here is what I want. The record of this boy's admission to the Chapter House. All evidence of how they treated him. The log of all contacts with him. Use evidence bags to secure the log and whatever else you may find. You know how to maintain chain-of-custody. As soon as your shift at the fire station is over, take all these things to Window Rock. Deliver them personally to Chief Joe. Will you do that?"

"Yes, Doctor."

"One more thing, Johnny. I suspect Family Services will try to keep this death quiet, since it appears the boy may have been left alone for many hours before and after death. Still, people will learn of it. Some will avoid the Chapter House, thinking the boy's *ch'įįdii* inhabits it. If you hear any hint of ghost sickness, please call me. There are no more true Medicine Elders, although the men who pretend to be may bring comfort to some. Ghost sickness may be real or it may be psychosomatic. Even in that case, it is real. One of Spencer and Chuchip's friends is a fledgling Medicine Elder. He can conduct a Holyway Ceremony.

Dr. D. smiles at the young EMT. "Remember, Johnny Highrock, you are part of Naatáanii. He is with you as he is with others."

168

Dr. D leads Chuchip and Spencer from the Chapter House for the drive back to Folio. Customarily, Dr. D would nap during the drive. This morning, he takes the front passenger seat and shows no sign of being sleepy.

"Full rigor." Dr. D says once Chuchip reaches the highway.

Chuchip and Spencer do a quick game of Even-Odd with their fingers, and Spencer takes the question. "Probably dead at least twelve hours, but not more than twenty-four to thirty-six hours. That would be from the time the EMTs got there, which was eleven o'clock last night. No wonder Family Services wanted to move him. He had been lying in bed, dead, since noon yesterday, maybe longer."

"Did you notice that the door could be locked from the outside?" Dr. D asks.

"Yes, sir, as soon as I saw you take pictures of the knob with your cell phone," Chuchip answers. "You think he was maybe locked in and nobody checked on him?"

"What can we do at the autopsy to help determine that?"

"Stomach contents and their condition," Spencer says.

"Run the gut – check contents of small and large intestines, too," Chuchip adds.

"Blood sugar level. And BUN – blood urea nitrogen – would be high if he were dehydrated," Spencer says, and abruptly changes the subject. "If the chief can approve a forensic autopsy, why did you want the FS rep to sign the release?"

Dr. D's reply sends shivers through both his assistants. "I want to ensure a record for the inquest of Mr. Grumpy's presence and his responsibility. I think we will find the manner of death to be homicide."

In the three hours it takes to reach Folio, they outline a detailed plan for the autopsy. Dr. D know the autopsy will challenge the boys' courage and he hopes the routine of this clinical discussion will create a safety net for them.

"We will begin with imagery. Spencer? The absolutely sharpest images you can get. Do an MRI and CT scan first, then break the rigor and get X-rays from every angle. Chuchip? You will assist and learn to use that expensive MRI Spencer bought. It's going to be a challenge to arrange this boy for the X-rays, but less of a challenge than debriding his bones for examination."

Both Dr. D and Chuchip ignore Spencer's denial that the three million-dollar MRI is his and that he had anything to do with its purchase.

~~~~~

The external examination confirms the EMT report of lividity and finds no ecchymosis – bruising. The initial internal examination finds no endocranial hematoma and intact frenula of both lips.

"See how the lips are still connected by central, tiny bridges of tissue to the upper and lower jaw? Each bridge is a frenulum; two make up frenula," Dr. D explains.

"I thought the frenulum was where the foreskin connected with the body of the penis," Spencer says.

"Shows what you know, brother," Chuchip says. "Not so important after you were circumcised; more important in those of us who have been left intact."

X-rays show multiple broken bones and breaks that hadn't been reset properly. The rape kit is negative. "We found no evidence he was abused – other than being left to die in a locked room."

"But the broken bones?" Spencer asks. "They're what we've seen before."

170

"Yes, however, given the quality of your X-rays, it won't be necessary to debride his bones," Dr. D says, sharing his assistants' relief.

Chuchip uses a baseball stitch to sew up the Y incision they had made for the internal examination.

"We will send fluids and samples of the organs to the lab in Denver," Dr. D orders. "Based on white cell count, BUN, and emaciation, I suspect COD is dehydration complicated by leukemia, but the death certificate will read *pending* for both cause and manner of death until Denver sends the results. We will keep him in a freezer until we know more.

"Good job, both of you, from the crime scene through the autopsy."

~~~~~

The next day, Spencer displays images on the HDTV in Dr. Deschene's office. "Femurs show them best, but they're on the humerus, radius, ulna, tibia, and fibula – all the long bones."

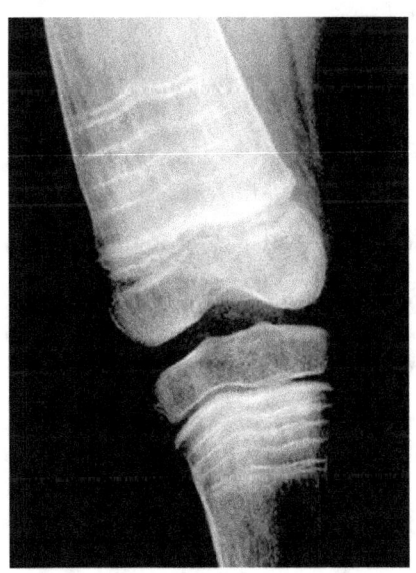

Spencer points to bright lines transecting the bones and parallel to the epiphysial plates – the places near the end of the long bones of the arms and legs where growth occurs.

"The lines are Harris lines – growth-arrest lines – created at times the body was stressed, usually from malnutrition or disease.

"One of the best ways to determine a child's age at

171

death is bones. This child's bones grew in ways that can be measured. But," Spencer raises his finger before Chuchip or Dr. D can speak, "there's something odd about his bones, so we may not be able to use bone growth, including teeth, to estimate age. Even knowing that, I estimate he's about eight years old and there are at least six clear growth-arrest lines in his long bones.

"That's about one per year. It's something tied to the calendar, and I'll bet it's the She Rains – the spring rains – washing chemicals from the mines."

Dr. D challenges Spencer. "A good observation, but can't those lines be attributed to normal growth spurts?"

Spencer doesn't fall for Dr. D's challenge. "Not in a child this young, I don't think," he replies. "In adolescents and post-adolescents, perhaps."

"Write them up that way. What about the other imagery?"

"The images of the long bones show they are warped from multiple breaks that didn't heal properly. The tendons and ligaments seem to follow the curves in the bones. I don't think we can say whether asymmetric pulls warped the bones or the asymmetric tendons and ligaments simply followed the remodeling of the bones after breaks.

"We'll never know for sure, but all signs of abuse are negative except for the broken bones," Spencer says. "Chuchip and I stayed up last night and did some work with the mass spec.

"He had low levels of lead, zinc, cadmium, and arsenic. They can interfere with calcium uptake leading to weak bones. This is what Nurse Toon told us about, and what we found in Tonilih."

"One thing Niyol's analysis didn't cover is time," Spencer says. "He looked at location, age, relatives. But not the time of onset. All the entries in Niyol's data base had dates—"

"Call Chief Joe," Dr. D interrupts Spencer. "Tell him about the growth lines and your hypothesis about annual pollution and the need to analyze dates in the records from Tonilih. Ask Chief Joe to summon Niyol. When Niyol calls, you will explain what we want.

"Meanwhile, for *Ashkii Anashdloh*, Laughing Boy, we will list cause and manner of death as 'pending' until we receive results of tox screens. Chuchip, please write up the autopsy. Spencer, write up the crime scene investigation and include how long he lay dead undiscovered, and the initial lack of cooperation by Family Services." Dr. D concludes. "Once again, excellent work, both of you."

Chapter 18 Visions

Dr. Deschene arrives home to discover a strange car in the driveway. His curiosity is answered when he reaches the kitchen to see Susan, with a fruit smoothie, and Doli Tabahaa holding a cup of chamomile tea.

Dr. D kisses Susan before greeting Doli. "Ya´ateeh, Doli, I didn't know you were visiting."

"Ya´ateeh, Nastas. I came to see you, but visited Susan, first. She's offered to put me up for a few days."

"And she's probably told you the sex of our child," Dr. D grumbles when he takes a soda from the refrigerator."

Both Doli and Susan laugh, proving in Dr. D's mind that Susan has shared the secret.

Dr. Deschene offers to spare Susan the chores of cooking and cleaning up, but she and Doli are adamant. Together they prepare a Three Sisters Bowl with hominy, tepary beans, and squash. Doli reconstitutes the dried beans in a pressure cooker and grinds herbs and spices while Susan peels and cubes the acorn squash.

"Before I met Susan, before she came here, I existed on Bilagáana TV dinners and the Three Sisters," Dr. D says. "But I never made a bowl this good. Thank you, both."

"Doli has things to tell you, and I must rest." Susan kisses Dr. D's forehead before leaving the kitchen. Dr. D and Doli sit at the table with coffee.

Doli begins the discussion. "My friends at the University of New Mexico have seen the metadata on symptoms and syndromes you provided. They are excited to have this to add to their studies – and, for two of the graduate students, for their doctoral theses. But, the results of their own water testing disappointed them. The water of the San Juan had cleared and testing at Four Corners showed the river is pure."

Dr. D understands. "The She Rains are over for the year. Water is no longer being washed from the old mines into the river."

"That is their conclusion." She chuckles. "They are not unhappy. This will justify extensions of several grants for at least another year."

"Spencer found Harris lines in bones of a child recently autopsied. These growth-arrest lines appear to represent annual events. You remember Niyol," Dr. D says. "He has just completed a new analysis of the data we collected from medical records at Tonilih." He hands Doli a folder. "He sent this just an hour ago."

Doli opens the folder and reads the first page. "Oh, this will make my friends happy. It shows a clear link between rainfall and polluted water. The university people will want to collect their own medical data, too. Do you suppose…?" She leaves hanging the question of patient privacy.

Dr. D chuckles. "Nurse Toon would appreciate a couple of university interns working in the records room. She didn't ask my team to sign confidentiality agreements, but the Council sent us. My guess is that university employees would also pass muster."

Doli closes the folder and focuses on the most important question. "What has the Council done to ensure pure water to the people there?"

"They have encountered the same test results as your friends. If the river is pure, there is no need to provide water to the Tonilih area. You should ask Susan for details. She's working on an article for *The Navajo Post* and by now, she knows more than I do."

~~~~~

Park Ranger Alberto Hermano pauses often to check his handheld GPS display. The trail he follows is not marked by signs with the names of trees and the Park Service mantra: "Take nothing but pictures; leave nothing but footprints." This trail is barren of footprints. Based on the elevation gain and the distance in miles, the trail is rated "Very Strenuous." It doesn't offer any good opportunities for selfies, so is not popular with tourists.

Alberto reaches what might be a fork in the trail and stops to take a picture with his phone. His supervisor expects him to return with a list of places to post trail guide signs. He checks to be sure the picture and GPS coordinates were saved, then steps onto the right-hand fork. At that moment, the ground shakes. *Earthquake*, Alberto thinks. Small earthquakes of magnitude 3.0 or so and linked to fracking, occur several times a week, and are so far are only a nuisance. This time, a small stone Alberto hadn't seen rolls under his foot. He loses his balance and puts out a hand to brace himself against a tree. The instant his hand touches the tree he feels a pulse of energy run through his arm, his heart, and then his feet. He falls; his head hits a rock, and he loses consciousness.

When Alberto wakes, he is lying beside the tree, a couple of feet away from the trail. *What the—*

He stretches his finger toward the tree and touches its bark before jerking the finger back. *Nothing.* He puts his palm on the tree. A sense of death overwhelms him, but he presses his hand against the tree.

No, he decides. The tree isn't talking to me. But something is telling me something.

Thoughts and images flow into his mind. Images of trees and the wildlife that depend on them – all dying but not knowing why they die. Alberto feels tears run down his cheeks. Here, a Piñyon pine, a hundred years old, withers, loses its needles, becomes a dry husk of its former glory. Here an eagle is dying after feeding on a squirrel, poisoned by acorns from an oak tree.

Other scenes flash through his mind. The cycle of death always begins with a tree whose roots reach deep into the soil and take up water – and poison.

The sun is half-way to the western horizon. Alberto has little time to reach his headquarters and even less time to think about what he saw.

Alberto downloads the pictures to the server and sends his notes to his boss by internal email. He's sitting at the computer terminal when his boss finds him. "Alberto? Is something wrong? You misspelled every other word in this report. That's not like you."

"Fell … tripped on a tree root … hit head." Alberto's voice is slurred. He slumps over the terminal.

~~~~~

Cheveyo, a Hopi whose name means *Spirit Warrior*, walks along a line of telephone poles. Cheveyo's task is three-fold. First, he numbers the poles consecutively so repair crews can identify them. When he reaches a pole, he selects from the four-inch aluminum numerals in a pouch at his waist and tacks the appropriate numerals to the pole. Then, he inspects the copper wire that runs from the top of the pole to the ground – a primitive lightning rod. Last, he uses a machete to chop weeds from around the base of the pole. He has just finished whacking weeds when his cell phone rings.

The call is from Dr. Deschene. Cheveyo's boyfriend, Alberto, has been injured and is on his way to the hospital, and Dr. D wants Cheveyo to be there.

Cheveyo's boss is understanding, but warns him, "I'm paying you for numbering poles and I want that line completed before the summer is over. Be honest with your time card and don't let me down. As long as you do that, you can take as much time as you need."

The woman had withdrawn from the same church that disfellowshipped Cheveyo. She took a role as his surrogate mother after his family abandoned him. Yes, the line needs to be cleared and numbered, but the task is more make-work than essential.

~~~~~

When Alberto wakes, he is lying in a hospital bed where Cheveyo stands vigil. Alberto runs his tongue over dry lips. Cheveyo sees this and hands him a cup with a bent straw. "Not too much … doctor's orders."

"What happened? Why am I in a hospital, and how did you get here?"

"Actually, you got here." Cheveyo's feeling of relief chokes his voice. "Your people said you fell and hit your head. The Park Service flew you here – it's the closest hospital with a new MRI machine. You can thank my friend Spencer for that," Cheveyo says. "You are in the Navajo Western Regional Hospital in Folio. That's why I'm here. Dr. Deschene recognized your name and called me."

Before Alberto can say anything, Dr. D enters. "Glad to see you are awake. Cheveyo told you how you got here? Good. We did two scans – CT and MRI. The CT scan suggested slight bruising to your brain. Together with the MRI, I got a clear picture.

"You experience a brain bounce, what we call *coup and contra coup*. You speak French, don't you?" Dr. D, who speaks Navajo, Hopi, Spanish, and English laughs, and sees Alberto's smile. "Your right temporal bone – Doctor D touches the side of his own head – hit something hard. Your brain bounced against the opposite side of your skull and was bruised just a bit. There was some subdural hematoma – a little blood under the membrane that covers the brain. You were unable to consent, but Chevyo holds your healthcare power of attorney. Under the circumstances, he agreed, and I performed a minor surgery to drain the blood and relieve the pressure. The surgery went well, but we will need to watch you for two or three days."

"My boss … I've got to—" Alberto begins.

"I have spoken to your supervisor. You are on medical leave until I say otherwise."

After Dr. D leaves, Cheveyo takes Alberto's hand. "You spoke while you were unconscious. I am the only one who heard. You must tell your story to a Medicine Elder."

"Why?"

"Our Elders are keepers of knowledge and teach us Creator's wisdom. They can understand and explain what you saw."

~~~~~

Two days pass before Dr. D allows Alberto to have visitors.

Cheveyo explains what will happen. "The two Medicine Elders who will visit are my brothers, although one is Navajo and one is Hopi. They are the last Medicine Elders of their Nations. They are my friends, and know we are of two spirits and are joined as one. A boy who they are teaching will be with them."

Alberto gasps and then lets out a deep breath. He trusts his friend and partner. "Please ask them to come in."

Gaagii, Chatima, and Gahtsoh greet Alberto and offer the grip of a warrior, with hands grasping wrists. Alberto responds

181

to their handclasps and thinks, *At least they haven't stereotyped me.*

Gaagii gives him no time to think further. "Our brother, Cheveyo, tells us someone gave you a vision in the forest. We study to become Medicine Elders and teachers. Will you tell us your story?"

Their honesty and directness put Alberto at ease. He tells them what he learned from the tree, while watching the others carefully. They do not grin or exchange knowing looks, but pay close attention, and nod encouragement when they catch his eye.

"What do you think?" Alberto challenges when he finishes his story.

Now Gaagii looks at Chatima before speaking for both of them. "Earth Mother gave you a great gift. Not only a vision but also the wisdom to seek understanding of what the vision means. *Ahéhee'*, thank you for sharing it with us."

"But what *does* it mean?" Alberto asks. "Cheveyo said you would know."

"I think our brother may have greater confidence in us than we have ourselves," Gaagii replies.

Cheveyo stands and clenches his fists. "No, brother. Do not think; feel!"

Gaagii tenses but relaxes when Chatima touches his shoulder. "He is right. We must enter his dream." He turns to Cheveyo. "Has Dr. D said Alberto could exercise on the hospital grounds?"

Cheveyo stutters his confusion. "Yes, but—"

"Soon, it will be dark. Come."

Chatima finds Alberto a robe and scuffs – cheap hospital slippers. The four young men and one boy make their way to the hospital grounds. In one corner, landscapers have planted drought-resistant yew and low manzanita shrubs. Gaagii leads the adventurers to a clear spot in the center of the vegetation.

"One day, they will install a fountain here. Meanwhile, it provides a place for a ceremonial circle. Please sit."

Gaagii and Chatima draw the circle, while Gahtsoh lays a small fire in the center. Alberto, alarmed, looks toward the hospital, but sees only a blank, brick wall.

Chatima sees Alberto's surprise. "They were foolish when they landscaped the one place on the grounds that cannot be seen from a patient room." He tosses corn pollen on the fire and begins to chant. Gaagii adds mountain smoke to the fire and joins the song.

The sun has set. Trying to conceal them, a mist forms low to the ground and crawls over the group sitting around the fire.

~~~~~

In the morning, an orderly finds them sleeping sprawled on the ground around the ashes of the fire. The man knows to call Dr. Deschene. By the time he arrives, they are awake, standing, and brushing dirt from their clothes.

"Alberto, you are a patient, so I would prefer you sleep in a bed, and that all of you find breakfast before I have to order intravenous fluids. You won't like the needles. I have a new student nurse looking for an opportunity—"

"Dr. D, this was important," Gaagii interrupts.

"Yes, it was. Now, breakfast. But first, showers. You all smell of smoke."

~~~~~

The five wear scrubs from the pathology laboratory and are waiting in Alberto's room when Dr. D arrives. "What did you learn?" Dr. D. asks.

They look at each other until everyone focuses on Gaagii, who answers Dr. D's question. "*It has been revealed* that Earth Mother gave Alberto a vision. We do not know if she selected him because he is a two-spirit boy and might understand the vision, or because there were no Athabascans nearby. It does not matter. Earth Mother touched him. Last night, we shared that vision.

"Something is poisoning the land around the Canyon of the Ancients. There is chemical death in the water. It begins in the trees, and moves through the entire eco– eco–..."

"Ecosphere," Alberto fills in.

Dr. D returns their stares. "We know there are poisons in the water and suspect the old mines. The She Rains, the spring rains, are flooding mines and washing chemicals into the rivers and wells. There are many investigations underway, and you must keep this secret for now, but I will ask Chief Joe to visit to hear Alberto's story."

Chapter 19 Code Breaker

Niyol slams his hand on the desk. The keyboard of his computer bounces. "I'm not getting anywhere with this data. I need a break!"

Chief Joe stands in the doorway of the police computer lab beside a woman whose nametag reads "FBI" in large blue letters. They are the only ones who see and hear Niyol's frustration. "Perhaps you need a new task, Nephew."

The chief's words calm Niyol, who looks up from his desk. "Yes, Uncle." Niyol then sees the woman and his smile brightens. "Ya´ateeh, I know you, Ms. Winder. Does this mean we will work together again?"

SAIC – Special Agent In Charge – Gabrielle Winder does not answer directly. "Last summer, I asked you to penetrate a computer used by the Russian Mafia after the NSA could not."

"Yes, ma'am."

"If you had encountered any of the NSA's code-cracking software, and if you had copied it, you could use it to decrypt something for me." Niyol's face echoes SAIC Winder's grin.

Chief Joe fills in what Ms. Winder hasn't said. "You and your friends found jars filled with water at Gahtsoh's grandfather's hogan. The labels had a symbol for poison and letters of the Navajo alphabet. The letters are meaningless, but we think they are a code and we hope you can break it."

Niyol's grin grows wider. Then he presses his lips into a tight, thin line. "You bet, Chief, Ms. Gabby. I'll get on that right away."

It takes Niyol less than an hour to break the code. It is no more complicated than the "magic decoder ring" he got in a Cracker Jack box, years ago. Easy to use and easy to break. But the meaning of the revealed Navajo words remains a mystery neither Niyol nor the NSA software can interpret.

"Chief, I've got a list of words on the labels – only ten different words – the Navajo names for Antelope, Beaver, Bear, Buffalo, Cougar, Coyote, Eagle, Rabbit, Raven, and Wolf. It's a list of spirit guides. Not every word is on every label."

Chief Joe takes the list from Niyol and shares it with the FBI agent.

"They're in alphabetical order – in English," Ms. Winder says. "What are the Navajo words, and what about word frequency? Can you list them as most common to least common?"

"On the flip side of the paper, ma'am. In Navajo and English. There are two groupings. Antelope, Beaver, Bear, Rabbit, and Wolf appear most often and with about the same frequency. The others appear less often."

"Perhaps Gahtsoh can shine light on this," Chief Joe says. "Take Ahote and a patrol car. This is official. When you return, draw *per diem* and reimbursement for fuel you put in the car."

~~~~~~

A strong wind from the south blows sand and dust over Highway 264, turning the two-hour trip into three. It is late afternoon before Niyol and Ahote arrive at the trailer near Kykotsmovi Village. Chatima welcomes the visitors while Gaagii pours coffee for everyone. Niyol explains what he has done, and then reads aloud the words he discovered written with the letters on Ton Yah's labels.

186

When Niyol reads in Navajo, Gahtsoh closes his eyes and hears his grandfather singing a song with only ten words – the names of spirit guides. He sees himself as a young child touching each finger in sequence, from one to ten. It is his grandfather's first teaching song. In the words Niyol reads, Gahtsoh hears numbers.

"It's the wrong order," Gahtsoh says, and sings the names from his grandfather's song. "They're numbers, one through ten."

He asks Niyol to start over, and calls numbers as Niyol reads the words from a label. *Náshdóítsoh*, Cougar is 1; *Shash*, Bear is 10.

Niyol matches the numbers to the words decoded from each label.

"Still doesn't make sense."

"What if Bear, *Shash*, is zero instead of ten?" Gaagii asks.

"What are you thinking?" Niyol asks and then re-writes the first label to find the answer. "It's GPS coordinates, 37000667109045880. Look, 37 is latitude; 109 – it should be minus 109 – is longitude."

He scribbles for a few minutes. "All the labels have a pattern that starts with 37 and has 109 in the middle. The rest of the numbers are decimal fractions of latitude and longitude. Ahote, please feed these into Google Maps." He reads off the first set of numbers.

Ahote switches the display of his tablet to satellite imagery and zooms in on the first point. "Two trailers, hogan, stock tank, sheep pens just north of the Four Corners Monument."

Niyol converts the words from the labels into GPS coordinates, and hands the paper to Ahote, who studies more satellite imagery. "The coordinates are all in the Tonilih Chapter and at settlements or farms with windmills and stock tanks. Six are the same places you took water samples when you were at Tonilih."

Gahtsoh's eyes widen. "Grandfather had a handheld GPS unit. We didn't find it in the hogan. He used it to mark the jars because he thought something in the water was causing sickness."

Someone may have killed him for that, and not for the peyote, Niyol thinks.

~~~~~

Niyol is exuberant when he reports to Chief Joe and FBI Agent Gabby Winder. "The words are numbers, and the numbers are GPS coordinates of locations around Tonilih where Ton Yah took water samples. Six were the same as places Dr. Deschene, Chuchip, and Spencer collected water samples. The others were in the Tonilih area, but they didn't visit them. Spencer said the samples in Ton Yah's bottles match the samples he took. He's going to send—"

"When did you see Spencer?" Chief Joe interrupts.

"We drove everyone to the hospital to see him and Chuchip as soon as—"

"Your *per diem* form and your trip report will interest me," the chief interrupts again. "Go on, please."

Niyol does not blush or hesitate. He knows he has done the right thing and that the chief will agree. "Spencer will send samples from the bottles to the same lab that analyzed the samples he took at Tonilih. Besides the duplicates, there will be four new data points. Gahtsoh believes Ton Yah suspected the water was causing illness. And that whoever trashed the hogan looking for peyote took his GPS unit.

188

"Ton Yah probably didn't realize the GPS unit would have stored in memory these coordinates as well as the coordinates of his peyote patch," Ms. Winder says. "We must wonder if someone killed him for the peyote or because his water-sampling was known to those poisoning the water."

"Chief," Niyol says, "we know most of the reservation rests on a sand and gravel aquifer. It gets charged mostly from rainwater, the northern rivers, and streams. Most of the wells on the reservation take water from the aquifer. We can't learn any more from Google satellite images. Someone needs to visit. And I need to see those maps of soil and geology and elevation in that meeting room at the Council House."

Chief Joe assigns tasks and agrees to get the maps Niyol needs.

"Two-hundred-kilometer radius of Tonilih," Niyol says.

Chief Joe makes a note. "We need our own samples of water from the places Ton Yah sampled but Dr. Deschene didn't. I will ask him to have someone meet you at Tonilih and arrange an escort from the hospital."

Chief Joe reminds them Ton Yah and Martin Begay were murdered, and orders Niyol to be careful. "May Creator watch over you."

~~~~~

Spencer's face turns more pale than normal after he opens the express delivery envelope from James Holomon University. He hurries to Dr. Deschene's office to report. "Fracking chemicals. The things I couldn't identify are chemicals used in fracking. The Holomon lab matched the ones in the wells near Tonilih and in the lungs of the drowned man. Even Holomon didn't have names for all of the fracking chemicals. Ashley said some were proprietary. The oil and gas companies are very secretive about them. What the EPA doesn't know can't hurt the oil companies."

"Ashley?" Chuchip raises his eyebrows.

Spencer's complexion cannot hide his blush. "She was in my chemistry class last year. Got an internship at James Holloman for the summer. We had a couple of classes – never mind.

"I still don't know what these chemicals do. But I'll bet Wikipedia can help us find out." He offers the report to Dr. D.

"Fax a copy of this report to Chief Joe. Tell him we'll send more information when we have it. And put a copy in the files."

Spencer and Chuchip split the list of chemicals and spend an hour on computer terminals. Chuchip looks up from his screen, signaling he has finished his list, and Spencer starts the printer. They pull pages from the output tray as fast as the printer can spit them out.

"Atrazine, that's a pesticide. And 1,4-dioxane is an organic chemical that irritates the eyes and respiratory tract. Toluene can cause confusion, nerve damage, muscle weakness, loss of vision and hearing. Polycyclic aromatic hydrocarbons – like the chimney sweeps who were the first cancer cluster – can cause skin, lung, bladder, liver, testicular, and stomach cancers."

Chuchip takes up the litany. "Benzine, which can cause cancer or leukemia, and dizziness, weakness, headaches, nausea, and vomiting. Diesel fuel. Wait! Huh? What?"

"I looked that up," Spencer says. "Diesel fuel and other chemicals containing diesel fuel are fracking fluids. So is kerosene."

"Fracking fluids include chemicals that cause lymphoma and leukemia. And they really do a number on the liver."

"And weaken children's bones."

"We have solved it," Chuchip says.

190

"No, brother, we have taken a step toward the solution. Cadmium, lead, and mercury were used in the old mines, but the fracking chemicals? The closest fracking wells are in the Canyon of the Ancients," Spencer says. "Which is next door to the Tonilih Chapter.

"The drowned man? In his lungs and stomach, fracking chemicals but not the old mining chemicals – cadmium, lead, and mercury. He got the pure stuff, which means he got it at the source."

~~~~~

Thirteen people sit in a circle on the dirt floor of an ancient kiva whose roof had disappeared long ago. The kiva was abandoned, having served its purpose, but still is a place of power. One member of the Eastward Kiva is absent. Susan Calvin is seven months pregnant and in no condition to be climbing over rubble. Two people who are not members are present – Gahtsoh and a young man in a US Park Service uniform.

Chatima, whose name means, *Caller*, stands and walks to the center of the circle where he has laid sticks for a small fire. He ignites the fire and begins the meeting. "We assemble to hear Cheveyo's friend, Alberto Hermano, who has important news for us."

Since non-kiva members are present, he abbreviates the opening ceremony. Chatima sprinkles mountain smoke on the fire and returns to his seat. Gaagii stands and asks Creator to guard and guide them.

Alberto stands and takes Gaagii's place beside the fire. "I am Hispanglo – my mother was from Mexico, my father from Canada. I lived with my mother's people in Mexico until I was ten, then among the Navajo. If I were Athabascan, you would

191

call me a two-spirit boy. Cheveyo is more than my boyfriend; he is my life-partner. He told me I might say this and said you understand."

When Alberto pauses, Chatima speaks for his brothers. "Cheveyo is our brother. We are blessed by Creator to have a brother and now a friend of two spirits. We honor him and you."

A chorus of "*Aho*" – I agree– echoes from the sections of kiva walls which still stand.

Alberto turns his hands so that his palms face forward. "*Gracias. Muchas gracias.*

"I do not know if it is because I am of two-spirits or because I have lived in the forest for so many years, but I had an experience and saw things that Cheveyo said I must share with you."

He tells of the time he stumbled, held on to a tree, and felt the tree's pain and the poison at its roots.

"I think I know the source of the poison. You know how fracking – hydrologic fracturing to extract oil and gas from deep underground – works. What most people don't know is that some water – which includes hazardous chemicals and carcinogens – injected in the wells can travel miles through fractures in the rocks, and can reach aquifers that carry the chemicals tens or hundreds of miles. Most people don't know that some of the injected water and chemicals return to the surface in what the oil companies call 'flowback' or 'produced water.' The law requires the companies to dispose of this water without contaminating the water table. They usually do this by pumping it back into the well where it joins other poisons in the aquifers.

"I am sure some operators are trucking the flowback away from sites in the Canyon of the Ancients and dumping it somewhere. I followed a tanker truck that left a well and traveled on US 160 toward Four Corners. It drove like it was heavy –

slow to climb grades. It turned onto a private road after the driver crossed into Arizona. My headquarters has lots of maps, including one that shows an abandoned gold mine at the end of that road. It's on the reservation. The truck was empty when it got back to the highway."

Niyol crosses his arms across his chest. "It's not enough they are pumping crap into the ground, but they're dumping it, too?"

"Niyol, Brother," Chuchip says. "This sounds like a conspiracy theory – the Bilagáana are poisoning the downtrodden Indians. Are we sure—"

"This Indian is sure," Niyol interrupts. "And this Indian has read the paper scientists from Yale University and the National Institutes of Health published – on the NIH website. They found fifty-five carcinogens in fracking chemicals, including twenty proven to increase the risk of leukemia and lymphoma."

"I'm glad you said *increase the risk*," Dr. D says. "Cancer is complex but environmental factors, including chemicals, may open the door to cancer."

Before Niyol can object, Dr. D lifts his hand, palm toward Niyol. "Spencer? This calls for additional tests on some of our autopsied people. We will plan that, tomorrow. You and Chuchip will prepare samples for James Holloman University."

"Isn't it dangerous to follow the tanker trucks?" Chatima asks Alberto

"Not really," Alberto says. "I don't use a Park Service vehicle, and my truck is like every other pickup around here – a rattletrap with sun-blistered paint. I've taken video, too, and plan to take more."

Gaagii adds sticks to the fire as words carrying ideas and plans fly through the smoke while Chatima watches the sky. The discussion slows and he speaks. "*Woman Who Rotates* has watched us but now tires. She will soon be lost in the dawn when *Tsohanoai* brings the sun.

"Alberto Hermano, thank you." Gaagii looks at his brothers. They know his question; he sees their agreement. "Alberto, you are brother to our brother Cheveyo, and so you are our brother. We believe you, we trust you, we hope you believe and trust us. Will you allow us to take this information to Chief Joe?"

Alberto assents. The fire is now embers, barely hot enough to ignite the mountain smoke Gaagii sprinkles when he offers a prayer of thanks to Creator.

Chapter 20 Fracking

Dr. Deschene reads aloud from the fax papers Spencer brings to his office – the tox results from Laughing Boy. "Blood tests show very poor liver function, but we suspected that. We know the old mining chemicals can cause this. The proximate cause of death is kidney failure due to dehydration. I'm tempted to enter manner of death as 'homicide,' but I do not have enough proof. I will say *pending* in order to keep this open.

"Please call Chuchip and set up a video conference with Chief Joe."

After the conference begins, Dr. D describes the results of Laughing Boy's tox screens and manner of death.

"What about the fracking chemicals," Niyol, who sits beside Chief Joe, asks.

"Only traces of chemicals either from old mining or from fracking appear in Laughing Boy's blood. We don't know for sure he lived in Tonilih," Dr. D answers.

"The company probably does some legitimate cleanup of fracking chemicals," Niyol says. "It's an expensive process and they would do it only for show. It's cheaper to truck the flowback and produced water, and the remains of purification, to an old mine and dump it, like Alberto saw."

"That's the hypothesis," Spencer says. "Fracking chemicals seep through an aquifer between Canyon of the Ancients and Tonilih. Other chemicals come from the old mines."

"And the She Rains wash the chemicals into the aquifer," Niyol says. "The fracking chemicals and the flowback being dumped may carry also old chemicals into the aquifer. We need to test the mine Alberto identified."

"Don't forget, Ton Yah was killed by a military sniper rifle, and they have a range of several miles," Chief Joe reminds them. "And the man who drowned was murdered, and his lungs and stomach were full of those chemicals. Whatever you do, tell me beforehand. Be cautious and be quick."

~~~~~

Edward Hightower, District Supervisor for the U.S. Park Service and the man responsible for the Canyon of the Ancients National Monument, reads Alberto Hermano's original report and the revised report. He looks at the young man's personnel file, including the notes he, himself, had made two years ago when he first interviewed him.

As he reads the report, Hightower thinks about the hunting trips he has taken with his friend, Chief Joseph of the Navajo Nation's police and the chief's nephew, Tommy. He thinks of the stories Chief Joe told around their campfires, and recalls how seriously the chief and Tommy treat the ceremony that accompanies each kill and the respect they show to the dead animals and for all life.

Then, he calls Alberto's supervisor.

"Martin? It's Ed Hightower. I just read Ranger Hermano's reports – both of them. The doctor at the hospital in Folio assures me there were no drugs in his system when he got there. I can't believe everything he wrote was because of a knock on the head, either. Would you object if I interviewed him, myself?"

Alberto's immediate supervisor has no objection and offers to send the young man to Hightower. "He's at his desk, drawing up a trail map and a list of signs based on his aborted hike. He'll have to go out again and finish. That will be an overnight trip."

Minutes later, Alberto knocks on the door of the District Supervisor's office. Through the glass and past the gilt letters spelling the man's name, he sees Supervisor Hightower look up and gesture for him to enter. "Sir? You wanted to see me? I'm okay to return to duty, aren't I, sir?"

"Yes. The doctor – Doctor Deschene – sent his okay by email. He said except for an extra hole in your head, which was healing, you can return to unlimited duty."

Hightower chuckles at his own humor. "Have a seat, please. I do have questions, and this may take a while."

When Alberto is seated, the man continues. "Your supervisor reported that you were at your desk after filing a report filled with mistakes. You didn't lose consciousness, but you were incoherent, as was your report. Your supervisor told me some of what he heard."

Alberto gasps when he realizes what had been in the original report and what he might have said. "Sir, I—"

The District Supervisor's raised hand silences the young man. "You are not in trouble, but you said some things that are puzzling. You said you *felt* the trees stressed by poison and you *saw* the poison moving in the ecosystem from the trees to animals. A tree told you all this."

"Sir, I was babbling—"

"You wrote the same things in the original report."

The man looks at papers on his desktop. Alberto feels sweat forming on his forehead and upper lip. He knows the papers include a printout of his report.

"You and I know that trees don't talk – not even to Park Rangers and not even to report on the poisons the oil and gas company is pumping into the ground. Yes, we know about that. The president opened more and more national parks – even those sacred to the Athabascans – to drilling and fracking. Last month, his puppets have ruled that drilling may begin near Chaco Canyon."

The man picks up a different paper, one with the White House logo at the top and an illegible, spiked signature at the bottom, and then drops it onto the desk. "You know, don't you, they will do offset drilling, guiding the drill heads under the lands of the Navajo, stealing the oil."

Alberto nods his understanding, and Hightower continues. "The Supreme Court ruled pumping waste water below ground is not exempt from clean water regulations. But, the oil companies still do it. They are protected by their allies in the Congress and bribes to those charged with enforcing the law.

"What I do not know is whether your experience with the Park Service and powers of observation led you to this conclusion, or whether as our neighbors, descendants of the First Peoples of this continent, believe as a two-spirit person you have a unique perspective about life in general and the natural world, in particular."

Alberto feels ill, and stutters, "Sir, I —"

"Son, I keep interrupting you. I am usually better than this at talking to people. Do not be so afraid – yes, afraid. I see you sweating and your face is the color of your green uniform. The Park Service does not discriminate based on anything not directly related to the job and your ability to perform it. But I want to know more about what you saw and felt. Do you think you can continue?"

Alberto takes a deep breath, lets it out, and begins. "Sir, I was mapping a hiking trail when I stumbled. I reached out to brace myself on a tree and felt an electric shock. I've thought about that. It was probably just the rough bark on my skin. At the hospital, they bandaged abrasions on my hands. I fell and hit my head, and was unconscious for awhile."

The young man continues to describe his experience, his feeling that the tree told him things, even though he had fallen and was no longer touching the tree. "I cannot say where those thoughts and ideas came from, but I told my friend and his friends about them. They're all Navajo or Hopi, and they all think it was Earth Mother speaking to me through the tree."

Alberto keeps talking before the supervisor can interrupt. "Sir, I did something you should know. I did it on my own time and with my own truck but … well, I followed tank trucks from Fracking Site CA-2 across the state line and onto the Navajo Reservation. They turned onto a private road, and I couldn't follow them there, but our maps show that road leads to an abandoned gold mine. The trucks were heavy going in and light coming out. I think they were full of flowback and dumped it in the old mine. I told my friends and they are going to tell the Chief of the Navajo police."

Alberto and the District Supervisor sit quietly for several minutes before the supervisor speaks. "Thank you for telling me these things. Will your friends be discrete?"

"Yes sir. At least two of them are police deputies, and I think Dr. Deschene is their leader."

After Alberto leaves, his boss pulls a heavy, three-ring binder from the bookcase. He flips through pages until one catches his eye. After reading the page, he makes a note, and then repeats the process. Then he picks up the telephone.

"Sam? I want you to check two of our old monitoring wells. Get samples. And be careful. There may be unregistered mining and illegal dumping at the Rocky River Mine. You ready to copy?" The Supervisor reads coordinates of two wells. One is downhill from the mine; the other is outside the fence of Fracking Site CA-2.

~~~~~

Miles away, Susan Calvin arrives in Dr. D's office at the Navajo Western Regional Hospital.

"I spent the morning at Dr. Nez's office," Susan says, naming her obstetrics doctor. "His Medical Assistant did an abdominal ultrasound. For two hours, with Dr. Nez and Dr. Yazzie there for the second hour."

"That's the long and short of it," Doli Tabaha, who has followed Susan into Dr. D's office, says. Her pun on the names – Nez meaning 'tall' and Yazzie meaning 'little one' – is lost on Susan. Although she can converse in Navajo, her vocabulary is still limited.

Dr. D frowns at Doli. "Dr. Yazzie is a cardiologist." He turned to Susan, "Is something wrong?"

"No, dear," Susan assures her husband. "Your sons are both fine."

Dr. D's breathing stops briefly, then he blurts, "Sons?"

"Yes, dear. May I sit? Although I've been lying on my side for two hours, my feet are not happy."

After Susan sits comfortably with her feet on a hassock, she smiles at her husband. "You can thank Doli for that information. She told me your young friends would need time to prepare and perform the necessary ceremonies, and that you would need time to find two appropriate names." Susan could not reveal that Dr. D's young friends were, with him and her, members of the Eastward Kiva Society. But she feels Doli is on the cusp of understanding.

Before Dr. D can assimilate Susan's news, Chuchip enters the office, holding papers. "Dr. D. … uh, uh … Ms. Susan, Ms. Doli. Uh, this just came in from Chief Joe. It's something from the Park Service."

Dr. D's initial fear for Susan and his child – now, his children – having been relieved, he is not reluctant to turn elsewhere. He knows his original role in the conception of the boys is about to be expanded. And, he knows he will need help and advice.

Dr. D scans the papers. "The Park Service checked two monitoring wells, both of which were removed from the normal inspection schedule by someone in the Denver Headquarters of the EPA. One was near the mine where Alberto saw illegal dumping. The other was near a fracking site in the Canyon of the Ancients. The analysis of the chemicals from both locations gave identical results, except the concentration of chemicals near the fracking site is greater than that near the old mine. This may be the confirmation we need that fracking chemicals are the villains."

Doli takes a sheaf of papers from her dispatch case. She unfolds one which becomes a map of the Tonilih region. "This provides a detailed analysis of well water from thirty sites in the Tonilih Chapter tested by university people. The map is a summary and much easier to understand than all these pages of reports." She explains that the concentration of chemicals in the water is stronger in the east, near the Canyon of the Ancients, and weaker toward the west, farther from the Canyon.

"This is explained by the geology of the aquifer.

"You will see that a PE – a Professional Engineer – has signed and sealed each page. The originals, in my safe, are also notarized."

"You have something in mind," Dr. D says.

"What we have here is not enough to prosecute, but it may be enough to get search warrants. But I need power and publicity."

"I agree it is time for publicity," Dr. D says. "Susan has all the information we have gathered. It does not include individual patient names, and her knowledge predates what we discussed with the Council President and the Drug Enforcement Administration. Our agreement of secrecy does not bind Susan, however, she understands the ground rules we agreed to, especially that the fracking chemicals are not yet public knowledge. And, as Chief Joe once said, 'If you want more Piñon nuts, shake the Piñon tree.' It's time to shake the tree.

"And speaking of Chief Joe, we need to bring him up to date. Chuchip will set up a video conference. He's become quite adept with the computer system." Chuchip's embarrassment at Dr. D's praise almost causes him to fumble the connection.

Chief Joe appears on the monitor with SAIC Winder and Officer Niyol. After a brief discussion, the chief and Ms. Winder agree that Susan will write an article for *The Navajo Post*. The article will focus on the diseases being treated at the Tonilih hospital. She will describe the contaminated water around Tonilih. She will be careful to exclude any danger to NAPI, after Niyol explains to her the soil and geology maps.

"See," Niyol explains. "Sand, soil, and now caliche covered this volcanic dike. It's invisible, but it separates the aquifer under Tonilih from the rest of the reservation. This is why the effects of contaminated water are limited to that corner of the reservation. Here," he points to a spot on the map, "here is the mine that's the source of the old chemicals. It's owned by the same British bank that's blocking a right-of-way for a water pipeline from Lake McIntire to the Tonilih Chapter. They're part of the conspiracy."

Dr. D has been listening. "We don't know that, yet, Niyol. If Susan were writing for the *Tattler* or another foxprop outlet, she could intimate that, but she's writing for legitimate media."

"Yes, sir," Niyol says. "But I know it's true!"

Niyol agrees to the terms of Susan's article, but no one knows just how hard the Piñon tree will be shaken, or what Susan will say to a former journalism school classmate.

Ahiga is an orderly at the hospital, but his job is "PRN" – medical-speak for "as needed." He is happy when his phone rings at 8:30 one morning even though the caller ID puzzles him. It is not the hospital – it is Dr. D's home number, and the caller is Susan.

"Ya´ateeh, Ms. Susan. Does Dr. D need something?"

"No, Ahiga. I need something. Were you called in to work, today?" They both know that if the hospital hasn't called by 8:30 AM, there will likely be no call."

"No, Ms. Susan. Looks like—" The young man doesn't say the other thing they both know – no call, no pay.

Susan fills in the blanks for Ahiga. "Dr. D doesn't want me to drive and at nearly eight months pregnant, I'm not sure I can fit under the steering wheel. Do you still have a friend who's a gig driver and will he rent you his van for the day? I feel big enough to need a van."

Thirty minutes later, Ahiga arrives in a Ford Transit van, and helps Susan into the passenger seat. "You're sure, Ms. Susan, I won't get in trouble with Dr. D?"

"I promise. Besides, he left for Window Rock and won't be back until after supper since they'll stop at the Tuba City Diner on the way home."

~~~~~

A sign in front of a modern Quonset hut – pre-fabricated steel erected on a slab of concrete – in Greenbriar, Arizona marks the offices of *The Four Corners Tattler*. Ahiga pulls the van into a handicapped spot in front of the building. "I don't have a handicapped plate or hanging tag, Ma'am, but you shouldn't have to walk so far." He sounds nervous.

Susan digs a red and black placard from her purse. "I do." She grins as Ahiga hangs it from the rear-view mirror. "It's the only thing I've found useful about being pregnant in the heat. Please remind me to tell Nastas, no more September babies."

Ahiga blushes at her words and then helps Susan from the van.

The *Tattler* office occupies the entire building, with no walls except for two small rooms in the rear corners, likely the restrooms. Ahiga follows Susan to the desk closest to the door. A woman, seated at the desk and focused on a computer screen, looks up when Susan says, "Good morning."

"Sorry, sweetheart. We're not buying stories of unwed mothers. Now, if you were taken up in a flying saucer—"

"My dear," Susan interrupts, "if these children were those of a space alien, my visit could not be more important than it already is." She takes a pasteboard rectangle from her dispatch case. "Here is my card. Please give it to Mr. Nez."

The woman, who is not after all a receptionist, glances at the business card and gasps when she reads it. "Miss ... Miss ... are you really? ... Of course, you are ... Oh, my God!

"Henry!" her voice echoes from the steel walls. "Henry, get your butt up here!"

Mr. Henry Nez, Editor of *The Tattler*, insists that Susan take his chair while Mr. Nez sits in a folding chair beside his own desk. The staff of the newspaper isn't sure who Ahiga is and choose to be cautious. They give him a folding chair beside their boss.

"Miss Calvin, I'm not sure whether to be honored or confused," Henry Nez says.

"Mr. Nez … please call me Susan and may I call you Henry?" Without waiting for an answer, Susan continues. "I still write as Susan Calvin, but I am now Susan Deschene. You know my husband, Dr. Nastas Deschene, of course. And, Henry, I do remember you from the Columbia University School of Journalism, from which we both took degrees. It's good to see you, again."

"Susan, I … uh … we have gone different ways."

Susan's laugh is not mocking, but draws Henry and Ahiga into her humor. "Ahiga, Henry is concerned I think less of him because he is editor of *The Tattler* and not a war correspondent for *United Press Universal*. Henry," she turns to her host, "your newspaper brings both entertainment and news to people who otherwise would be in darkness and ignorance. Nastas has said that you never lie. You only ask questions. You must remember what we heard during our first course in our first year: 'Doubt everything, for doubt leads to questioning and only questioning leads to truth."

Henry Nez drops his head toward the floor for a moment and then sits up. "Only you, Susan, could understand. Now, what can I do for you?"

Ahiga does not understand all that transpires. Susan and Henry talk about mining, drilling, chemicals, international corporations, and sources which cannot be named. Ahiga is not sure either Susan or Henry have reached any agreement, but he knows Susan is happy and energized on the trip home.

Chapter 21: Shaking the Piñon Tree

HEALTH SERVICES RESPOND

Special to *The Four Corners Tattler* by Susan Calvin

Folio, Arizona

Lymphoma and leukemia are both cancers. They have other things in common. The number of cases of both these diseases in the Tonilih region is higher than it should be. ...

Tests of well water made in early summer in the Tonilih Chapter found chemicals known to cause cancer, including lead, cadmium, ...

The danger was limited to Tonilih ...

The Navajo Nation's Council began trucking in pure water and distributing it throughout Tonilih ...

Investigators from the Nation's coroner's office and police department, working with people from the Council and researchers from the University of New Mexico suspect the contamination may be caused by chemicals washed from old mines by the She Rains, the spring rains which have been heavy for the past several years.

~~~~~

The North American headquarters of a multi-national oil and gas company does not receive *The Four Corners Tattler*, but subscribes to an electronic clipping service. An employee of that service recognizes Susan's name from the time she was an investigative reporter for *The Washington Standard* and sends a copy of her article to the Denver headquarters of Saramco. The article is first read by an intern in the Public Relations office who forwards it to his supervisor.

<< Tonilih closest part of Navajo reservation
to Saramco operation Canyon of Ancients possible
connection >>

The intern's supervisor forwards the clipping and the intern's message to the Director of US Operations, with her own question.

<< Should we refer this to a geologist given
possible contribution of the Canyon operations?" >>

The Director's reply is terse.

<< Not necessary >>

~~~~~

Chief Joe's phone shows a call from U.S. Park Service District Supervisor Edward Hightower. Chief Joe greets his friend. "Have you decided you can hunt a javelina as well as a Navajo?"

"I've been practicing. And I think my aim is as accurate as yours, Joe."

Chief Joe *harumphs*. "I should never have shown you that compound bow. The season is closed until Hunter's Moon. But you know that. Something else brings your call."

"Yes, Joe. One of my people, a Hispanglo but with special ties to your people, has an interesting story to tell."

Chief Joe smiles to himself. "I know, for your ranger has friends—" Chief Joe can't speak about the Eastward Kiva, so he equivocates. It's a way of lying without trampling the truth "—he is friends with my nephew and his friends."

"You know what he saw, then?" Hightower asks.

"I do. And although it's early for javelina, the bass are striking near Moki Steps. Can you get away for a few days?"

The two men plan a fishing trip and end the call. Chief Joe places a call to Dr. Deschene. Although the doctor's primary sport is golf, he is also a fisherman, and the chief easily persuades him to join the trip.

~~~~~

Introductions are unnecessary, since Ed Hightower and Nastas Deschene have often discussed Alberto's treatment and return to duty.

"Are you sure I can't stay with you?" Hokee grumbles while helping load the Beaver aircraft with packs, food and water, and fishing gear. "You know it was me who talked you into repairing the floats. Besides, is this fishing trip official?"

Chief Joe sees behind Hokee's grumbling and takes him aside. "Hokee, we tease you about the Beaver being your airplane—" Chief Joe holds up a finger to stop whatever Hokee is going to say. "But it really is. It was seized in a drug raid, that much is true. I auctioned it off – and your uncle and his friend bought it. They created a corporation – in your name – which leases it back to the police with the understanding you will be the pilot. Dr. D and Superintendent Hightower and I are paying for this trip. The leases are how your uncle pays insurance and maintenance costs. Now, are you sure you can get us to Moki Steps?"

Hokee stands silently and then runs his fingers across the blade of the propeller. "Mine?" he whispers.

"Yes, but you must tell no one. I have broken a promise to tell you this. Your uncle knew I might have to, someday."

Hokee lands in the waters of Lake Powell and water-taxies into Overlooked Canyon, the ravine that leads to Moki Steps. After the men unload their gear, Hokee taxies back to the river from which he will take off.

Dr. Deschene confronts Chief Joe. "You told him. I could tell by the way he handled the plane."

"I had to, brother. He questioned our honesty. That was one of the conditions I set with his uncle."

"What did you tell who?" Ed Hightower asks, while shrugging the backpack onto his shoulders and fastening the waist belt.

"When we get to camp," Joe says, and strikes out along the north shore of the canyon toward Moki Steps.

The purpose of their fishing is not to set records for number or weight of bass, but only to provide enough for their meals and some to take home. All three men are adept at cooking and smoking the fish, leaving them time to talk.

"The boy who flew us here. You said something important to him," Ed says to Joe.

"Not a boy any longer. A young man with a commercial pilot license and instrument rated. He's the only one who flies the Beaver, although I never send him out at night or in weather, even though he is trained for it, but..." Chief Joe's voice silences. He doesn't want to admit he's afraid for Hokee.

210

"He and a dozen or so others were kicked out of their scout troop and disfellowshipped by church and family. You know that Hokee means *Abandoned*, right? His maternal uncle, on whom responsibility for him would rest, was on active duty in the Air Force, mostly in the Middle East. I don't think the man even knew the boy had been born. When Johnny Bidziil retired after twenty-five years – as a Chief Master Sergeant – he hooked up with Hokee and made sure he finished the flight training he started in high school. How they got together is their story to tell, but don't ask them. Get to know them and wait until they offer."

Chief Joe then explains what he told Hokee about the airplane and the corporation that owns it. "The corporation is a *Native American small business*, which helps me cut through the paperwork to give them the lease."

Ed Hightower reels in his line and then casts again. "Those contracting rules apply to me, too. Let me know, please, if there's an opportunity for the Park Service to lease the plane – and pilot."

Chief Joe chuckles. "Already did, Ed. You'll get the bill for transporting Alberto from your headquarters to the Folio hospital."

Before he cast his line, Chief Joe taps Ed's shoulder in a coup strike. Ed is not disappointed. He knows the gesture not as a coup by Chief Joe, but a sign of trust and friendship.

They build a small, smokey fire over which they hang strips of fish. The smoke will preserve the fish long enough to get them home. Their supper is fresh fish and tepary beans, cooked over a pressurized white-gas stove.

Over supper, Chief Joe outlines the problem that brings them together. "We know but we cannot prove that poison from old mines seeps into the wells of our people. We know but we cannot prove more poison comes from the fracking sites operated by Saramco in the Canyon of the Ancients. And we know that powerful interests in Washington protect Saramco."

Ed Hightower adds, "And, a Park Ranger, Alberto Hermano, has videotaped trucks which contain flowback chemicals which are dumped in an abandoned gold mine on Navajo territory."

Dr. D weighs in. "We need more."

Chief Joe knows the law of the Navajo and of the Bilagáana that surround them. Superintendent Hightower knows the scope and limitations of the powers of the US government. Dr. Deschene knows the etiology of the diseases and the relationship of the chemicals found in the homeland of the Navajo. It does not take long for them to create a plan.

~~~~~

Two weeks plus miles of travel and hours of analysis and planning later, Spencer, Gahtsoh, Gaagii, Chatima, Cheveyo, and Chuchip join Dr. Deschene and a dozen police officers in Chief Joe's briefing room. Doli Tabahaa follows Superintendent Hightower and Alberto, both in Park Service uniform. Alberto's head jerks and his eyes flick from side to side until he sees the person he seeks. When he catches Cheveyo's eyes, he smiles and relaxes. Chief Joe enters, escorting FBI Special Agent in Charge, Gabby Winder. The chief signals Niyol to begin.

First, Niyol puts a map of the Navajo Nation on the large display screen.

"The Colorado Plateau Aquifer underlies much of the Navajo, Hopi, and Ute territories. On most maps, it appears as a continuous stretch of gravel and sand. It is not continuous. There are many volcanic dikes – on the surface and underground – that break up the aquifer. Such geologic formations have isolated a section of the aquifer that underlies the Canyon of the Ancients

National Monument and a corner of the Navajo Nation. The Canyons Monument is administered by the U.S. Park Service, although the Canyon of the Ancients technically belongs to the Bureau of Land Management.

"That confusion of control allowed the current Bilagáana president to open the Canyon to fracking, despite the Canyon being the richest archeological site in the Western United States – and contained within a Ute reservation."

Niyol zooms the view into the corner of the Navajo reservation that lies in Utah, inserts a flash drive into the computer, and presses a key. Points of light, all near Tonilih, appear on the map. Beside each are the chemical symbols for the elements found in the water – *Cd* for cadmium, *Pb* for lead, *As* for arsenic, *Hg* for mercury and *X* for unknown. Niyol explains. "These data come from water samples taken by the Park Service, researchers from the University of New Mexico, and the Navajo Police and crime scene investigators working for the nations coroner." He names the elements represented by their symbols.

"We know some of these chemicals are used in gold mining. The area was mined until the mid-20th century and then abandoned by the mining companies. They left behind at least three hundred mines capable of polluting the rivers and the aquifer. The drainage from the old mines works its way through the rocks and contaminates the aquifer with toxic chemicals."

"Why now?" One of the police detectives asks.

Niyol gestures to Spencer, who takes the question and puts up a series of slides with a NOAA logo. "It's raining more in the Four Corners region. The She Rains are filling old mines with water, which then seeps into the aquifer. But, that's only part of it. The mines aren't the only source of chemicals." Spencer nods to Niyol who calls up information from another flash drive. A list of chemicals scrolls up the screen to disappear at the top. "These were unknown until we got help from James

Holomon University. These chemicals are from samples taken from the San Juan River and in the wells around the Tonilih region."

Niyol re-starts the scrolling. His throat tightens, making his words snarl from his mouth. "These are fracking chemicals. The Bilagáana president is destroying one national monument after another. He opened the Canyons of the Ancients National Monument and the San Juan National Forest to fracking. Last month, he opened the land around Chaco Canyon to fracking and drilling. It didn't take any time for the Saramco oil and gas company to inject chemicals into the ground."

Dr. Deschene's words are as terse as Niyol's. "Many of these chemicals are poisons; some are carcinogens." A buzz of voices fills the room.

Chief Joe stands, silencing the room and then introducing the two Park Service men. "Superintendent Ed Hightower is in charge of U.S. Park Service activities in the Canyon of the Ancients. The person with him is Ranger Alberto Hermano, who provided videos showing illegal dumping of fracking chemicals from Colorado into an old mine on Navajo territory."

Alberto's videos raise as many eyebrows as had the lists of chemicals. Then, Dr. Deschene stands. "Officer Niyol, please display the map I gave you … Thank you. The red dots represent deaths from cancer – primarily lymphoma and leukemia – and other serious diseases including stillbirths and miscarriages among young, healthy women. The orange dots represent living people with lymphoma, leukemia, or other diseases including high liver numbers or kidney damage, convulsions or loss of muscle coordination, symptoms resembling stroke, and dementia. Many of these people will die from their illnesses. Yellow dots represent people with peripheral neuropathy, cardiac dysrhythmia, and other debilitating diseases. Green are

214

people with symptoms which are easy to treat – people who complained of nausea, diarrhea, and stomach cramps. A group of children with what looked like rickets, but which are bones weakened by pollution, are in this group.

"All these diseases and conditions are directly linked to pollution in the aquifer. You all have heard that *correlation does not prove causation.* The fracking companies deny they are responsible for earthquakes in Oklahoma and will deny they are responsible for this poison and the cancers, here. However, we can provide a positive link between these chemicals and the diseases and conditions caused by pollution in the aquifer."

FBI Agent Winder raises an eyebrow and speaks softly to Chief Joseph. "Trucks full of fracking chemicals crossing a state line? A polluted river that flows through three states and your territory? They give a new meaning to 'crime crossing state lines.'"

What she doesn't acknowledge is that an article in *The Four Corners Tattler* shook up a federal judge enough to issue the search warrants Ms. Winder requested.

Chapter 22 Gahtsoh and Hatałii

There is no greater joy
than to have an endlessly
changing horizon, for each
day to have a new
and different sun.
Athabascan Wisdom

Gaagii and Chatima watch Gahtsoh struggle to climb the trail to *tsebida 't'ini'ani*, the rock shelter in the cliff wall above the Chetro Ketl Great House. A backpack holds sticks for a fire, water, and food – dried mutton and fruit, and flat bread. The mid-afternoon sun turns the sky white with heat on this day of the full moon. Gahtsoh retreats to the cool shadow of the shelter until the sun passes behind the hills in the west, then builds his fire circle on the ledge.

It is still light when the old man steps onto the ledge. He carries a bundle of sticks. "We will need a long fire," the man says and sits across the fire circle. He nods approval when Gahtsoh lights the fire and sprinkles tobacco and corn pollen on the flames. After the smoke has risen, the old man sings a song Gahtsoh recognizes as the song that spirit voices sang just before he first met the old man.

The old man makes a sign of endings and again begins the song. Gahtsoh finds it easy to join and to understand. It is not a calling or a summoning or a song of power, but a story – the story of his people before the Bilagáana arrived. The story becomes dark as Hispanic explorers come seeking gold and bringing the missionaries of the Catholic church who destroyed the writings of aboriginal civilizations to the south and who try to suppress the sacred knowledge of the Navajo and Hopi. The story tells of the conquest by the Bilagáana Army. The song grows darker when it tells of elders who hold ancient knowledge driven to hide in the mist. They are safe there, but the mist hides their knowledge too deeply and much is lost.

The old man's voice stops, but Gahtsoh continues the song. The boy sings of the children taken from their families to a place called Carlisle, where those who survived were forbidden to speak their own language or wear their traditional clothes, but were forced into the Bilagáana mold. He sings of excesses of the Bureau of Indian Affairs and the incursion of Protestant churches, of those who robbed his people of their property, their history, their culture, and their dignity, and who still seek to keep his people in penury.

Gahtsoh knows of poisoned water and diseases and weaves these into his song. When his voice fades, the old man again signs completion. "You know the story, and you know more than I do. When I wake to come to this place, I see the Great House as it is, but I also see it empty and in ruins. I thought this was a foreseeing. Now, I understand. I see the Great House as it was for me and as it is for you. The story you tell will happen after my time. We both have thought we were from different times, different worlds. I think we must now accept the truth of that."

The old man sits silently, occasionally feeding a stick into the fire, while Gahtsoh thinks about what he said. "You come from before I was born; you live in my past," the boy says.

"Yes," the old man says. "I do not know how much more time I will have with you. Listen and learn." The old man and the boy spend long hours by the fire, hours much longer than the hours of that night. The man teaches Gahtsoh song after song, including the drum beats that accompany each.

Night flees and rosy clouds of dawn gather above the canyon wall.

"My time has come," the old man says. "This is the last time we will meet."

"But *Hatałii*, there is still so much for me to learn!"

"You live in a new world and need new knowledge. It is time for the Athabascans and their descendants – the Navajo, Hopi, Ute, Apache, and all their brothers and sisters to rediscover Creator and relearn their past. It is time for them to find and reveal the knowledge of the Elders, long hidden in the mist. You will be part of that, with Rabbit as your spirit guide." The old man pauses, chuckles, and continues speaking. "We know Rabbit as Clever One. He and others will teach you the rest of what you need to know."

The old man's eyes bore into Gahtsoh's spirit. "Of the monument rocks on the plateau above the Great House, only one bears your name. Beneath the rock is a talisman. You will climb the mesa and retrieve the talisman."

~~~~~

A small group meets in Chief Joe's office. SAIC Gabby Winder requires each person to sign an agreement not to reveal anything heard in the meeting. "These agreements are effective for the rest of your lives. Do you understand?" Gabby polls each person before handing Niyol a flash drive. "Do not download this but only display it."

Niyol nods his understanding and inserts the flash drive into the computer. He sees the .m4v files and opens an app to play them. Even the unperturbable Dr. Deschene gasps when he realizes what he is seeing. It is a video, taken from high above

219

the Canyon of the Ancients. The camera zooms in to show a truck parked near a fracking well. A hose runs from the truck to the wellhead. A figure, foreshortened by being seen from above, disconnects the hose. He and another get into the truck and drive away. The camera follows the truck.

"That's Cortez," Alberto says. He's going south on 491 … Just crossed the border. He's interstate now … Turning on the road to the mine. That's as far as I've been able to follow them." But the camera follows the truck until it stops. Two figures jump from the cab and pull the hose to an opening in a hill.

"Mine adit," someone says.

"We can't see the back of the truck, but we're sure that man is opening a valve to empty the truck into the mine. These images were taken three nights ago. I had a task force enter the mine the morning after. They found puddles of flowback and identified them by their chemical signatures."

"How did you get the video? It was at night, right?" Niyol asks. "It couldn't have been a satellite. A satellite would have moved unless it was in geostationary orbit, and if it were, it would be over the equator and the view would have been oblique, not overhead."

Gabby finds it hard to keep from smiling. She and Niyol have collaborated on matters much more secret than this. "That's correct; but you're looking in the wrong direction."

Niyol's face freezes. Then he laughs. "You got me, Ms. Gabby. But I'll figure it out."

"That's not all," Gabby reports. "We raided the Denver headquarters offices of SARAMCO. We found emails and letters that prove senior management knew about fracking chemicals leaking into the aquifer and illegal dumping of flowback. Warrants are being prepared. We will arrest a score of people, from the *suits* in Denver to the roustabouts and roughnecks at the wells in Colorado – and at least two truck drivers."

~~~~~

After the meeting, Hokee corners Special Agent in Charge Gabby Winder. "I know how you got the videos."

The confidence in his voice assures Ms. Winder that the boy really knows. She pulls him into an empty office and closes the door.

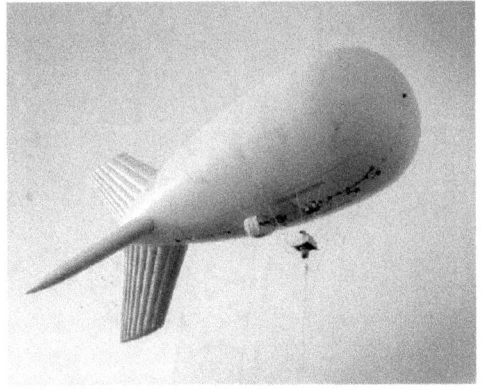

"An aerostat," Hokee says. "A tethered blimp filled with helium. Aerostats along the US-Mexican border carry radar to detect drug smugglers. The NOTAM – Notice to Airmen – warning us away from the Canyons of the Ancients used the same words they use to warn pilots away from those. Not very smart, wouldn't you say?" Hokee crosses his arms over his chest and grins at Gabby.

"That NOTAM went out to every flight service station in the Four Corners region. Other people would have reached that conclusion."

Hokee's eyes flick from side to side as he thinks. "It's not the aerostat that is secret. It's that the aerostat took the video – no, more than that. It's that the aerostat *can* take video. That's the sec—"

Before the boy can finish the sentence, Gabby hits his shoulder lightly with a clenched fist, a coup strike. In response to Hokee's open mouth, Gabby asks, "Does that mean you will keep this secret?"

Hokee grins his understanding and agrees. Then, the FBI agent describes the program that lofted helium-filled balloons carrying radar and look-down cameras over the Navajo and Ute territories. "That would have violated a treaty between the US and the Navajo and the Ute, except it was agreed at the highest levels of your governments and mine.

"You have discovered more than we anticipated."

"It's just science," Hokee says.

Chapter 23 Gahtsoh
and Earth Mother

"This is something I must do, and I must do it alone," Gahtsoh tells his teacher-uncles, Gaagii and Chatima. "It has been six months since my grandfather was murdered, something less than that since I found both my spirit guide and – well, something else – an ancient Medicine Elder. They both taught me many things, but—" the boy's voice breaks. "But I've not done anything to prove myself. Do you understand?"

Gaagii and Chatima exchange looks through hooded eyes. Gaagii speaks for them both. "Yes, Gahtsoh, we understand. Knowledge is worth nothing unless it is shared and used. Your teachers have filled you to bursting with knowledge, with songs, with prayers, with ceremonies. But you've done little with that knowledge. You know it is time for you to do something. We understand; what can we do to help?"

"I must visit the mine used to dump the chemicals, the mine where ancient chemicals combined with new ones to create death. I must…"

The boy hesitates. "I'm not sure what comes next, but I think I must stop the danger to Earth Mother."

"But the Bilagáana police   FBI and DEA, even their EPA – have shut down the fracking and the dumping," Gaagii says. "What else is there?"

"The She Rains," Chatima says. "*Tó Neinilii* will send them again next spring. It's not just evil people, it's the rain that poisons Earth Mother. The rain is not evil, but *Tó Neinilii* is a joker and a trickster. He is powerful, and not even Rabbit can change the rains. I'm sorry, brother, but—"

"Not the rains; something else," Gahtsoh says. "I do not know what it is, but I will feel it when I reach the mine."

Gaagii and Chatima take Gahtsoh to the Rocky River Mine, which had been flooded with fracking chemicals and water from the She Rains – chemicals and water that flowed through the aquifer under Tonilih, chemicals that caused disease and killed. Although no one was dumping fracking chemicals – at least, until lobbyists for the multinational oil and gas companies could get past the bad publicity and re-write the environmental regulations – the old mine remains a source of contamination. Gahtsoh leaves Gaagii and Chatima and walks slowly to the old-new fence – old to mark the property, new to include un-rusted gates and electronic locks.

Lurching in his braces, carrying nothing but his crutches, Gahtsoh approaches the gate.

"Go no closer." A voice behind him startles the boy.

"The very ground is poison, and there is no need for you to go within the fence."

Gahtsoh turns to see a young man wearing blue jeans, moccasins, and a doeskin vest. The beads of his necklace – turquoise, garnet, obsidian, and shell – shine in the sunlight.

The young man grins. "Did you think I would not be here with you?" He sits, legs crossed, near the gate.

Gahtsoh remembers what Rabbit had said: "Like Life and Death, I do not follow a schedule or a pattern, but I always know how to find you." The boy opens the links in his braces so he can sit and then lie on the ground. He stretches out his hands, presses them onto the dirt, and feels Earth Mother's heart. He sings the Song of Power – the last song the ancient Medicine Elder taught him. When he reaches the end of the song, he hears a deep rumble. A cloud of dust rises from the opening of the mine as the entire hill drops. Deep underground, tunnels collapse, sealing forever the poison that lingers.

Gahtsoh feels Earth Mother's relief and watches a heron fly over the tumbled rocks that mark what had been the entrance to the mine, and then circle clockwise above him.

~~~~~

Niyol and Spencer sit in the hospital cafeteria. It is long after suppertime, but coffee is always available. "Your parents – they are mining engineers, geologists, right?" Niyol asks.

"Yes. That's why the Navajo government hired them."

"They would know how to close an abandoned mine, right?" Niyol presses.

"Um, yes. That's become more important as the environmental movement gains traction."

"So, they would have known where and how to set explosives in the Rocky River Mine?"

"Yes, but that would have been illegal, since the FBI has it sealed as a crime scene."

"And the mine was owned by a British bank," Niyol says.

"And Doli has convinced the bank to open the right-of-way for a water line between Lake McIntire and Tonilih rather than being sued for the pollution."

Hospital employees in the cafeteria see, but do not understand, the high-fives exchanged between a Navajo and a Bilagáana.

~~~~~

A black SUV carrying Special Agent in Charge Gabby Winder stops at the guarded gate to the fracking site. The guard

225

steps from the boxy building and slouches toward the vehicle. Without waiting for the driver to say anything, he growls, "Private Property. Turn around and leave." He puts his hands on his gun belt and hitches it up over his belly.

Ms. Winder steps from the rear door holding a document. "FBI. This is a search warrant signed by a federal judge. Stand fast, keep your hands where we can see them."

Ignoring her orders, the man reaches for the pistol in his belt. Before he can unsnap the safety strap, Gabby has a nine-millimeter pistol in her hands with the barrel pressing into the flab at the man's chin. "Wrong move. Hands in the air."

The guard's face pales and his raised hands quiver. He has the courage to speak. "I need to call—"

"No, you don't need to call anyone. All you need to do is open the gate." By this time, two more black SUVs have arrived. An agent jumps from one and takes the man Agent Winder has subdued. He pushes the guard into the building and watches the man open the gate.

The warrant authorizes the FBI agents to search the facility, including private vehicles. In one truck, they find a sniper rifle and a box of seven point six two NATO cartridges. The serial number of the rifle matches a number on the search warrant. The truck is a dually, and one of the rear tires matches casts taken where Ton Yah was murdered and where he grew peyote.

The next day, a pond of flowback is drained and a thermos found in the muck is identified as belonging to Martin Begay, a man whose drowned body was found under a desert powerline. Fracking Site CA-2 is shut for months while crime scene teams from several federal and state agencies work. Frank Falco, Assistant United States Attorney, has no difficulty convincing a federal judge to convene a grand jury which quickly indicted three men for murder and seventeen others for violations of the Clean Water Act. More than 200 civil suits for wrongful death would take years to crawl through the courts.

~~~~~

In the lobby of a glass and steel skyscraper in the Denver business district, Gahtsoh shifts his weight to the crutch on one arm and presses the button to open the powered exit door. He lurches down a handicapped access ramp and walks to the Hummer waiting at the curb. The beads of his necklace – turquoise, garnet, obsidian, and shell – shine in the noon sun. When he reaches the vehicle, he hands a dispatch case to FBI Special Agent in Charge Gabby Winder. "Fifteen copies of *The Tattler* delivered, as ordered, ma'am."

On the top floor of the building, the fifteen members of the Board of Directors of Saramco North America wave copies of a newspaper as they yell at one another. A question mark at the end of the headline is deliberate:

SARAMCO LEGACY?

Below the headline is a picture of a girl-child. She is wearing a beaded blouse and a skirt that reaches to her knees. Below the skirt, old breaks in her shin bones make bumps in her skin. Her arms show similar warping and bumps. She stands beside a grave marker with another girl's name and dates of birth and death separated by only seven years. The photo caption reads,

"Desba Nez stands at the grave of her sister, who died from leukemia. According to Navajo health experts, this was caused by chemicals in the water from the family's well. Desba, herself, has seven breaks in her bones.

Chemicals found in the water prevented her bones from absorbing enough calcium. Her bones were brittle and could not heal properly despite medical care.

Desba and her sister are just two of hundreds of Navajo children and adults maimed or killed by these chemicals. Can the chemicals in the wells of Tonilih be traced to SARAMCO fracking in the nearby Canyon of the Ancients? Scientists at universities and among the Navajo are working on that question. SARAMCO had not responded to our calls as of press time."

The Director of US Operations and Chair of the Board understands better than most what is at stake. How did the newspaper get a copy of the internal email that admitted a connection between Saramco fracking and poisoned water? Did someone leak a copy? The Director remembers that the last message in the thread was from she, herself, denying any need for an investigation.

She raps her gavel, nearly breaking it, before the angry voices of the other directors quiet. "Can we sue the newspaper?" she asks.

"Yes, but we would lose," the board's counsel says. "Look at the question mark on the headline. This newspaper makes no claims and assigns no blame except as questions. Besides, if we sued them, they would fold – and start over with a new name. They have no assets to seize."

"What can we do to mitigate the damage?" That question is more difficult and the board debates it for nearly an hour before the Chairwoman calls time. "We have nearly emptied the oil and gas fields in the Canyon of the Ancients. The best solution seems to be to shut down all operations there. We still have the operations near Chaco Canyon. Fred? You're in charge of accounting. Calculate our losses and determine how we can use them to offset taxes on profitable operations. Mai Lin, get your people in Washington on this. We need some immunity from liability. See what our people in the Congress can do. Meeting adjourned."

~~~~~

Dr. Deschene invites Gahtsoh, Gaagii, and Chatima to visit the linguist. "He has some interesting things to tell you."

What the linguist says surprises Gaagii and Chatima. "Dr. Deschene was correct that the way Gahtsoh sings is with his tongue toward the back of his mouth. When Gaagii and Chatima sing, their tongues are in the front of their mouths. The vowel sounds have changed, much like the Great Vowel Shift between Middle English and Early Modern English."

The linguist sees blank looks on his audience's faces, and laughs. "I doubt you share my keen appreciation of this. In simple terms, Gahtsoh sings these songs in a way the language might have been spoken hundreds of years ago. It is almost as if this were the Navajo language at the time of the Emergence."

Gahtsoh knows this is true. He knows the old man, although a spirit, was real and was both a link to the past and a warning of the future. Gahtsoh knows he must tell his story, but only to three Elders: Gaagii, Chatima, and Dr. Deschene.

~~~~~

Eleven members of the Eastward Kiva Society sit in the hogan just completed in one corner of Dr. Deschene's back yard. "We needed a place to meet," Dr. D says. "But the ground is nearly solid rock. This is no place to excavate for a traditional kiva."

The twelfth member, Gaagii, waits outside with Gahtsoh. A lone drumbeat signals them to enter. Gaagii sits beside Gahtsoh on a log while Chatima, *The Caller*, speaks the invitation.

"Gahtsoh, you see here the members of the E′e′aahjigo Kiva Society. We are a secret group, because we are Navajo and Hopi, male and female, Athabascan and Bilagáana. Earlier, Gaagii asked you to keep our secret. Even without knowing what the secret is, you agreed. Thank you.

"Creator led you to us. Becoming a Medicine Elder is a process and is more than learning songs and drumbeats. You must also learn the old ways. Gaagii and Chatima have been your teacher-uncles. They tell us you have other teachers, and we are glad, because The People have lost much of the old knowledge. Tonight, we offer you a place among us – a home. We offer you a place of safety where you can learn from us and teach us. Will you join us?"

In answer, Gahtsoh struggles to stand from the log, and then lurches on braces and with crutches toward the fire. He sprinkles on the fire the last of his grandfather's mountain smoke, rescued from Ton Yah's hogan. As the smoke rises, Gahtsoh sings the Song of Thanks to his new brothers.

~~~~~

The inquest into the death of *Ashkii Anashdloh*, Laughing Boy, conducted by the Council Representative for Four Corners, finds the manner of death to be negligent homicide, and "Mr. Grumpy" attends a Tribal Court, where he has the obligation to confront his actions, to acknowledge his conduct, and to make right.

The boy's body is never identified or claimed. The next summer, after the boy has been a year in a freezer at the hospital

230

Pathology Lab, Dr. Deschene orders his funeral. On a Saturday, the entire Eastward Kiva, along with Chief Joe, Johnny Highrock, and Frank Falcon, travels to the Canyon of the Ancients. They erect a platform among the trees and place Laughing Boy's remains there before asking Earth Mother and Father Sky to accept him.

"Why do we do this? His spirit has long been with Creator," one of the newest members asks.

"To complete the cycle," Gaagii says. "You remember funerals before we were disfellowshipped. 'Ashes to ashes, dust to dust.' They believe we are made from clay and would become clay. That's what they said, but clay is not living. They embalmed their bodies to keep them from turning into clay, then buried them in coffins to show how wealthy they were and put the coffins inside crypts to protect them even more. We know we are one with all the cosmos, and with all life. We do this so that this boy's body will be taken up by new life."

The forest is too dry to risk a fire, so Gahtsoh lifts his grandfather's calumet in which mountain smoke smolders and carries his Song of Farewell to Creator.

~~~~~

In one of the sacred places in the Athabascan world of 1492, a Medicine Elder sits facing a small fire. The fire provides little light and less warmth. The man reaches into a pouch and throws mountain smoke onto the fire to take his prayers to Creator. Then he throws corn pollen, and the fire responds by flaring brightly for a moment. The Elder throws herbs from the pouch onto the fire.

In the smoke that rises he sees clouds attached to canoes holding many men. The clouds pull the canoes to the lands of the Athabascans, and the old man sees that those who inhabit

231

this world will not be able to resist the newcomers, nor their weapons and diseases. He knows his people's history and magic must be preserved until these invaders are fragmented, fighting one another, arguing over riches and religions and rulership.

Moonlight and firelight merge to bathe the old man in the four sacred colors. He dreams, and sees the future. He sees Gahtsoh, and knows he and the boy are separated by more than five hundred years. *I must prepare him so he can prepare my people.*

He opens his medicine bag and removes the talisman given him by his own teacher. It is a silver disk engraved with symbols important to a Medicine Elder. Feathers, corn, lightning, and a dome with a ladder protruding represents a kiva.

He grimaces from the pain in his knees, hips, and ankles, but stands erect. He moves from the rock shelter behind the Great House to climb the ramp that leads to the mesa above Chetro Ketl and connects this sacred place to others by hundreds of miles of straight and undeviating roads.

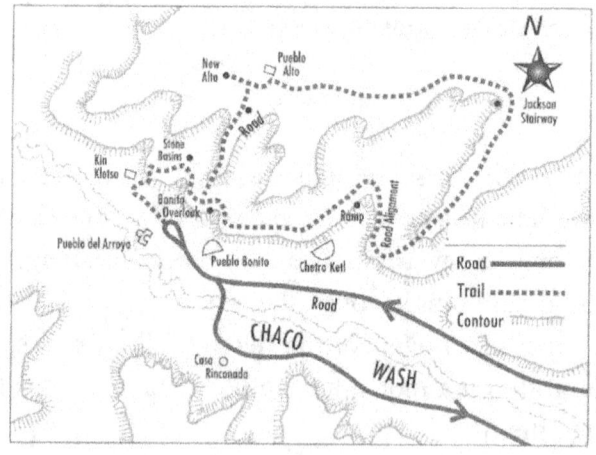

When he reaches the place of the pictographs, he points to a particular stone and then raises his arms. The stone lifts from the ground. He places the talisman under the stone. The stone drops, sealing the talisman's hiding place.

The old man dies then, knowing his task as a teacher has finished although it will not begin for many years. Before a day passes, scavengers arrive. Male coyotes rip limbs from the Elder's body and drag them away to eat in solitude. The female coyotes and pups gather to savage what is left. Flies lay eggs and hungry maggots attack the scraps. Beetles arrive, feed and multiply. In less than a week, the flesh is gone and the bones are scattered, but the essence of the old man remains, to sleep until a certain boy arrives.

~~~~~

The sun is high in the sky when Gahtsoh reaches the plateau and finds the rock which bears his name. The rock is a rectangular stela, as tall as Gahtsoh and about two feet in width and breadth. A geologist could tell him it weighs at least two metric tons. Perhaps it is best Gahtsoh doesn't know this. The boy braces himself with one crutch and pushes with the other arm, but there is no movement. He strains, pushes, moves to another side of the rock and tries again. His sharp cry of frustration crackles through the dry desert air. A rabbit's ears stand erect and twitch. The desert blurs for a moment as a small cloud in the otherwise cloudless sky passes across the sun. A young man wearing blue jeans, moccasins, and a doeskin vest steps into the sunlight and lends his strength. The beads of his necklace – blue-green turquoise, yellow garnet, black obsidian, and white shell – shine in the sun.

Another push, and the stela shifts and then crashes away, revealing an indentation where it had stood. Gahtsoh unlocks his braces, kneels, and digs at the compacted dirt in the indentation until he sees a glint of sunlight on metal. He scrabbles at the dirt, tearing a fingernail. He slices a fingertip on a sharp edge and his cry punctuates the silence. More cautious now, he removes a silver circle just larger than the palm of his hand. There is something more. Below the silver circle is an eagle feather. It is the one from Ton Yah's medicine bonnet which Gahtsoh had given the old man. There is no question in the boy's mind. He had helped his grandfather assemble the bonnet; he had selected this feather to give to the old man.

Holding the feather in his hand, Gahtsoh turns to Rabbit. "This was his." He knows Rabbit understands both the statement and the underlying question.

"And it will be the first in your own medicine bonnet. But that will not be today."

Rabbit presses Gahtsoh's hand closed on the talisman. Gahtsoh hears his spirit guide's words, but only in his mind. "The talisman and the feather are symbols of your coming status as a Medicine Elder. They are only symbols; they hold no power or magic. Both power and magic will come from you and from your connection with Earth Mother and with Creator." With these words, Gahtsoh's Spirit Guide vanishes.

Hágoónee´

Author's Afterword

Like its predecessor, "The Cry of the Innocents," this narrative occurs on an Earth Analogue different from the one in which you are reading. The Athabascans are the descendants of the First Peoples of the American continents, known today by many names including Apache, Diné (Navajo), and Hopi. Their names and languages are used herein. The Hispanglos are people, primarily from Europe, who brought disease to the Americas and took slaves from these peoples beginning in 1492. The geography and geology of this place and the history and culture of these peoples are similar to, but not identical with, places and peoples with whom you may be familiar.

The history, culture, and legends of these people were likely corrupted by the Hispanglo missionaries and the soldiers and settlers who, with the blessing of the Pope, decided that white Europeans had the right to the entirety of the American Continents. Too many modern scholars make profound pronouncements *ex cathedra* (or, more accurately, *ex umbilicum* – from their belly buttons) that the commonality of some Athabascans' legends and the Bible prove the truth of the Bible. The real reason for the commonality, which so few seem willing to acknowledge, is that the missionaries corrupted the history of the original inhabitants of this continent.

While the ceremonies and customs described herein may resemble ceremonies and customs from Earth Analogue III (the one in which you are reading this), they are pure fiction, as are the capabilities of the aerostat.

237

In this reality, Page, Arizona (renamed "Folio") is once again part of the Navajo Reservation. In our reality, Page was part of the Reservation until a 1958 land-swap made it a federal autonomous territory.

Water in an aquifer moves based on underlying geology and the makeup of the material (gravel, sand, and the like) in the aquifer. In the Ogallala Aquifer, water moves less than meter per day. No aquifer I know of acts quite like the one in this narrative. This is, however, the only liberty taken with science. The forensic and medical science, and the science linking certain fracking chemicals to cancer, are real.

Acknowledgements

This narrative would not have been possible without the time, talent, and energy of Beta Readers Mary "Lani" Clancy; Richard Moore, MD; Charles Robinson; Charlotte Elizabeth Robinson; and Robert Viens.

I am especially indebted to development and line editor, Rebecca Watts for her support, energy, and talent.

These people did their best to steer the manuscript in the right direction. Where that occurred, give them credit; where I didn't do that, blame me.

Constructive comments may be sent through the "Contact" menu at www.PaulLentzAuthor.com.

Characters and Glossary

_____, Gahtsoh: (*Rabbit*) Nickname of a Navajo boy crippled by polio, who wears braces on both legs and crutches strapped to his arms. Given name, Tsela, *Stars Lying Down*. Born to Bitter Weed Clan, born for Roan Horse Clan. Age 13 when the narrative begins. Lives with grandfather in a hogan near Many Farms. [Gahtsoh is more correctly a hare rather than a rabbit; however, time has erased that difference.]

3-Tesla MRI: Rating for the most powerful Magnetic Resonance Imagery machine used in routine medical diagnosis. More powerful machines exist, but are used almost exclusively for research.

Aboriginal: Meaning "from before the beginning." It is used herein to define the first people to "discover" the American continents and specifically those who were the first inhabitants of what is now the Four Corners area of the United States. See also "Athabascan."

Acromion: Greek: *highest shoulder*. Plural, acromia. The bony point of the scapula atop the humerus. Starting point of the Y-incision of an autopsy.

Adit (Mine Adit): A horizontal entrance or shaft into a mine.

AGL: Above Ground Level.

Ahéhee´: (Navajo) *Thank you.*

Aho: (Navajo) *Yes, I agree.*

239

Ahote: (Restless One) Hopi member of the Eastward Kiva. Officer in the Navajo Nation Police Force.

Antigen: Any foreign substance that causes an immune system response.

Animas River: The River of [Lost] Souls, so named by Juan Maria Antonio Rivera, a Spanish explorer, around 1765 CE. The river is 126 miles long and originates at Animas Forks at an elevation of 11,120 feet. It flows southward to Farmington, New Mexico, where it joins the San Juan River.

Ante-mortem: Before death.

Apothegm: An "old saying" that is not a law of nature but which may contain a kernel of truth worth considering, pursuing, and discussing.

Ashkii: (Navajo) Boy or young male.

Ashkii Anashdloh: Laughing Boy. Name given to an unidentified, dead child by the EMTs who first encountered the body.

Atahalne (Ata´halne´): Navajo male name, "*He Who Interrupts*." Member of E´e´aahjigo Kiva. Name given by his friends to Tommy Chee, member of the Eastward Kiva Society and nephew of Chief Joseph of the Nation's Police.

Athabascan: Technically, this applies only to Alaskan and Northern Canadian natives and others descended from those who spoke the Athabascan ethnolinguistic group of languages. It is used herein (perhaps incorrectly) to describe all "Native Americans" and "First Peoples" who likely migrated over the Bering Strait during the last ice age, including those on the Pacific coast of California, Oregon, and Washington, the Maya, Toltecs, and Aztecs, and others, as well as those in and around the Four Corners area of the Southwestern US.

Atsa: (Navajo) Eagle. Name given to Spencer Hansen when he was inducted into the Eastward Kiva.

Autolysis: "Self-digestion." The destruction of cells or tissues after death by their own enzymes. Occurs when cells' lysosomes release digestive enzyme into the cytoplasm due to the cessation of active processes in the cell. The corneas begin to cloud from autolysis within 3-4 hours of death. Certain other organs normally undergo autolysis at fairly predictable intervals.

Autopsy: AKA *post-mortem (examination),* or *necropsy.* Medical examination of a body by a Medical Examiner, Pathologist, Forensic Pathologist, or similar qualified person(s).

Avatar: A visible manifestation of a deity or spirit. A symbol that represents something of power.

BCE: Before the Common Era. See also "CE."

Begay, Martin: Murder victim.

Begay, Mary, RN: Gahtsoh's nurse at the Navajo Western Regional Hospital, Folio, Arizona.

Bidziil, Johnny: ("Strong") Navajo. Retired US Air Force Chief Master Sergeant. Friend of Sam Little Crow. Inveterate airplane watcher, Folio Municipal Airport, Arizona. Maternal Uncle of Hokee.

Bilagáana (bill-la-GAH-nah): Navajo name for white people or people of Caucasian descent. May specifically refer to an Anglo-Saxon. Sometimes, but not always, used in a derogatory way.

Bitsé siléí: The foundational essence of the Navajo Way of Life. *Bitsé* – that which is in front or ahead. *Siléí* – foundation; that which lies before. *Bitsé siléí* – the very beginning, nothing better before it. [See Navajocourts.org/harmonization/bitsesieli.htm]

Bois d'arc: The Osage orange, nicknamed "bow wood" by French trappers and traders when they saw it being used to make bows (and war clubs).

Bone Remodeling: The process by which mature bone tissue is "resorbed" and new bone is formed ("ossification"). The process occurs normally and naturally as a person grows and following injuries to the bone. The time of a remodeled injury may be determined by the amount of growth; bone grows over fractures at a regular and predictable rate.

Born to/Born for: Navajo children are born to the mother's clan and born for the father's clan.

Borstal: A youth detention center in the United Kingdom and some Commonwealth countries.

Breath of Creator: The wind, especially a cold wind.

Brooks, _____: Drug Enforcement Agency (DEA) Agent.

Burn, Degrees of Burns: There are many systems for categorizing the degree of burns. The National Institutes of Health MedlinePlus uses three different systems. Here is one with four categories.

First Degree Burns: Reddening of only the outer layer of the skin, sunburn is an example

Second Degree Burns: skin is red, may slough, is blistered. Affects first two layers of the skin.

Third Degree Burns: All dermis is converted to carbonaceous ash, subcutaneous fat is exposed (yellow), muscle tissue is exposed (burgundy)

Fourth Degree Burns: Flesh is charred to the bone (black flesh, white bone).

Cadaveric spasm: Muscular stiffening which occurs at the moment of death and persists into rigor mortis. AKA postmortem spasm.

Caliche: Sedimentary rock that covers many deserts including the High Plains in the US. It consists of a thin layered cement of calcium carbonate binding sand, clay, gravel, and silt. It is usually found on the surface but may be below the surface. Caliche prevents flow of surface water into underlying aquifers.

Calumet: A pipe in which tobacco or herbs are burned or smoked as part of a ceremony.

Calvin, Susan: Investigative reporter who worked for a major eastern newspaper. A Bilagáana and the only woman known to be a member of a kiva society. Wife of Dr. Nastas Deschene, q.v.

Cancer Cluster: A disease cluster in which a relatively high number of cancers of the same or related types occurs in a group of people linked by geography. There are documented cases of work-related cancer clusters as well as clusters associated with specific environmental substances, however, these are rare. [See web pages of the National Institutes of Health at cancer.gov]

Canyon de Chelly: National Monument located just east of Chinle, Arizona, and part of the Navajo Reservation.

Cartelé(s): (car TELL ā, car TELL āz) Member(s) of a Mexican drug cartel.

Catafalque: A wooden framework to hold a body or coffin often while the body lies in state or is being transported.

Cause of Death (COD): Factor(s) such as a specific disease or injury that caused or contributed to causing a person to stop breathing and their heart to stop beating. The origin of a sequence of events that occur without significant intervening causes. See also "Manner of Death."

CBN: See "Contraction-band necrosis."

CE: Common Era, Year of the Common Era. See also "BCE."

Chatima (Cha´tima): *(The) Caller* Hopi Member of the Eastward Kiva Society. He studies to become a Medicine Elder.

Chaco Canyon: The Center Place found by the Hopi after they emerged into this world. Promised to them by Earth Mother. The precise location of the Center Place is Pueblo Bonito, the largest of the Great Houses in the canyon. The houses and kivas in the canyon were constructed between 850 CE and 1126 CE. Having served their purpose, the houses and kivas were abandoned and are returning to the earth.

Chee, Tommy: Nephew of Navajo Nation Police Chief, Joseph White Eagle. Also known as Ata'halne' *(He Who Interrupts)* of the Eastward Kiva Society.

Chelation Therapy: Treatment to remove heavy metals from the body. Drugs such as disodium ethylenediaminetetraacetic acid (EDTA), succimer, dimercaprol, edetate calcium disodium, deferoxamine, and penicillamine are injected through an IV or ingested orally. The drugs bind to the metal(s) and are voided in urine.

Chetro Ketl: The largest of the Great Houses at Chaco Canyon.

Cheveyo*: (Spirit Warrior)* Hopi. Two-spirit boy; member of Eastward Kiva Society. He works for the telephone company in Farmington.

Chief Joseph White Eagle: Chief of Navajo Nation Police. Maternal uncle of Tommy Chee. Adopted Tommy after he was disfellowshipped from his scout troop, church, and immediate family. Honorary uncle of all members of the Eastward Kiva.

Chįįdii: A ghost, the spirit of a dead person. *Chįįdii* are believed by some people to linger around a dead person's body or possessions and to cause illness ("spirit sickness"). A *chįįdii* may summon skin walkers (q.v.) to avenge their death, especially if that death was unjust.

Chuchip: Hopi member of the Eastward Kiva; autopsy technician and fledgling crime scene investigator working for Dr. Deschene (pathologist and Navajo nation's coroner).

CIA: Central Intelligence Agency. A real agency of the US Government.

Clans: The four original clans of the Navajo people are Kinyaa'áanii (The Towering House clan), Honágháahnii (One-walks-around clan), Tódich'ii'nii (Bitter Water clan) and Hashtł'ishnii (Mud clan). There are now more than 100 clans, each with a unique identity. Each person belongs to four clans: the mother's, the father's, the maternal grandfather's, and the paternal grandfather's, and belongs to the tribe by virtue of clan membership.

Clinical Autopsy: An autopsy done for the purpose of studying disease or an illness believed to be the cause of death. A clinical autopsy may be ordered by the Coroner (Dr. Deschene) or the hospital administrator. Compare to **Forensic Autopsy**.

CO: Carbon monoxide. A product of incomplete burning.

COHb Carboxyhemoglobin: Carbon monoxide compound which forms in red blood cells when carbon monoxide is inhaled. A blood test for COHb is useful during an autopsy to assess the degree (if any) of carbon monoxide poisoning.

COD: See "Cause of Death."

Concho belt: A belt for a man or woman decorated with oval or round disks of silver and inset with turquoise, coral, or another semi-precious stone. A small one might be worn through belt loops; a large one would likely be worn on the outside of trousers or skirt.

Contraction-band necrosis: Microscopic damage to the fibers of the heart muscles commonly seen in cocaine-related death. It is the result of uncontrolled cell death (the necrosis) unique to cardiac myocytes. While a number of conditions or treatments can cause contraction-bank necrosis, an absence of myocardial fibrosis points to cocaine abuse.

Corn Pollen: Corn pollen is a fine, yellow powder collected from the tassels of a mature corn plant by a woman and subsequently blessed by a medicine elder. It is one means of communicating with Holy People. (See also "tobacco.") A small, leather bag of pollen may be given to a person traveling outside the nation's boundaries to protect them while away.

Correlation Coefficient: A statistical measure that shows the strength of the relationship between two variables. Value can range from -1.0 (indicating a perfect negative correlation) to +1.0 (a perfect positive correlation). A value of 0.0 indicates no relationship between the variables. The closer the value to zero, the less likely there is a relationship.

Cortical bone: the dense outer surface of bones that protects the internal bone. Also known as **compact bone**, it makes up about 80% of bone mass in adults.

Coyote: (*mą'ii*) A Totem Animal and Spirit Guide. Also known as Anger. With Magpie and Buzzard, one of the traditional tricksters. (See also "foxprop.")

Crepitant rales: A peculiar crackling sound audible in the lungs with inspiration in pneumonia, tuberculosis, and other lung diseases. May also be heard when lungs removed in the autopsy of a drowning victim are prodded.

CSI: Crime Scene Investigation. Usually refers to a multidisciplinary team who collect and preserve evidence at a crime scene.

CT Scan: Computer (assisted) Tomography, also CAT Scan. Non-invasive radiological scanning technique employing multiple X-ray beams from different directions to create cross-sectional images.

CV: *Curriculum vitae*. An academic's résumé.

Debride: To remove damaged tissue from a wound or burn during treatment; to remove flesh from bones during an autopsy. See also "Thermal maceration."

Decon, decon station: Decontamination; decontamination station with showers, eye wash stations, and other means of cleaning persons accidentally exposed to chemical spills, radiation, etc.

Deschene, Dr. Nastas, MD, Fellow, College of American Medical Examiners, Diplomate American College of Forensic Pathologists. Navajo. Pathologist at Navajo Western Regional Hospital. Coroner for the Navajo Nation. Spencer Hansen addresses him as mentor and uncle.

Desert Coyote (*Canis latrans*): A mammal somewhat like a small-to-medium dog (adults weigh about 7-11 kg, and are about 90 cm long, plus tail) which lives in most environments in the North American Continent, including urban. The range of the desert coyote is about 25 to 30 square km for a pack of 5 to 10 animals led by the alpha mating pair. They are primarily nocturnal. Females and cubs feed together; males drag food apart from one another before they eat. The dens of dessert coyotes may be a burrow, under a rock outcropping, or in a copse of brush. They may hunt alone for small game or in packs for deer.

Diné Bahane´: The Navajo Creation Story, which describes the prehistoric emergence of the Navajo into the current world in the area known as Dinétah, the Navajo traditional homeland.

Dinétah: "Among the people." The traditional homeland of the Diné (Navajo People). It is located between the Four Sacred Mountains, q.v.

Diné Bikéyah: The traditional Navajo country; The People's Land.

Diné dodiyinil: The Holy People.

Dził nát´oh: See "Mountain smoke."

Eastward Kiva Members: (E´e´aahjigo "Eastward Kiva")

Hopi: Ahote ("Restless One"), Cha'tima ("The Caller"), Cheveyo ("Spirit Warrior"), Chuchip ("Deer Spirit")

Navajo: Ahiga ("He Fights"), Ata'halne' ("He Who Interrupts") AKA Tommy Chee; Gaagii ("Raven"); Hokee ("Abandoned"); Niyol ("Wind)

Later additions: Spencer Hansen, Atsa ("Eagle"); Chief Joseph White Eagle (uncle to Tommy Chee and honorary uncle to all the young men); Dr. Nastas Deschene, Susan Calvin.

Ahote and Niyol have become regular police officers. Niyol is an accomplished computer hacker.

Gaagii and Chatima are studying their cultures' traditions to become Medicine Elders. They share a trailer south of First Mesa, in Hopi territory.

Hokee is a pilot. He becomes a regular police officer and flies a de Havilland Canada DHC-2 Beaver with Nations Police markings.

Cheveyo is a Two Spirit boy. His boyfriend, Alberto Hermano, is an Hispanglo Park Ranger in The Canyons of the Ancients National Monument.

Spencer Hansen is a medical student who has completed his first year at an eastern college. He is Dr. Deschene's protégé.

Chuchip has been hired as an autopsy technician by Dr. Deschene.

E´e´aah: West ("where the sun goes down").

Elder: See also Medicine Elder. One who has a great deal of knowledge and understanding of the traditions and customs of a community. Within a community, an elder is someone who has the respect of the community and is therefore considered to be an elder. It should be clearly understood that not all elders are spiritual leaders, not all elders are old, and not all old people are elders.

EMT: Emergency Medical Technician or Emergency Medical Team. Persons trained in first aid and some medical procedures, often part of a municipal or Chapter fire department.

Enrolled: Term used to indicate a person who has proven his or her right to membership in a particular tribe or nation, and who can show he or she is, indeed, a member.

EPA: Environmental Protection Agency. A real agency of the US Government.

Even-Odd: A game in which two players, on a count of three, display from one to five fingers on one hand. The players fingers are added, to create a number that is either even or odd. Before displaying fingers, one player will declare "even" or "odd." He will win or lose depending on whether the total number of fingers is even or odd.

Everpure: Fictious grain-neutral spirit, 190-proof ethyl alcohol.

Fajada Butte: Also known as Banded Butte for the visible rock layers, including a layer of lignite coal. AKA *tse dighin*, Holy Rock. The butte rises to a height of 135 meters (442 feet) above the floor of Chaco Canyon. Years ago, a spiral petroglyph, called the Sun Dagger was shown to track the solstices and equinoxes, as well as the 18.6-year lunar cycle. In Earth Analogue III, the rock on which the petroglyph was pecked has shifted and no longer serves as an observatory.

Falco, Francis (Frank): Assistant United States Attorney, Flagstaff, AZ.

Falcon, Francis (Frank): Emergency Medical Technician (EMT) at Four Corners Chapter; assistant to Johnny High Rock.

False Dawn: The light that by about an hour precedes the sun breaking the horizon.

Federal Bureau of Investigation (FBI): A real agency of the US Government.

Flowback: Water containing fracking chemicals and naturally occurring substances (salt, radium, for example) that return to the surface with oil or gas and which must be properly disposed of.

Folio, Arizona: Fictitious town on the western edge of Navajo territory.

Footy: Soccer.

Forensic: As used here, means the application of science to criminal investigation.

Forensic Autopsy: An autopsy done when the cause of death is known or suspected to be a crime. A forensic autopsy may be ordered by the Chief of Police and is required when someone dies in official custody, regardless of the cause of death. The forensic autopsy is conducted to determine the cause of death, mechanism of death, manner of death, and time of death. A forensic autopsy is much more invasive than a Clinical Autopsy, however every effort is made to ensure the body can be viewed at an open casket funeral. AKA Medicolegal Autopsy. Compare to **Clinical Autopsy**.

Four Corners: The place where the borders of the states of Arizona, Colorado, New Mexico, and Utah come together. A town on the Navajo Reservation near that location.

Four Corners Tattler: A tabloid published in Greenbriar, Arizona, just west of the Navajo Reservation. The newspaper reports legitimate news as well as "the weird and fascinating" and is targeted at Native Americans in the region.

Four Sacred Mountains: See "Sacred Mountains."

Four Sacred Times and Colors: Dawn (white shell, east); midday (blue-green turquoise, south); evening twilight (yellow garnet, west); night (black obsidian, north).

Foxprop: Disparaging term for political propaganda. From the *kitsune,* a fox of Japanese legend – a shape shifter – and the legends of the Quechua, a fox of the Andes – a scoundrel.

Frenulum (plural, Frenula): A fold or ridge of tissue that supports or checks the motion of that to which it is attached. Examples include the fold of skin below the tongue, the connection between upper and lower lips and the gum, and between the foreskin (or remains thereof) of the penis and the glans. A torn frenulum may indicate a severe blow to the face, or other abuse

Fracking (Hydraulic Fracturing): A process in which chemicals, water, and often sand are injected deep into Earth to break up rock and release oil and gas.

Fracking chemicals: Many of the more than 100 chemicals used may be found at the FractFocus Chemical Disclosure Registry.

Fry Bread (recipe):

3 Cups Flour, 2 tsp Baking Powder, ½ tsp Salt; 1½ cup hot water; Oil for frying

In a bowl add flour, baking powder and salt and stir to mix evenly. Add hot water and stir with a spoon. You can also mix with your hands. Dough will be sticky. Form into a ball and allow to sit covered for 45 mins. Separate dough into 12-16 balls; using the palms of your hands and fingertips, press each ball into a circle and work with your fingertips to a thin round circle about 4-5 inches in diameter. Heat oil in Fry Pan over medium/high heat OR Instant Pot on Sauté until it reads "hot." Add one piece of bread at a time in hot oil and allow to cook until golden brown and then flip. About a minute on each side (variable for how hot the oil is heated). Remove from oil and allow to drain on paper towels.

Gaagii [Gáag´íí] (*Raven*): Member of the Eastward Kiva Society. He is the medicine elder who is most able to see into the mist. [The "type species" of raven is *Corvus corax.* There is little to distinguish ravens and crows except some difference in size, tail-feather shape, and sound.]

Ginsel: Oil-field roughneck slang for "new guy."

Glyphosphate: Glyphosate is a non-selective herbicide, meaning it will kill most plants. It prevents the plants from making certain proteins that are needed for plant growth. Glyphosate stops a specific enzyme pathway, the shikimic acid pathway. The shikimic acid pathway is necessary for plants and some microorganisms. (http://npic.orst.edu)

Gold King Mine Spill: A real event (2015 AD) in which an Environmental Protection Agency (EPA) contractor released three million gallons of waste water containing 875,000 pounds of arsenic, cadmium, lead, and other heavy metals into the Animas River.

GPS: Global Positioning System. Location system incorporated in many cell phones, sometimes without the owner's knowledge.

Ha´aa´aah: East, "where the sun comes up."

Ha´a´aahjigo: Eastward, toward the East.

Hágoónee´: A word commonly used in parting, meaning okay, alright or "Things are settled. See you later."

Hansen, Spencer: Bilagáana [non-Athabascan]. Medical student at a college in Boston, protégé of Dr. Deschene. Spencer was a member of a scout troop until he was judged too irreverent, and was disfellowshipped. He joined with others who shared his beliefs and who had formed the Eastward Kiva Society with Navajo and Hopi members in defiance of both nations' beliefs. As a Nordic blond, Spencer stands out from the aboriginal members of the kiva.

Ha´tchi: *You have spoken well.*

Hatalii: Traditional title of a Navajo Medicine Elder or "Singer." Name given by Gahtsoh to his Teacher.

Hatsóí ashkiígíí: Grandson, son of one's child.

Hawiovi: Hopi male name, *Going Down the Ladder*. ("Down," along with "Up" and the four cardinal compass directions – North, South, East, and West – are sacred directions.) Member of the Hopi Police and of the Native American Church.

Hermano, Alberto: US National Forest Service Ranger assigned to The Canyon of the Ancients. Boyfriend of Eastward Kiva Society member, Cheveyo.

High Rock, Johnny: Emergency Medical Technician at Four Corners Chapter House; former autopsy technician who worked for Dr. Deschene.

Hightower, Edward: District Supervisor of the Forest Service unit with responsibility for the San Juan National Forest and, by tasking from the Bureau of Land Management, The Canyons of the Ancient National Monument. Supervisor of Alberto Hermano.

Hispanglo: Slang term often used by Athabascans to describe those from Europe, including Spanish Catholic missionaries, and the largely Anglo-Saxon US Army who drove the Athabascans into reservations and who surround them at the time and in the Earth Analogue of this narrative.

Hogan: A traditional Navajo home.

Hokee: Navajo name, *Abandoned*. Member, Eastward Kiva Society, pilot.

Holyway Ceremony: One directed to the *Diné diyiini*, the Holy People, to restore health to someone by attracting good.

Homeland: Short for "Homeland Security," a real agency of the US Government.

Hópituh-shínumu ("peaceful all people"): A more complete name of the Puebloans usually called Hopi.

Hózhó: There is no English translation. "Beautiful harmony and peace" come close, but don't quite make it.

Humvee: High Mobility Multipurpose Wheeled Vehicle (HMMWV; colloquially, Humvee): A family of light, four-wheel drive, military trucks and utility vehicles.

Hyponytremia: Severe lack of sodium in the blood. Can result in seizure and death. [https://www.ncbi.nlm.nih.gov/pmc/articles/PMC4712283/]

Innominate: Unnamed or unclassified. For example, the innominate bones of the pelvis are each composed of three fused (and named) bones: the ileum, the pubis, and the ischium.

INS: Immigration and Naturalization Service. Real agency of the US Government.

James Holomon University: Fictitious school whose forensic anthropology department pioneered the recreation of faces using information gleaned from partial remains. They are the site of a sophisticated forensic chemistry laboratory.

Javelina (Peccary): A hoofed mammal resembling the pig, found in the Southwestern area of North America as well as Central and South America. They are usually between 90 and

130 cm long and adults weigh between 20 and 40 kg. Some grow much larger.

Jeeshóó: Buzzard. A carrion-eating bird (several species); also, a person who benefits from others' suffering.

Juvie: Nickname for the part of the Department of Family Services that deals with juveniles.

K´é: The Navajo kinship system which has words for self, siblings, parents, aunts, uncles, and grandparents. It is based on clan affiliation, and every person who is a member of the tribe/Nation is a member of one of the many clans.

Kettle: Birds "kettling" are flying as a group in a circle. A kettle of vultures and buzzards is centered on something dead on the ground. (They do not circle things that are dying – they cannot know if death is near.)

Kiva (KEE vuh): (1) A structure used for social and ceremonial purposes. May also be a residence. Usually circular but may be square, hexagonal, octagonal, or keyhole-shaped. Often roofed, with a ladder leading from the roof to the floor. May be subterranean or built inside a rectangular structure on the surface. May have entrances at the four cardinal directions. May have holes in the wall through which the sun will strike various points inside the structure on different days of the year. Size varies significantly. (2) Kiva Society. A group of (usually) men bound by tradition.

Kót´é: *It is so.*

LED: Light-emitting diode. A source of bright light of different colors, including white.

Lensatic compass: AKA "military" compass, but also used in the sport of Orienteering. A compass with a cover holding a sighting wire, a rear sight, and illumination (phosphorescent markings or tritium lights).

Little Crow, Sam: Navajo. Retired US Air Force Senior Master Sergeant. Friend of Bidziil "Johnny" Two-Horses. Inveterate airplane watcher at Folio Municipal Airport.

Lividity: AKA *Livor mortis*. An unnatural color of the skin. As used herein, lividity is coloration caused by red blood cells settling in lower parts of a body because of the pull of gravity on a cadaver after death. It begins in as few as 20-30 minutes after death, and is usually noticeable about two hours after death.

Lymphoma: A group of blood cancers that start in the lymphatic system, which is a part of the body's immune system. Lymphoma may involve lymph nodes, the bone marrow, the spleen, thymus gland, and the blood. Enlarged lymph nodes, fatigue, and weight loss are symptoms.

Mą'ii: Coyote. A Spirit Guide; a trickster.

Magnetic Resonance Imagery (MRI): A medical imaging technique that employs magnetic fields to provide insight into anatomy and physiological processes of the body.

Man Who Rotates: The asterism also known as The Big Dipper – *Náhookòs Bikà'*.

Manner of Death: The way a person died. There are six standard manners of death used on death certificates in most jurisdictions: homicide, suicide, accidental, natural, iatrogenic (caused by a medical treatment or complications), and idiopathic (unknown). "Pending" may be entered as Cause or Manner of Death when additional investigation, information, or test results are needed. **Natural** is the most common manner of death and accounts for about 30 percent of all deaths that reach a pathologist.

Mass Spec[trometer]: Mass spectrometry is an analytical tool that is used to determine and describe the chemical identity of molecules and compounds.

Mastoid process: The bones behind each ear where muscles are attached. Generally larger in males than females and one way of determining sex of a skeleton or burn victim.

Medicine Elder: A Medicine Man or Woman, Shaman (in Asia), Witch Doctor (European name for African traditional healers), who engages in spiritual healing and perhaps physical healing with herbs, simples, compounds, tinctures, etc. Elders are considered repositories of history and culture.

Mercaptan: AKA ethyl mercaptan, methanethiol. An organic chemical, CH_3SH. A colorless gas with a distinctive putrid smell released from decaying organic matter and present in some natural gas deposits.

Mescaline: Trimethoxyphenethylamine. A naturally occurring psychedelic alkaloid, a hallucinogen similar to LSD and psilocybin ("magic mushrooms"). It is found in peyote cactus. **Side effects** include nausea, vomiting, anxiety, paranoia, fear, elevated blood pressure, increased heart rate, increased respiration rate, changes in vision, headache, dizziness, and hallucinations. It can be detected in urine for 2-3 days, in blood up to 24-hours, in saliva for 1-10 days, and in hair follicles for up to 90 days.

Mesothelioma: A malignant cancer that most often affects the lungs and which may often be caused by exposure to asbestos fibers.

Microtome: Device which slices things (e.g., samples of organs and tissues) very thinly to make microscope slides.

Mineral King Mine: Abandoned mine located in southwestern Colorado. The spill of tons of hazardous chemicals by a contractor for the US EPA is true and well-documented.

Mountain smoke: *Dził nát'oh*, traditional "tobacco." It is a blend of plants (none of which are tobacco) found in and around *Dinétah*, usually on mountains. The plants must be harvested in their season and are collected with special songs, prayers, and offerings. When smoked reverently, it helps rejuvenate the mind and heal the body. When thrown onto a fire, the smoke speeds prayers to Creator.

MRE: Meal Ready to Eat. Field rations produced for the Bilagáana military. Although labeled "ready to eat," many include a chemical heater for the entrée.

MRI: See "Magnetic Resonance Imagery."

Mutton: The meat of a mature sheep and one of the fattiest meats in existence.

Naatáanii: ("Great leader" or "Great teacher.") One who follows the four basic rules of leadership: thought and planning, following the plan, creating change that accords with the plan, improving the plan to ensure continued success.

Naabah, Hashkem: Navajo man, operator of a food truck, dealer in illegal drugs and alcohol.

Nahasdzáán: The world; the earth. Note the inclusion of *asdzáán*, which imbues the meaning of "woman" or "female."

Náshdóítsoh: Cougar or Mountain Lion. A Spirit Guide and symbol of protection and healing. Guards the Sacred Mountain of the South, *Tsoozil*.

Náhookòs: North.

NATO: North American Treaty Organization. Among other things, it sets standards such as caliber for weapon systems used by member nations.

Nava hu *or* ***nabahoo***: See "Navajo."

Navajo: Official name of the people whose territory was outlined in the 1868 Treaty of Bosque Redondo. This geographic area is known as *Naabeehó Bináhásdzo* in the Navajo Language. The official name of the tribe was designated the "Navajo Nation" in 1969. The name, Navajo, originated in a Tewa-puebloan phrase, *nava hu* or *nabahoo*, meaning "place of large planted fields."

Navajo Taco: The best food ever created, consisting of a puffy slab of blue corn fry bread (q.v.) topped with ground meat (e.g., mutton or beef), beans, greens (e.g., lettuce, spinach, dandelion), clotted cream (cream cheese, sour cream), spices, and topped with "red or green" sauce, to taste.

Navajo Western Regional Hospital: Fictitious hospital in Folio, AZ, on the Navajo Reservation, which is operated by the Navajo Nation, and at which Dr. Nastas Deschene is the pathologist. Although labeled, "Navajo," it is owned by a 501(c)3 (non-profit) corporation governed by a board of directors.

Nez, Herman: Family Services employee at Four Corners. Also known as "Mr. Grumpy."

Nihalgai: The Glittering World or the White World; the one on which the Navajo and other Athabascans now live.

Nilch´i: Wind, as a sacred wind, or wind from Creator. See also "Breath of Creator." This has been corrupted by some Xtian missionaries to mean "Holy Spirit" (Holy Ghost), one of the three faces of their godhead.

Niyol (*Wind*): Member of the Eastward Kiva Society. Computer hacker and police officer in the Navajo Nation Police.

NOAA: National Oceanic and Atmospheric Administration. Home of the US National Weather Service. A real US government agency. One of many attacked by an anti-science political agenda.

NOTAM: Notice to Airmen.

NSA: National Security Agency. A real agency of the US Government.

Occipital Bone: A trapezoidal bone located at the lower back of the skull.

Per diem: ("per day") Reimbursement for expenses (food, lodging, transportation) incurred while away from home or home station on official business.

Perforated septum: A hole or fissure in the wall that separates the two sides of the nose. In the absence of inflammation and tumors, this may suggest significant use of cocaine or methamphetamine due to reduced blood flow as well as numbing of the inside of the nose.

Peri-mortem: At or near the time of death.

Peyote (*Lophophora williamsii*): Also known as Devil's Root, Divine Messenger, Magic Mushrooms, and other names. Peyote is a small, low-growing cactus, buds of which may be chewed or used to make a tea. The chemicals released, mescaline and other psychoactive alkaloids, are hallucinogenic. Possession is illegal except for members of the Native American Church. It is most common in Mexico and southwestern Texas. The alkaloids in the cactus are bitter and protect the plant from being eaten. Peyote buttons found at archeological sites in

Mesoamerica have been carbon dated to nearly 4,000 BCE. See "Mescaline."

Piñyon Pine: A common tree of southwestern North America, especially the Four Corners region. The nut of the tree is a staple food of Native Americans and of local Bilagáana food.

Post-mortem: After death.

Produced water: All water produced as a byproduct of oil and natural gas extraction. This include natural occurring water brought up by the well, water injected to increase the amount of oil or gas produced by a well ("waterflooding"), and water containing fracking chemicals, and waste water from fracking including flowback (q.v.). Produced water is an industrial waste and its disposition is regulated. Treatment is specified by the Environmental Protection Agency before the produced water can be injected underground or discharged into surface waters (streams, lakes, for example).

Reduction(s): Places resembling concentration camps into which early Spanish missionary-priests, first Franciscans then Jesuits, concentrated the local aboriginal population and required them to build churches and rectories, and forced religion on them.

Remodeling: See "Bone Remodeling."

Rocky River Mine: Fictional abandoned gold mine in the Tonalih region.

Sa´ah naaghai bik´eh hozhon (SNBH): "That according to which harmony exists," a philosophy involving each one's personal and moral character. Sa´ah evokes the Navajo emphasis on life and that death of old age is a goal. Naaghai calls to mind the completion of the cycle of life. Bik´eh simply means, "according to." Hózhó is "harmony, order, and balance," and reflects a state of harmonious relationships with one's surroundings.

Sacred Mountains: Dził Diyinii Dįį´go Sinil. The Four Sacred Mountains are: (1) Blanca Peak (to the east), also known as Sisnaajiní, the dawn or white shell mountain. (2) Mount Taylor (in the south), Tsoodził, "turquoise mountain," or "blue bead." (3) San Francisco Peaks (in the west), Dook´o´oosłííd, "the summit which never melts" or "abalone shell mountain." (4) Hesperus Mountain, to the north. Dibé Nitsaa, "big sheep." None of these appear within the Navajo Reservation.

Sage, sagebrush: As used herein, refers to *Artemisia tridentata*, an aromatic shrub which provides food and habitat for many desert mammals and is used by humans as firewood and in religious ceremonies. Small bundles are used for "smudging," the spreading of smoke from a bundle of sage that has been ignited and then snuffed out until only smoldering.

Saramco: Fictional oil and gas fracking exploitation company. A multinational corporation with North American headquarters in Denver, Colorado.

Scattergun: Essentially, a shotgun, although there are some minor technical differences.

Shash: Navajo, "The Bear." An animal with holy power which may become a Spirit Guide.

She Rains: *Níltsą bi´ááḍ.* The soft, female spring rains associated with a warm front. Compare to *Níltsą bikạ´*: He Rains, the hard male-rains as from a violent rainstorm associated with cold fronts and orographic or convection thunderstorms.

Shidá´í: A boy's maternal uncle.

Shimá yázhi: A person's mother's sister; a maternal aunt.

263

Shinálí: Paternal grandfather.

Shiprock: Town in the northeastern Navajo Territory. For the geological feature, see *Tsé Bit´a´í*.

Shizhé´é: A person's father.

Sitsilí: Younger brother.

Shiye´: A man might call his son or nephew this.

Skinwalker *(yee naaldlooshii)*: Navajo medicine elder ("shaman") who has achieved great power and can transform into an animal, usually for some evil purpose (murder, e.g.). Popular Bilagáana (non-Navajo) culture often incorrectly equates "skin-walker" to "ghost" or "zombie."

SPIO: Superparamagnetic iron oxide particles. Used as tracers in examining cancerous lymph nodes.

Spirit Guide (Totem animal): The animal that appears to a boy during Spirit Quest (q.v.) and which will guide his life thereafter. The animal will be a teacher and mentor, and lend its characteristics to the boy. Not all characteristics are obvious, especially to the untrained. For example, Raven is a trickster, a thief, a joker, and sometimes a liar, but Raven can also see the truth in a person, can see into a person's heart Some common totem animals are Wolf, Coyote, Bear, and Eagle.

Spirit Quest: The term used to describe the Vision Quest as practiced by the principal cultures of this narrative.

Stela: (stē´ lah) An upright stone column often inscribed and sometimes serving as a gravestone.

STOL: Short Takeoff and Landing. Features of an airplane that allow it to take off and land on shorter-than-normal runways, or unimproved landing places.

T'áá'áko: Navajo for "It is right," "It is agreeable," "OK," or "Fine."

Tabahaa, Doli: Navajo lawyer and advocate for children. Office in Fairfax, Virginia. Friend of Dr. Deschene and Susan Calvin Deschene.

Tattler; The Four Corners Tattler: Weekly newspaper with offices west of the Navajo Reservation in Greenbriar, AZ. Editor, Henry Nez, classmate of Susan Calvin Deschene at the Columbia University School of Journalism.

Temporal bones: The bones located on both sides of the skull above and just behind the ear.

Theodolite: Surveying instrument usually set on a tripod and used to measure both vertical and horizontal angles with great accuracy.

Thermal maceration: Using heat and a solution of water and chemicals, often a detergent, to debride (remove flesh from) bones.

Three Sisters: The three sisters are corn, beans, and squash. They are often grown together with the corn providing something for the beans to climb, the beans providing nitrogen for the soil, and the squash shading the soil from the sun to slow evaporation of moisture.

A "Three Sisters Bowl" is a traditional recipe using those ingredients. Here is one recipe.
½ C dried hominy
½ C dried tepary beans
1 small peeled acorn squash, halved, seeds and membranes removed
light oil for sautéing
salt
1 small white or yellow onion, thinly sliced

1 T chili powder
2 T chopped, fresh sage
½ C dark greens (dandelion, kale, spinach)

Cover beans and hominy with water and soak overnight or refresh in pressure cooker at high pressure 15-30 minutes until *al dente*. Simmer for about 1 ½ hour. Drain hominy and beans. Reserve 1 1/3 C cooking liquid. Roast squash at 425 degrees (slice in half; put cut side down on a baking sheet). Cut into 1-inch chunks. Sautee onion and spices; add reserved cooking liquid, hominy and beans, squash and greens. Season to taste with salt.

Tilly Hat: A wide-brimmed, canvas hat, usually khaki in color and with cord to hold it onto one's head.

Tó Neinilii: Spirit Person whose domain is rain. He is also something of a trickster (as are many of the *gods*).

Ton Yah: Medicine Elder born to Tall House Clan, for Silent Walker Clan; grandfather of Gahtsoh.

Tonilih: *Running Water*. Fictional Navajo Chapter and community north of Four Corners, site of a cancer cluster.

Toon, Bertha: Charge Nurse at the Tonilih Comprehensive Health Care Facility.

Totem animal: See "Spirit Guide."

Toxicology: Testing of tissue and fluids, etc. to determine if the person were chemically impaired in any way (e.g., drugs whether prescription or recreational, alcohol, etc.).

Trabecular bone: The porous bone found at the ends of the long bones (e.g., femur, radius and ulna, and humerus).

Tsé Bit´a´í: (Rock with Wings). Geologic feature – the remains of an ancient volcanic throat – that rises 482.5 meters

(1583 feet) from a flat desert. Located about 15 km south of the town of Shiprock. The Navajo name is a reference to the legend of a great bird which brought the Navajo to their present lands. [That would be before the Bilagáana army drove them there.]

Tsebida ´t´ini´ani: "covered hole," refers to any of the rock shelters ("sealed concavities") in the cliff behind Chetro Ketl, one of the Great Houses in Chaco Canyon.

Tsela: Navajo boy name meaning *Stars Lying Down*. See "Gahtsoh."

Tséyi´: Navajo, literally *within the rock*; *canyon*. The word was coopted by the Bilagáana as part of the name of Canyon de Chelly (pronounced de-SHAY).

Tsohanoai: Navajo spiritual figure (Sun god) who carries the sun on his back across the sky.

Two Horses, Bidziil: ("Strong") Navajo. Nickname, Johnny. Retired US Air Force Chief Master Sergeant. Friend of Sam Little Crow. Inveterate airplane watcher, Folio Municipal Airport, Arizona. Maternal Uncle of Hokee.

Two Spirits: Said of someone who possesses both male and female characteristics. Often used to describe homosexuals or lesbians, although more broad interpretations are possible. Two-spirit persons are honored in many Athabascan cultures.

United Press Universal (UPU): Fictitious newsgathering and distribution organization headquartered in London.

Vision Quest: "Vision quest" is a Bilagáana term for the rite of passage from childhood to adulthood for older boys and young men, which is part of some Athabascan (q.v.) culture. It may involve multiple ceremonies conducted by elders of a particular tribe or nation and usually includes several days of

267

fasting. This latter rite is done alone and at a sacred site. The objective is for the youngster to receive a vision that will help him understand his purpose in life. Visions may include symbolism from nature – usually animals. Visions must be interpreted by elders.

White Eagle, Joseph: Chief of Navajo Nation Police. Uncle of Tommy Chee.

Winder, Gabrielle (Gabby): FBI Special Agent in Charge (AAIC) of the Phoenix, AZ Field Office who works closely with Chief Joseph and the Navajo Nation's Police.

Window Rock: A geologic feature overlooking the Navajo Tribal Park and Veterans Memorial. The town in which this is located.

Woman Who Rotates: The constellation also known as Cassiopeia – *Náhookòs Bi'ááá*.

Xajiinai: A hole in the La Plate Mountains in southwest Colorado, from which the Navajo emerged into this world, and where they were taught to live in balance with Earth Mother, Father Sky, and the elements including humankind, animals, plants, and insects. The Navajo conduct ceremonies to keep this balance, and believe when these ceremonies cease, the world will cease.

Ya´ateeh: Navajo. "Greetings" (literally, "It is good.")

Yupköyvi: Hopi name for Chaco (Canyon).

Zygomatic bones: The pair of bones that form the cheeks and the outer side walls of the orbits (eye sockets).

Bibliography and References

This book was not intended to be a scientific paper or a student's publication; however, it did involve a great deal of research. The following is provided for readers who may wish to pursue some of the included subjects.

Bateson, John. "The Education of a Coroner: Lessons in Investigating Death." Kindle Edition. 2017.

Craig, Emily, Ph. D. "Teasing Secrets from the Dead: My Investigations at America's Most Infamous Crime Scenes." Kindle Edition. 2004.

Kristofic, Jim. "Navajos Wear Nikes: A Reservation Life." Kindle Edition. 2011.

Maples, William R. and Michael Browning. "Dead Men Do Tell Tales: The Strange and Fascinating Cases of a Forensic Anthropologist." Kindle Edition. 1994.

McCreery, Nigel. "Silent Witness: The Often Gruesome but Always Fascinating History of Forensic Science." Kindle Edition. 2014.

Melinek, Judy, MD. "Working Stiff: Two Years, 262 Bodies, and the Making of a Medical Examiner." Kindle Edition. 2014.

Roach, Mary. "Stuff: The Curious Lives of Human Cadavers." Kindle Edition. 2003.

Shepherd, Richard. "Unnatural Causes: The Life and Many Deaths of Britain's top Forensic Pathologist." Kindle Edition. 2018.

Smith, Sir Sydney Alfred (Emeritus Professor of Forensic Medicine, Edinburgh University). "Mostly Murder." 1959.

Zinn, Howard. "People's History of the United States." Kindle edition. 1980, 2003.